DARK ANGELS
Revealed

✠

DISCARD

To all those who wait in lines at theaters and bookstores for the next glimpse of our favorite dark angels. And to the actors, writers, and artists who share with us these beautiful dreams.

Text © 2011 Angela Grace
Design © 2011 Fair Winds Press

First published in the USA in 2011 by
Fair Winds Press, a member of
Quayside Publishing Group
100 Cummings Center
Suite 406-L
Beverly, MA 01915-6101
www.fairwindspress.com

15 14 13 12 11   1 2 3 4 5

ISBN-13: 978-1-59233-457-5
ISBN-10: 1-59233-457-1

Digital edition published in 2011
eISBN-13: 978-1-61058-053-3

Library of Congress Cataloging-in-Publication Data
Grace, Angela.
 Dark angels revealed : from dark rogues to dark romantics, the most mysterious and mesmerizing vampires and fallen angels from count dracula to Edward Cullen come to life / Angela Grace.
   p. cm.
 Includes bibliographical references.
 ISBN-13: 978-1-59233-457-5
 ISBN-10: 1-59233-457-1
1. Vampires. 2. Vampires in literature. 3. Vampire films. I. Title.
 GR830.V3G73 2011
 398.21—dc22

                                                              2010049439

Cover and interior design: Monica Rhines

Printed and bound in China

DARK ANGELS
Revealed

FROM DARK ROGUES TO DARK ROMANTICS,
the secret lives of the most mysterious & mesmerizing vampires and fallen angels

from Count Dracula to Edward Cullen

ANGELA GRACE

FAIR WINDS
PRESS
BEVERLY, MASSACHUSETTS

Contents

Chapter Four: Dark Guardians

Chapter Five: Darkest of the Dark

"Who will take care of me, my love, my dark angel, when you are gone?"

—Claudia to Louis, Interview with the Vampire

The word *angel* can have many meanings, both literal and figurative. The modern image of the vampire includes a variety of dark beings who qualify as fallen or compromised angels, but who nonetheless often act heroically, giving supernatural protection to human beings—or who are simply perceived as angelic by the spellbound humans upon whom they feed. The dark angels within this book can be found all around us today, in books and media, in all their fascinating complexities and contradictions. Lestat, that handsome devil from *Interview with the Vampire*, explains it best: "Evil is a point of view. . . . God kills, and so shall we; indiscriminately . . . for no creatures under God are as we are, none so like Him as ourselves, dark angels not confined to the stinking limits of hell but wandering His earth and all its kingdoms."

Chapter One
Dark Romantics

Romeo's got nothing on these guys. The dark angels in this category trade everything for love. They give their lives to pursue the ones who've won their hearts. If Jack from Titanic were a vampire, he'd definitely be one of the dark romantics.

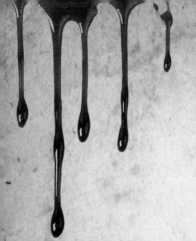

EDWARD CULLEN: THE DARK ROMEO

Indisputably the most popular (and romantic) of all current vampire icons, Edward Cullen is the undying creation of author Stephenie Meyer in her best-selling novels Twilight *(2005),* New Moon *(2006),* Eclipse *(2007), and* Breaking Dawn *(2008). In the blockbusting screen adaptations of Meyer's books, Edward is indelibly portrayed by British actor Robert Pattinson.*

Who couldn't love Edward Cullen?

Well, the truth is that vampire fans either love or loathe him; there seems to be no middle ground. For some, it's the fact that he sparkles rather than disintegrates in sunlight or that he's so polite and charming when they would prefer an ultimate bad-boy type. To others, Edward's old-fashioned moral compass makes him seem an impossibly perfect hero, who gives young women the absolutely wrong idea when it comes to finding love in real life. Edward couldn't possibly be more misunderstood.

Unlike the naysayers, those of us who adore him recognize all his charms. Rather than being easily swayed by a pretty face, Edward appreciates a female with deep thoughts and genuine emotions. As a member of the old-school preternatural, he's a wonderful return to the vampires who saw themselves as serious romantic monsters, instead of just partying the centuries away. He's like Anne Rice's Louis from *Interview with the Vampire*, without all the exhausting self-torture and bouts of clinical depression, or Shakespeare's Romeo without the self-sabotage.

His High Points . . .

Falling in love with Edward is easy enough. He's a hundred years old, stands six foot two, and is capable of crushing vehicles, taking down large prey, and running from one country to the next in an evening. He also has impeccable taste, is well read, and composes music to rival the masters. And he's a romantic, which leads to an abundance of heart-throbbing scenes in the series—an unforgettable prom, secret bedroom trysts, and eventually a spectacular vampire honeymoon—all of which leave us wanting more.

Edward, as seen in the film *New Moon*, is James Bond-ish with his impeccable style and secret identities. The two also share a love of expensive cars—like Edward's Vanquish.

When it comes to true romance, selflessness is perhaps his most moving characteristic. One example of this is in the testosterone-charged tent scene in *Eclipse*. Although his warm-blooded werewolf rival Jacob Black is intent on torturing him with his ability to interact with Edward's passionate teenage love interest Bella Swan on a human level, to physically warm her in the freezing cold when the undead Edward cannot, to have a physical relationship with her, and to grow old with her (as Edward also cannot), it is Edward who rises above it and has the strength to admit his own limits. "You don't have the faintest idea how much I wish I could do what you're doing for her, mongrel," he says. Edward loves Bella so much that he endures everything Jacob can throw at him with little resistance, all just to keep her warm.

After winning an exhaustive competition against Jacob's underhanded attempts to steal Bella away, Edward has the empathy and selflessness to recognize Jacob's pain at the wedding. He knows, even without the use of his profound mind-reading gifts, how much Jacob means to Bella. Giving his new wife the gift of a private moment and a dance with Jacob is perhaps Edward's most endearing scene. It's more than most human men would endure, and requires a level of emotional maturity and genuine love.

. . . and His Crashing Lows

Edward frequently flirts with tragedy once Bella comes into his life. Part of the struggle for safety is Bella's inability to avoid danger. As Edward tells her in *Eclipse*, "If we could bottle your luck, we'd have a weapon of mass destruction on our hands." Even her boyfriend choice is the most dangerous one possible, because Edward can barely stop himself from sinking his teeth into her every moment they are together in the beginning, which would blow the carefully created cover of a human doctor and his family that the Cullens have created (see "The Cullen Family: Dark Clan"). In *Midnight Sun*, he describes how irresistible she smells to him, saying, "Her scent hit me like a wrecking ball, like a battering ram. . . . In that instant, I was nothing close to the human I'd once been; no trace of the shreds of humanity I'd managed to cloak myself with remained."

After he overcomes the mouthwatering scent of Bella's blood, his instincts to attack her, and the risks the Cullen family takes to welcome her into the fold, there's the problem of the other vampires. When vampire drifters who drink human blood, unlike the animal-blood-drinking Cullens, wander into the family's supernatural baseball game, Bella's scent and Edward's protective response drive the thrill-seeking James, a vampire with a gift for tracking, to start a deadly game of cross-country hide-and-seek with Bella as the prize. Although Edward saves the day, James's death sparks a hunger for vengeance in his redheaded lover, Victoria, who spends much of the saga trying to rip Bella's throat out. If the other vampires coming to his home in Forks, Washington, weren't enough of a problem, the brush with death and the Volturi in Volterra, Italy, surely tops it off.

Edward fighting James in the ballet studio in *Twilight*. Unlike some dark angels, both vampires have a reflection in mirrors and can tolerate sunlight.

While these confrontations are motivated by external factors, two of Edward's near-tragic scenes happen simply because of his love for Bella. In *New Moon*, when Edward leaves Forks and goes into hiding so that he can save Bella from dying at the hands of the Cullens or from being turned into one of them, his unspoken heartbreak is worse than Bella's. He might have fooled her into thinking that he actually didn't care, but true fans know he was leaving to protect her from future threats, such as the triggering incident, a paper cut at Bella's eighteenth birthday party that filled the room with the scent of blood and caused Jasper, Edward's newest adopted brother, to attack her. Even though we're not shown his months of depression, we come to understand his suffering through his family and then his attempt to die at Volturi hands, after he's criticized Romeo's similar actions so harshly, in *New Moon*.

Then, when Bella leaps into his arms, Edward's joy makes the level of his previous heartache obvious by contrast alone. He is so happy just to see her that he says in *New Moon*, "You smell just exactly the same as always. So maybe this is hell. I don't care. I'll take it."

The other heart-wrenching scene occurs in *Breaking Dawn*. When Jacob sees Edward next to a pregnant, dying Bella, he describes Edward's shocking condition by saying, "His eyes were half-crazed. He didn't look up to glare at me. He stared down at the couch beside him with an expression like someone had lit him on fire. His hands were rigid claws at his side." Then, when they speak outside, Edward shows Jacob how he really feels and how dire Bella's situation is. Jacob is again surprised by the depth of Edward's pain, saying, "For a second I was just a kid . . . just a child. Because I knew I would have to live a lot more, suffer a lot more, to ever understand the searing agony in Edward's eyes. . . . This was the face a man would have if he were burning at the stake." It's almost impossible not to feel his desperation. Asking Jacob to father children with Bella so that she will give up the one she's carrying is unthinkable before Edward has to watch her wither away while a parasitic hybrid vamp-human baby grows inside her. It's only to save her life that Edward would ever make this bargain with the "dog," Jacob, exchanging a future mating and baby with Jacob as a bribe for Bella to abort the fatal pregnancy. It costs Edward, as it would any man, such a large part of his dignity. But he does it, all for love.

The Real Hero

Even though he is exceedingly romantic and caring, Edward isn't the pushover his critics claim him to be. In most of the saga, we see him doing his best to hold it together under horrendous circumstances. He's almost too good to be true, smiling and playing the diplomat when he should be snapping necks. But this is Bella's view, and her view only (at least until *Breaking Dawn*). She sees Edward in the best light possible, not as the centenarian he is, but as a hot high school guy. As we look closer, the true feelings behind that calm mask are easy to discern. Besides the numerous jabs he takes at Jacob and Mike, Bella's high school classmate, Edward exhibits some distinct signs of real emotion.

In *Midnight Sun*, a manuscript-in-progress posted on stepheniemeyer.com, we see the real Edward. Not only is he grumpy in the beginning, but he is also much more like the other vampires in his condescending opinion of humans, and he has a sinful sense of humor. When a man in Port Angeles, Washington, with a history of sexual assault is intent on adding Bella to his list of victims, Edward discerns his intentions telepathically, and behaves tellingly. Rather than being a sweet, passive vampire (as Bella sees him), he drops her off at home so that he can go back and deal decisively with the attacker.

Bet you didn't see that coming in *Twilight*!

The Mysteries of Edward

There are a few other questions most fans have about Edward that aren't answered in one way or another by the man himself. One that kept even Bella wondering is whether he and Tanya, his beautiful friend from the Denali clan in Alaska, ever "hooked up." Since it is widely accepted that Edward was a virgin in the beginning of the story, he couldn't have been with her in a sexual way. Still, the idea lingers that they had perhaps been an item. This question is answered when Tanya pursues him. Even though Edward is in Denali to avoid his feelings for Bella, which would be a prime opportunity to start a dalliance with Tanya, he has no interest in a relationship with her deeper than that of extended family.

And there's also no chance that he ever had a real interest in his beautiful, well-bred Cullen sibling, Rosalie, as Carlisle had once hoped he would. Edward makes his disapproval of her obvious with the many times he calls her shallow in *Midnight Sun*.

Then, some of us still wonder what Jacob and Edward were talking about in their partially silent conversation in *Eclipse*. In the tent, Jacob obviously asks something with his mind that Bella doesn't get to hear. Edward says, "Yes, I'm jealous of that, too," to which Jacob gloats, "Sort of evens the playing field up a little, doesn't it?" Edward all but answers this during another scene when he states, "With every fiber of my being, I ached to be a normal man, so that I could hold her in my arms without risking her life. So that I could be free to spin my own fantasies, fantasies that didn't end [in] her blood on my hands, her blood glowing in my eyes." Knowing this, and how Edward obviously can't have sex with Bella without risking her life, the answer is simple. Jacob *can* be a real boyfriend. Free of the bloodlust that Edward constantly battles in Bella's presence, Jacob can be almost human. He can kiss her without wanting to rip her throat out. He can do all the things Edward wants to do but without hurting her.

And possibly the greatest mystery of Edward and Bella's story is whether he was there with Bella when she was lying outdoors, reading, in *Twilight*. Yes, he was. The answer comes in *Midnight Sun*, in which he tells of stalking her under the guise of protection. It's also here that he sneaks into the sun beside her while she sleeps. It's a sweet scene that makes him even more endearing through his utter inability to see himself as anything but a "freak."

Overreaction? Edward? Nah!

Some readers also question why Edward left Bella in *New Moon*. In the simplest terms: to save her. Edward sees himself as a monster, a fallen angel. By the end of *Twilight*, he's fully in love with Bella, but more aware than ever of her fragility. Then, in *New Moon*, Jasper's frenzied response to her paper cut cements Edward's belief that by remaining in her life, he is putting her in even greater danger. He realizes that his family poses the greatest threat.

In the confrontation outside the Swan home after Jacob kisses Bella in *Eclipse*, Robert Pattinson (Edward) had a tough time grabbing Taylor Lautner's (Jacob's) shoulder after he bulked up for the role.

This includes the possibility of her being changed, which he believes would damn her soul to hell just as he believes his soul already has been. So, in a gallant attempt to save both her mortal life and her immortal soul, he leaves Bella to live her normal human life, obliging himself to a life of heartache and misery without his love.

Edward's leaving Bella is an overreaction, one among many. If there is a potential tragic flaw in Edward, that would be it. He can be a drama queen where Bella is concerned, but would we love him any other way? He wouldn't exactly be Edward without that passion, sprung from an overreaction to Bella's physical scent that sparked the entire saga. If he hadn't been so attracted to her blood, and so curious about his inability to hear her thoughts, she would have simply been another uninteresting member of the herd. Critics have questioned the superficial nature of this initial attraction, but it's no different from how most humans are initially drawn to their mates. The combination of physical appearance and chemical reaction often sparks lifelong love. For Edward, who's lived around so many exceptionally beautiful women for roughly a century, it takes something a bit more unconventional to attract him. All of these factors work together to create an ideal romantic hero. As with many of the characters in the *Twilight* world, most readers who meet the remarkable Edward fall quickly for his genteel ways. Levelheaded and wise, he can negotiate with the most impossible vampire leader and still open his heart fully to the fragile human girl who captures his attention. This combination of control and passion makes for the perfect modern romance hero, our dark undead Romeo, Edward Cullen.

❧ FACTS AND TRIVIA ☙

• Edward's birthday is June 20, the beginning of the summer solstice.

• As a human, Edward had green eyes, not the honey color of the vegetarian vampires.

• Although a fan of most music, he's not particularly fond of country.

• In *New Moon,* when Edward loses the vote to change Bella, he angrily breaks something in the living room of the Cullen home. Readers wondered what the object was loudly and persistently enough that Stephenie Meyer answered the question herself, stating that it was "a sixty-inch plasma TV that the Cullens had shipped in from Korea because it's not available in the States yet. [Edward's brother] Emmett was a bit annoyed."

❧ QUOTES ☙

"I decided as long as I was going to hell, I might as well do it thoroughly."—Twilight

"And so the lion fell in love with the lamb. . . . What a sick, masochistic lion."—Twilight

"You don't know how it's tortured me. The thought of you, still, white, cold . . . to never see you blush scarlet again, to never see that flash of intuition in your eyes when you see through my pretenses . . . it would be unendurable. You are the most important thing to me now. The most important thing to me ever."—Twilight

"Before you, Bella, my life was like a moonless night. Very dark, but there were stars—points of light and reason. . . . And then you shot across my sky like a meteor. Suddenly everything was on fire; there was brilliancy, there was beauty. When you were gone, when the meteor had fallen over the horizon, everything went black. Nothing had changed, but my eyes were blinded by the light. I couldn't see the stars anymore. And there was no more reason for anything."—New Moon

"I'll be back so soon you won't have time to miss me. Look after my heart—I've left it with you."—Eclipse

"You know that you nearly gave me a heart attack? Not the easiest thing to do, that."—Eclipse

"High school. Or was purgatory the right word?"—Midnight Sun

BILL COMPTON: SOUTHERN GENTLEMAN

The most charismatic television vampire since Barnabas Collins (see "Barnabas Collins: Love-Struck Angel"), Bill Compton began his star turn in HBO's hit series **True Blood** *when novelist Charlaine Harris introduced him in* **Dead Until Dark** *(2001), the first of her best-selling "Sookie Stackhouse novels," so-called for Compton's human (but telepathically gifted) love interest. More formally known as the Southern Vampire Mysteries, the eagerly awaited annual series now includes nine more novels featuring Bill:* **Living Dead in Dallas** *(2002),* **Club Dead** *(2003),* **Dead to the World** *(2004),* **Dead as a Doornail** *(2005),* **Definitely Dead** *(2006),* **Altogether Dead** *(2007),* **From Dead to Worse** *(2008),* **Dead and Gone** *(2009), and* **Dead in the Family** *(2010). On television, this very American vampire is memorably portrayed by British actor Stephen Moyer.*

A few of the dark angels are from the American South, but none of them embodies the Southern gentleman ideal like Bill Compton. His history parallels that of his Southern home. Born on April 9, 1840 (1835 in True Blood), Bill lived in Bon Temps, Louisiana, a farmer married to Caroline Isabel Compton. The two had children. When the War Between the States broke out, Bill fought, and, like the Confederacy, he was never the same. On November 20, 1868 (or, on his way home from the war in the show), the vampire Lorena changed him into a vampire, taking away his life much like the war destroyed the South.

Wars

The next war to rock Bill's Louisiana is the war between vampires and humans, which breaks out after the undead introduce themselves to mankind at a moment called the Great Revelation. Although it's much more like the Cold War than the Civil War, it is equally unhinging. Just after this war, Bill meets Sookie Stackhouse, a Bon Temps waitress with extrasensory powers. She, like Lorena, changes his life the way the Great Revelation does. She opens him up to a new world, helps him "mainstream," and shows him real love with another human

Bill, as portrayed by Stephen Moyer in *True Blood*, was a human farmer with two children before the Civil War.

woman. She also kills Lorena in *Club Dead*, rescuing Bill from the control Lorena has had on him through blood. In many ways, Sookie is his "anti-Lorena" and gives him back everything Lorena took away, including family via the Bellefleurs, Bill's long-lost relatives and part of Bon Temps's "old money."

It is also interesting to note the reversal of Bill's status as a person from pre-vampire to post-Reveal life. Before the Civil War, he was among the most powerful of all people in the South, a young white man. His power was born to him just as slavery was born to the slaves. The Great Revelation reversed this. Afterward, vampires, even in the tolerant United States, are not afforded human rights. In many ways, the Great Revelation freed Bill, just as the Civil War did slaves. But just as African Americans have had to continue fighting for rights, so too do the vampires, and the Vampire Rights Amendment is gaining ground.

Gentleman or No?

Bill's positions and occupations as a vampire are taken out of necessity and survival. Much like the chaos in the South after the war, vampire life is cutthroat. After "mainstreaming," he applies for the investigator position under Eric Northman (see "Eric Northman: Angelic Viking"), the sheriff of Area Five, a vampire-designated territory in northern Louisiana that includes the small town of Bon Temps, simply to stay close to his biggest competitor for Sookie's affection. Likewise, Bill's work for Queen Sophie-Anne Leclerq, vampire monarch of Louisiana, is done to win her favor and stay alive.

This power game leads to several high points for Bill. One is when he discovers his surviving great-grandchildren are the Bellefleurs, who've long since lost their family fortune. As an anonymous benefactor, he acts in kindness, donating money to repair their home and their dignity, all while they treat him with ill regard. It's not his only selfless act. When he kills other vampires to save Sookie, he is risking his unlife. He also makes several attempts to help the human population of Bon Temps, something most vampires would never do.

Bill's lowest point comes in the beginning of his relationship with Sookie, when the queen sends him to Bon Temps to seduce her and exploit her telepathic gifts. Eric subtly forces Bill to admit this in *Definitely Dead,* where the two men meet at the hospital to check on Sookie. The bedside revelation of his betrayal breaks Sookie's heart because, although every vampire subject is obliged to obey an order from the queen, Bill has kept it a secret for so long. His deceit is unfathomable, given the level of intimacy that Sookie allows him, and it will forever negatively mark his character.

Bill with Sookie during the first moments of his unforgivable betrayal—seducing her for Queen Sophie-Anne Leclerq.

Powers in the Blood

The vampires in Bill's world have supernatural strength, speed, stamina, and agility; enhanced senses; and other extraordinary traits. They are ageless, cold, and pale, and some can fly. Their healing abilities are astounding, allowing them to survive most injuries. The stake, however, will kill them, along with sunlight, decapitation, or complete exsanguination. Silver is also poisonous, but a cross is just a pretty adornment to a necklace, and holy ground just another piece of dirt. Holy water and garlic are basically allergens, more likely to make vampires wet or stinky than to do any harm. However, the old-school myth of vampires being forbidden from entering a home uninvited applies to this crew.

As for mental powers, a vampire has the ability to "glamour" humans, that is, to hypnotize them with his eyes, planting suggestions that the victim is bound to carry out. If he tells them to go home, eat a piece of pie, and forget everything that happened, that's exactly what they do. Likewise, a vampire is also compelled supernaturally to obey his maker's every order, just as Bill cannot resist returning to Lorena.

Vampires have a similar psychic bond with their human victims and lovers. Such a supernatural connection isn't unique to Bill's world, but it does make things interesting when Bill, Eric, and so many others are competing for control of Sookie. The link keeps Bill close to her, and perhaps helps make him more human.

"V" Junkies

Bill's blood, just as the other vampires', doubles as a highly sought after and highly addictive drug, with the street name "V." It temporarily gives the user such vampiric physical enhancements as strength, healing, stamina, and even beauty. On the downside, it can also cause a psychotic break in some users. Plus, there are rumors that the blood can raise the ghost of a corpse. Because V is so valuable and addictive, Bill and other vampires have to contend with black market dealers who try to trap and drain them for profit.

On a similar note, vampires have created a synthetic blood known as TruBlood to replace the need for human vitae. Typed the way that human blood is (O, A, AB, and so on), vampires can enjoy their preferred flavor in public. This allows them to live among the humans in a nonpredatory manner. However, vampires and V junkies agree that it isn't close enough to the real thing.

If you're wondering, Sookie says that Bill's favorite flavor is type O negative.

Family Ties

As with many Southerners, family is of the utmost importance to Southern vampires. Bill is no different. To understand the man (and vampire) is to know his family. Here's a quick look at Bill's lineage.

Bill's Human Family Tree

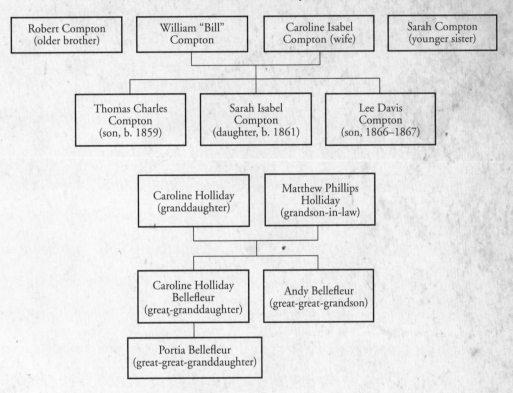

Robert Compton (older brother)	William "Bill" Compton	Caroline Isabel Compton (wife)	Sarah Compton (younger sister)

Thomas Charles Compton (son, b. 1859)	Sarah Isabel Compton (daughter, b. 1861)	Lee Davis Compton (son, 1866–1867)

Caroline Holliday (granddaughter) — Matthew Phillips Holliday (grandson-in-law)

Caroline Holliday Bellefleur (great-granddaughter) — Andy Bellefleur (great-great-grandson)

Portia Bellefleur (great-great-granddaughter)

Bill's Vampire Family Tree

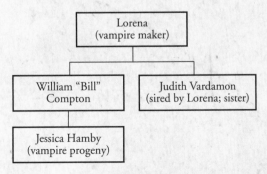

Lorena (vampire maker)

William "Bill" Compton — Judith Vardamon (sired by Lorena; sister)

Jessica Hamby (vampire progeny)

FACTS AND TRIVIA

- Throughout the Southern Vampire Mysteries, there are a number of inconsistencies. One is the precise effect of vampire blood on humans. A single drink can turn one person into a junkie and another into a psychotic mess, but drinking blood from Bill and Eric has neither effect on Sookie. Why? According to Charlaine Harris's website, it's all relative. She states that "the variables include the age of the blood (how long it's been out of the vampire), the age of the vampire, and the mental condition and previous drug use of the imbiber. Blood taken straight from the vampire does not necessarily make the drinker high, unless he or she is already an addict."

- What about blood bonds? If all vampire blood can bond humans to vampires, wouldn't this supernatural blood also link all those V users to the original vampire donors? No. According to Harris's site, "A blood bond may be formed when a vampire and a human exchange blood, though often it takes more than once. It also may depend on the emotional bond existing between them."

QUOTES

"I've been around long enough to know just about anyone is capable of just about anything."
—True Blood, *"Escape from Dragon House"*

"If you do that any more I'll have you whether you want to be had or not."—Dead Until Dark

"Sweetheart, I have always loved you and I will be proud to die in your service. When I'm gone, say a prayer for me in a real church."—Dead and Gone

"Know this: I will die for her. If you harm her, I'll kill you."—From Dead to Worse

"Sookie, most of us, vampire, human or otherwise, are capable of both good and evil. Often simultaneously."—True Blood, *"Scratches"*

"Oh, but you have other very juicy arteries. There is one in the groin that's a particular favorite of mine."—True Blood, *"Strange Love"*

"If Sookie is hurt in any way because of you, I will not stop until I drive a stake through whatever semblance of a heart you have left."—True Blood, *"Release Me"*

DANIEL GRIGORI: FALLEN ANGEL

Though not a vampire, Daniel Grigori has many of the attractive supernatural qualities often associated with the undead. One of the most popular recent teen-Goth icons, he is the central character in Kate Lauren's best-selling novel **Fallen** *(2009) and its sequels,* **Torment** *(2010) and* **Rapture** *(forthcoming, 2011). The series has been optioned for feature film production by Disney, an event eagerly anticipated by Daniel's fans.*

What would you do if an actual angel fell in love with you?

What if you and he were destined to fall in love over and over throughout time, with tragic consequences every time? That's Daniel's story. If his endless cycle of love and death weren't enough to make him a dark angel, then his fallen angel status surely is.

Daniel isn't just another gorgeous dark angel. Yes, he is attractive, according to his love interest, Lucinda (Luce) Prince. He has enchanting violet eyes and a touch that can set her on fire, and he is downright ethereal. But what most catches her attention is his trademark red scarf, an emblem of personal rebellion against the dress code and strict rules of the Sword & Cross reformatory school in modern Savannah, Georgia. Innocent rebellion infuses his very soul.

Going Biblical

Daniel's very name, both first and last, tells much about him. Both his first and his last name appear throughout the first and second books of Enoch and Jubilees, books not selected for inclusion in the Bible known as biblical apocrypha, and the book of Daniel. The name *Grigori* (for a category of angels) comes from the Slavonic Second Book of Enoch, where, as in the book of Daniel, these angels are known as watchers.

No actual photos of Daniel have surfaced at this time—his appearance is still vague. Pictured is one possibility.
A true fallen angel, he is even mentioned in books of the Bible.

We learn the most about the Grigori from the books of Enoch, supposedly written by the great-grandfather of Noah. In Enoch I, especially chapters one through thirty-six, also referred to as the Book of Watchers, these angels fall through their disobedience. On Earth, they mate with humans. Such pairings created the offspring Nephilim, hybrid angel-humans who oppose God's plan. The Nephilim are also mentioned in Genesis 6:4.

There are supposedly two hundred Watchers, though we only know the names of the twenty leaders. One of these leaders is Dânêl, aka Daniel. In Hebrew, the name *Daniel* means "God has judged." He is the seventh angel, and the one who taught the sun signs. This Daniel is, without a doubt, the Daniel of *Fallen*.

Cursed or Not to Be Cursed

As a fallen angel, Daniel is cursed by God. He chose the love of a mortal woman over the commands he was given, throwing away the power that he was given and his place in the heavens. But does he regret it? According to Daniel's interview with *The Undercover Book Lover* (theundercoverbooklover.blogspot.com), "I made a choice that was misunderstood. I chose love instead of . . . power. I don't want anything from anyone other than to be left alone with Luce." She is now his destiny, and all he needs, but given the chance to do it all over again, he might not. In the same interview, he also says that he would prefer to live without her if it would save her from the pain of reliving their love and deaths over and over because, as he puts it, "To say that I love her is an understatement."

Love and Rudeness

Still, Daniel comes under mountains of criticism from readers because of his rudeness, but they aren't thinking about it from his point of view. As Daniel puts it, "I've spent too many years agonizing over losing [Luce]. This time is different, and I won't let it happen again." So, determined to stop the next recurring cycle of love and death, he tries to avoid the girl.

When Luce resigns herself to his repeated rejections of her advances, it is as heartbreaking for him as it is for her. They're fated to be together. If Luce is unnaturally drawn to him, he is obviously going to have similar feelings. He, however, loves her enough to suffer through the rebuffs to save her, much the way Edward Cullen does when he leaves Bella in *New Moon*. Yes, he comes across as harsh, but it's necessary. After all, he knows what's going on. A little rudeness is tolerable when he's saving them both from the alternative.

Angelic Gifts

Daniel's powers differ from those of the vampiric dark angels. He has a powerful presence that allows him to be sensed before he is seen. The same could be said for many beings, but for Daniel it is an extra power. Then there's the way that he's always there to take care of Luce. If she's in trouble, you can bet that he won't be far behind. As Luce perceives it, he travels in "the shadows." But according to Daniel, the shadows are the "Announcers." In *Fallen,* he explains that they only gossip like a "demonic version of a clique of high school girls" about what he does, but one also pushes Luce down the stairs.

His wings could be considered yet another power. Most of the time they are invisible, but certain times they can be vaguely seen, as when he emerges from the lake in front of Luce and the water cascades down the otherwise unseen appendages. When fully visible, they are described as "glorious, blinding wings."

Like the other dark angels, Daniel is almost unkillable, and he has supernatural speed. Unlike most of the others, however, he also has the ability to materialize things, as demonstrated when he conjures white peonies, Luce's favorite flower.

FACTS AND TRIVIA

• Any fan of *Fallen* has seen that Daniel's only hobby appears to be sketching. But as he reveals in his interview with *Undercover,* he also enjoys the occasional round of karaoke.

QUOTES

"The only way to survive eternity is to be able to appreciate each moment." —Fallen

"I came here to get away; if you're not going to leave, I will." —Fallen

"I get to live forever. You come along every seventeen years. You fall in love with me, and I with you. And it kills you." —Fallen

LOUIS DE POINTE DU LAC: DARK BOHEMIAN

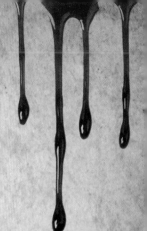

The vampire whose voice unforgettably tells the story in Anne Rice's novel Interview with the Vampire *(1976), Louis de Pointe du Lac is a member of an eighteenth-century French Louisianan plantation clan made undead by the vampire Lestat (see "Lestat de Lioncourt: Dark Rock Star"). The intermingled lives of Louis and Lestat, one of the most enduring of all vampire "couples," are also chronicled by Rice in her best-selling books* The Vampire Lestat *(1985),* Queen of the Damned *(1988),* The Tale of the Body Thief *(1992),* Memnoch the Devil *(1995),* The Vampire Armand *(1998), and* Merrick *(2000). On film, Louis was portrayed by Brad Pitt in Neil Jordan's screen adaptation of* Interview with the Vampire *(1994), and by actor Jim Stanek in the Broadway musical* Lestat *(2006).*

Louis is a classic romantic/bohemian dark angel. Although Dracula (in some of his incarnations) and a few of Louis's predecessors possess a certain level of self-doubt and self-loathing, Louis seems to have internalized it the most. He's dark and brooding, and his ongoing humanity counters any evil he actually manages to perform.

Drink from Me

When we meet Louis's human self, he is depressed over the death of his brother, Paul (or wife and child in the movie). Previously, Louis had spent much of his time caring for the family's indigo plantation, his widowed mother, and his younger siblings. Indulging his beloved brother Paul's religious leanings, Louis had built an oratory on the property where Paul had prayed fervently. The prayers had turned into visions of St. Dominic and the Virgin Mary, who had instructed Paul to sell the plantation, move to France, and become a missionary.

Louis had scoffed at the idea of real visions. This conflict had led to a heated discussion between Louis and Paul in Louis's room, where Louis again had refused to sell the plantation. Paul had stormed out of the room, hurt by Louis's refusal to believe in the validity of the visions. It was then, as Louis says in *Interview with the Vampire*, at the staircase just outside

Louis's room, that Paul had turned as if he had "seen something in the air. Then his entire body moved forward as if being swept by a wind." Paul had tumbled down the stairs, dying when his neck snapped in the fall.

Was it an angel or spirit? We are never told, but this moment hurtles Louis toward his "damnation" just as surely as if God had come down and sent him to hell. Louis, sure that his refusal has killed his baby brother, blames himself fully. This guilt over Paul's death dominates every aspect of Louis's life. As Louis puts it in *Interview with the Vampire*, "I felt that I'd killed him."

Louis moves to New Orleans, where his ensuing despondency turns to a suicidal lifestyle that brings Louis directly into the path of his angel of death and vampire mentor, Lestat de Lioncourt, in 1791. Previously sure that he wants to be free of his life, Louis changes his mind when Lestat offers to change him. The death wish he romantically entertained isn't quite as attractive when he actually stares death in the face. Changing his mind about what he wants after he gets it becomes a recurring theme with Louis throughout his immortality.

And Live Forever

Vampire life is far from glamorous or easy for Louis. More than once, he wishes he had died. As he tells Lestat, "You've condemned me to Hell." For a soul as gentle as Louis, life as a walking parasite is unacceptable. He is tortured by his own damnation and the need to survive by taking the lives of others. There is no solace, except in taking human blood, as he describes: "Her blood coursed through my veins sweeter than life itself. . . . I knew peace only when I killed and when I heard her heart in that terrible rhythm, I knew again what peace could be." But that escape from his pain comes with a price too high for Louis to accept: the deaths of others.

A child of the Enlightenment and Romantic era, Louis spends his existence in philosophical pursuits. Life, love, knowledge, and truth are the most precious things on earth to Louis through most of his bohemian existence. Even when he thinks he's lost all humanity, life is of the utmost importance. "How do we seem to you?" he asks one victim who requests the Dark Gift of vampire conversion in the film version of *Interview*. "Do you find us beautiful? Magical? Our white skin, our fierce eyes? 'Drink' you ask me. Do you have any idea of the thing you will become?" He is appalled by her yearning for something that he despises.

That Naughty Girl

Louis pursues love through three characters: Claudia, then Armand, and finally Merrick. The object of his love, the vampire child Claudia, is also Louis's emotional downfall. She is the thing that finally breaks him and takes away that human innocence.

Louis and his beloved Claudia, whom some fans argue is the object of a pedophile's affections because of Louis's love for her.

Once a six-year-old girl dying of the plague, Claudia comes into Louis's life when, starving from a life of feeding on rats, he wanders into a plague-stricken part of the city, discovers the girl, and feeds his frenzied hunger on her blood. Before he drains her completely, Lestat finds him and teases Louis for his choice of victims. Horrified and embarrassed by his own actions, Louis flees.

When it is clear that Louis cannot forgive himself, Lestat finds the child at a hospital for orphans of plague families and pretends to be her father so that he can bring her home to Louis. Since she is dying of the plague and weak from Louis's feeding, Lestat offers her his bleeding wrist and brings her into vampirism while a horror-stricken Louis watches.

Louis, as portrayed by Brad Pitt in the film *Interview with the Vampire*. Pitt became Louis in the minds of millions of fans, despite an initial public concern about the casting.

Although Lestat attempts to make Louis happy by turning Claudia, it backfires and strips away part of Louis's humanity. When Claudia asks what has happened to her, he tearfully responds, "I took your life. . . . He gave you another one." True to his nature, Louis can only focus on how he took her life, unable to acknowledge her already impending death.

There are brief moments of happiness with her, but Claudia eventually becomes the thing that destroys what remained of Louis's humanity. When life is almost bearable for Louis, sixty-five years into Lestat, Louis, and Claudia traveling and living as a family, Claudia decides that she can no longer tolerate life as a vampire trapped for a humiliating eternity as a child, never achieving the body of a woman that most girls look forward to.

Resenting Lestat for making vampires of both her and Louis, Claudia plots to destroy him. She poisons him, but after unsuccessfully dumping his body, Lestat returns. It is Louis who sets fire to their home (and Lestat) to allow their escape to France. Louis and Claudia find other vampires for the first time in their short existence in Paris, though Louis carries guilt for his part in Lestat's purported death. Sensing Louis's need for adult vampire companions and the others' disdain for her, Claudia prepares for a life without Louis and brings Madeleine, a beautiful French woman whom Claudia wants as her vampire mother and companion.

First, Louis is outraged by the request, but soon caves to the monstrous wishes of his child. Creating another vampire, damning another person, is no easier for Louis to accept than killing victims so that he can survive. Both actions make him less human and more the monster he saw in Lestat. In the movie, he tells Claudia what it has cost him to change Madeleine: "Bear me no ill will, my love. We are now even. . . . What died in that room was not that woman. What has died is the last breath in me that was human." But it isn't what finally breaks him.

Armand and the Theâtre des Vampires are.

Theater of Blood

Unlike the New World vampires—if there were any besides Lestat, Louis, and Claudia—the vampires in Paris hide in the open with their avant-garde productions at the Theâtre des Vampires, a theater in Boulevard du Temple, where they pretend to be humans pretending to be vampires.

Unknown to Louis upon their arrival, the theater had been part of Lestat's vivid life and unlife. As a human, Lestat had worked there as a laborer and then rose to local fame as an actor. Once a vampire, Lestat had purchased the theater with money left to him by his maker. Frustrated by the audience's fright at his unnatural abilities, Lestat had closed the theater.

Later, Lestat had met the Children of Darkness, a coven of Satanist vampires led in the old ways by an ancient vampire named Armand. Unable to change with the world around him, Armand had maintained full control until his followers came into contact with Lestat. Lestat's new ways had inspired the coven members and showed them a different lifestyle. Armand had lost control of the group and, frustrated by his disillusioned cohorts, had burned to death all but four: Eugenie, Felix, Laurent, and Eleni.

It was then that Lestat had turned his theater over to his vampire companion Nicholas (Nicki) de Lenfent and the four survivors. Nicki changed the name to Theâtre des Vampires and the troupe rose to fame with their acrobatic, supernaturally themed shows. Lestat later urged a forlorn Armand to join his former followers at the theater. He did so, eventually becoming their leader again and adding onstage feeding to the shows, much to the thrill of their gullible human audience.

Death of the Children

When Louis and Claudia arrive in Paris, they attend a show at the Theâtre des Vampires and meet Armand and his coven of actors. Shortly after, Louis becomes enamored with the charismatic coven leader. He is the mentor that Lestat never was, knowledgeable in all the vampire ways and customs, and fully willing to teach Louis. Furthermore, Armand loves Louis's sensitive ways, praising rather than demeaning him for them. Before long, Armand sets his sights on Louis.

Armand's coven, through their vampire ability to read minds, also discovers that Claudia, and perhaps Louis, killed Lestat. At least until Lestat arrives in Paris, seeking Armand's help. Intent on having Louis as a companion, Armand forces Lestat to tell the coven that it was Claudia who attempted to kill him, another vampire, which is a crime among their kind. The group destroys Claudia, who by vampire laws shouldn't have existed, because vampiric children are not capable of fending for themselves. They also kill Madeleine, who Armand had subtly pushed Louis into creating to drive an emotional wedge between him and Claudia. Louis avenges their deaths by killing Armand's coven and burning the theater, but Armand spirits Louis away before he can discover Lestat's presence in the city or the truth of his deceptions.

Louis survives the attack at the theater, but only in the flesh. As he puts it, "All my passion went with her golden hair. I'm a spirit of preternatural flesh. Detached. Unchangeable. Empty." As Armand later notes in his own book, *The Vampire Armand*: "[Louis] will not make others after his tragic blunders with vampiric children, Louis who is past questing for God, for the Devil, for Truth or even for love."

Once that perceived last bit of humanity is gone, Louis finally forgives Lestat for turning him. He believes himself free of any remaining human emotion until he meets Merrick Mayfair, a modern witch he falls in love with and convinces to bring forth Claudia's ghost. Against her instincts, Merrick conjures what may or may not be Claudia. The spirit mocks Louis and tells him that she never loved him, only manipulated him. The harsh rejection of what may or may not be her spirit is the final straw.

Louis turns Merrick into a vampire, then tries to commit suicide by sunlight, convinced the apparition was truly Claudia, expressing her true feelings. Fortunately, Merrick manages to summon Lestat, who has become one of the most powerful vampires of his time since he and Louis parted ways, and Lestat revives Louis by feeding him his powerful blood.

Night and Day

In an odd turn, Louis spends his afterlife giving advice to Lestat, who ignores wise counsel just as Louis ignored his own mortal brother's advice to sell the plantation and move, which would have saved him from vampirism. This happens several times, most notably before Lestat's rock concert that awakens the ancient Egyptian vampire goddess, Akasha (see "Akasha: Dark Queen"), and then before Lestat switches bodies with the scheming, supernaturally talented human, Raglan James, in *Tale of the Body Thief,* to regain mortal life for one day. Louis essentially becomes Lestat's conscience, and the only vampire who can penetrate his stubborn façade and touch the shriveled heart beneath.

He is the day to Lestat's night. If Lestat is the moon, Louis is the sun. The relationship between the two companions and the planets appears throughout the works. First, when Louis leaves his world of light on the first morning of his unlife. Louis recalls his last daybreak as a mortal: "I remember it completely, and yet I can't recall any sunrise before it. I watched its whole magnificence for the last time as if it were the first. And then I said fare-well to sunlight, and set out to become what I became." This starts the life of darkness with Lestat that lasts until Louis moves back to the New World after losing Claudia and becomes free of Lestat's influence in all its forms. There, the sun reenters his life, and he describes seeing it in an early motion picture as "a mechanical wonder [that] allowed me to see the sun rise for the first time in two hundred years. And what sunrises, seen as the human eye could never see them: silver at first, then, as the years progressed, in tones of purple, red, and my long-lost blue." This return of the sunrise to his world coincides with his embracing life free of Lestat. He learns to "shine" on his own, free of his dark companion.

But it doesn't last long. Louis returns to Lestat, bringing his newfound independence, but it can't stand up to his codependent devotion to his maker. "Louis, the watcher, the patient one, was there on account of love, pure and simple. . . . Louis would go where Lestat led him. Louis would perish if Lestat perished," one character observes in *Queen of the Damned*.

Boring Personality

Louis is hardly a boring vampire, but his humility keeps him from seeing this. "I'm fright-ened of myself," he says, sure that he is a monster. However, the descriptions given by others paint a vampire who is breathtakingly beautiful and gentle.

He appears to be twenty-five, the age of his change, and just as tall and lean. His eyes are generally described as emeralds or something equally stunning, and his skin is described as porcelain. Though gorgeous, he says in *The Vampire Lestat*, "They never knew what I looked like, really."

Perhaps Louis is incapable of seeing himself in the best light because, as Armand says, "He has no pride or vanity." He probably does believe the worst, as when Lestat says, "You whining coward of a vampire who prowls the night killing alley cats and rats and staring for hours at candles as if they were people and standing in the rain like a zombie until your clothes are drenched and you smell like old wardrobe trunks in attics and have the look of a baffled idiot at the zoo." But this is only said in frustration. Lestat recants his words later in his book when he says, "Even his unusual beauty and unfailing charm were something of a secret to him . . . the most beguilingly human fiend I have ever known . . . a compassionate and contemplative creature, always the gentleman."

Louis is very reflective. He contemplates everything from the meaning of life to Lestat's latest slight. Of all those he knows, he is the only one who seeks out others like himself in a search for his place in the world and the meaning of his existence. He's eager for truth in a world of lies, and he searches fearlessly. Armand describes him most accurately in *The Vampire Armand*:

Louis exacting his vengeance on the Theâtre des Vampires and Armand's coven for their murder of Claudia and her new companion.

A deadly and romantic vampire, the kind of night creature who hovers in the deep shadows at the Opera House to listen to Mozart's Queen of the Night give forth her piercing and irresistible song. . . . Sweet, dusty Louis, reading Keats by the light of one candle . . . standing in the rain on a slick deserted downtown street watching through the store window the brilliant young actor, Leonardo DiCaprio, as Shakespeare's Romeo kissing his tender and loving Juliet (Claire Danes) on a television screen.

Dark Gifts

In keeping with his overall personality, Louis is too modest to abuse his power, too kind to let it deceive all the humans around him. As one observer notes, Louis was "the gentle one . . . whose steps made a careless sound when he walked, who even whistled in dark streets so that mortals heard him coming." It's easy to imagine sweet Louis warning the humans of his presence as he moves along.

"His senses are finely tuned and vampiric," Lestat admits, noting that Louis couldn't read minds the way other vampires could. According to Lestat, the Dark Gift affected each person differently, but Armand notes in his book that because Louis had lived only two hundred years at that time he was still very observant and dangerous. Lestat then says that "when he puts a mortal into a trance, it's always a mistake." Armand adds to this summation of Louis's powers, or lack thereof, saying that Louis is "unable to read minds, or to levitate, or to spellbind others except inadvertently, which can be hilarious, an immortal with whom mortals fall in love . . . an indiscriminate killer, because he cannot satisfy his thirst without killing, though he is too weak to risk the death of the victim in his arms." Louis's inability to drink without killing is important. It haunts him throughout time, forcing him to choose between his own unlife and the life of each mortal he's considering for dinner. For such a gentle soul, this is an almost impossible task.

In *Tale of the Body Thief*, Lestat describes Louis as a stealthy hunter with an added benefit: "When he feeds it is painless and delicate and swift." Lestat also notes Louis's physical strength, speed, and agility, surprising for such an introspective vampire, because "with a gesture too quick for my eye he hurled me backward against the chair." Unlike some of the other dark angels, he is unaffected by crosses and stakes. In fact, "I can look on anything I like. And I rather like looking on crucifixes in particular," he says.

When no one else can quite put his finger on it, Marius de Romanus, the ancient Roman vampire who was guardian of the vampire queen Akasha, friend to Lestat, and maker of Armand, finds Louis's gift. "This one was so gifted, and yet not gifted at the same time. . . . The human tenderness, the human wisdom that no one could give another; the gift of knowing others' suffering with which Louis had probably been born." Louis's greatest powers, the ones that enamor all the undead who meet him, are empathy and compassion. It makes him priceless to the others and the most human of the vampires.

❧ FACTS AND TRIVIA ❧

• Louis's mortal birth year is definitely 1766 in France, though the day and month are something of a mystery. Anne Rice says she gave him her own birthday of October 4, making him a Libra. However, she also says March 4 is his birthday, making him a Pisces. It is probably safe to assume that the October birthday is his mortal birthday, while March is the date of his rebirth.

• Louis has a tombstone located in the St. Louis Cemetery in New Orleans next to his brother Paul's. There he sees his sister as she grows older, returning to take care of his grave.

❧ QUOTES ABOUT LOUIS ❧

"Something so refined about that one, even as he slipped beneath the floorboards, something about the way that he lay down as if in the grave; the way he composed his limbs, falling at once into utter darkness." —Queen of the Damned

"[A]nd there was Louis beside her, struggling gracefully to keep up. Louis looked so touchingly civilized in the wilderness; so hopelessly out of place." —Queen of the Damned

"The cold was biting at him a little, biting at his hands. He didn't like to put his hands in his pockets the way men did today. He didn't think it a graceful thing to do." —Queen of the Damned

"[He] lifted his right hand languidly, wholly unconscious of the seductive quality of this simple gesture, and ran his fingers back through his loose dark hair." —Tale of the Body Thief

"My old familiar gentleman friend, my tender enduring pupil, educated as truly by Victorian ways of courtesy as ever by me in the ways of being a monster." —Memnoch the Devil

"You are a vampire who never knew what life was until it ran out in a big gush over your lips." —*Lestat*, Interview with the Vampire *(film)*

BARNABAS COLLINS: LOVE-STRUCK ANGEL

The first major vampire icon to emerge from television, Barnabas Collins dominated the daytime soap opera **Dark Shadows** *from 1966 to 1971, appeared in the motion picture* **House of Dark Shadows** *(1970), and featured in two dozen paperback novels by Marilyn Ross in the 1960s and '70s. Most famously portrayed by Canadian actor Jonathan Frid (who returned to the role in a 2010 audio drama), Barnabas was also played by Ben Cross in a 1990 prime-time revival of the series, and will soon be reinterpreted by Johnny Depp in a big-screen adaptation by director Tim Burton.*

In the time-honored tradition of lovesick revenants, Barnabas Collins wanders the New England night in search of his long-lost love, Josette duPres. But it isn't a Faustian bargain with another vampire or a deliberate choice to become undead that steals his love and destroys his happiness. Unlike most of the other dark angels, Barnabas becomes bound to the night (and destruction) through his own human weakness.

In 1795, young Barnabas betroths the beautiful young heiress Josette, whom he'd met on his travels on the island of Martinique. They have an instant connection and begin a passionate romance—at least until Barnabas makes the horrible mistake of spending a night with Angelique Bouchard, Josette's maidservant, who happens to be a powerful dark witch. Thereafter, Barnabas is caught in the web of the scorned Angelique's wrath, and everything he tries to stop the unfortunate results of his own behavior only make things worse for him and those he loves.

Mistakes

Barnabas is capable of deep affection and gentleness, but he also has many weaknesses, including vindictiveness, as well as the prideful arrogance typical of classic fallen angels. We see these character flaws in action right from the beginning. Regretting the one-night stand, he rebuffs Angelique. The rejection sends her into a rage from which she employs black magic to choke and sicken Barnabas. When that fails, she secretly wreaks her vengeance by casting a spell that causes Josette to marry Barnabas's uncle, Jeremiah Collins. Desperate to regain Josette's affections and full of male pride that won't allow her loss to the uncle,

Barnabas, as portrayed by Jonathan Frid, spends his unlife seeking his beloved Josette—or a suitable replacement, such as Maggie Evans.

Barnabas duels with Jeremiah and kills him. Pride wins again; he is unaware that he was protected in the lethal confrontation by one of Angelique's charms.

But Angelique doesn't give up, and she manipulates him by casting yet another spell. This time the victim is Sarah Collins, Barnabas's younger sister, whom she sickens supernaturally. Then, to cure her of the incurable with an herbal potion, Angelique demands marriage from Barnabas. He agrees, against his father's wishes, but he tries to back out of the arrangement as soon as Sarah is better.

On their wedding night, Barnabas discovers Angelique's manipulations. Even after Josette, supposedly his true love, begs him to stay with her, he sends her instead to Boston and shoots Angelique, but he fails to kill her. Enraged, the spiteful witch propels him further toward his undead destiny, summoning from hell a vampire bat to avenge her. "I set a curse upon you, Barnabas Collins! You wanted your Josette so much, well, you shall have her, but not in the way that you would have chosen. You will never rest, Barnabas! And you will never be able to love anyone—for whoever loves you will die. That is my curse, and you will live with it through all eternity!" After the bat attack, Barnabas becomes fatally sick.

Vampire Life

Willie Loomis, a grave robber looking for the Collins family jewels, uncovers Barnabas and becomes his first snack and human servant. Rising from the grave as a vampire, Barnabas finishes the job and strangles Angelique as she tries literally to drive a stake through his heart the way she has figuratively done before. When she dies, she becomes a vampire, further complicating things.

Though dead, Barnabas doesn't leave his home, haunting the family he misses. But he scares his aunt Abigail to death, and his sister Sarah hides from him in the cold night, contracting the pneumonia that kills her. Even his mother suffers when, after figuring out what has happened to him, she kills herself.

The most painful of these failures again involves Josette. Hoping to keep her love forever, Barnabas decides to turn Josette into a vampire. She agrees until Angelique interferes again and convinces her through visions that she would be a monster. When Barnabas comes to her again, she runs from him and eventually throws herself from the top of Widow's Hill to her death.

Love Corrupts All

It isn't clear whether his mind is twisted by vampirism or by the centuries tucked away in the mausoleum, but either way, Barnabas is not quite the man he was before. Mixed among the modern Collins family members, Barnabas is still fixated on Josette. This love obsession becomes his vampiric ruin when he tries to recreate that love with someone else.

Maggie Evans, a Collinsport waitress, is his first victim because of her striking resemblance to Josette. Barnabas kidnaps her and brainwashes her into believing that she truly is Josette. Even though she escapes, she is traumatized into a regressed state and is placed in Wyndcliff Sanitarium. Barnabas next seduces and attempts to bite Victoria Winters, the governess of the eleven-year-old David Collins, last of the Collins descendants. Their affair continues for some time and endures a lot of time travel, until 1796, when Victoria meets Peter Bradford, a law student who unsuccessfully defends her against witchcraft accusations and with whom she falls in love. Maggie assumes Victoria's governess position and catches Barnabas's attention again.

He also falls for Lady Kitty Hampshire, a former governess at Collinwood who returns after the death of her husband. As the actual (not presumed, as with Maggie) modern reincarnation of Josette, she is engaged to Edward Collins but breaks off the engagement to pursue love with Barnabas. However, when she puts on Josette's wedding dress, Kitty steps through a time portal in Josette's portrait that ultimately leads Barnabas back in time, too.

True Love

These women all point to another of Barnabas's great weaknesses: being a hopeless romantic. He spends his life and unlife believing his true love is Josette, but she is, after all, the one he betrayed with Angelique. After so much conflict, he realizes that he loves Angelique, but it is only shortly before she dies and could easily have been brought on by the moment. Blinded by infatuation, Barnabas doesn't recognize true love when it comes to him in the form of Dr. Julia Hoffman.

Throughout the *Dark Shadows* story, Julia counters the effects of Angelique's actions even after Angelique warns her that "the pursuit of Barnabas Collins can lead to nothing but misery. He is a cold, harsh, unresponsive man." Julia simply replies, "Who made him that way?" Julia loves him despite what he is, and sacrifices everything not only to protect him but also to cure him.

"You'll be making a serious mistake if you pursue this, Professor," Barnabas warns her at one point. Because she knows his secret, he tries to drive her insane and kill her. But in the end, Julia's influence brings him back to a level of humanity that makes friendship possible and turns him into the better, more human version of himself. She becomes his best friend, her own real love for him forever unrequited. Barnabas remains focused on other objects of infatuation, choosing immature women over the one who could offer him a real relationship and denying his true feelings to himself.

Barnabas skulking around the manor at Collinwood.

Ghosts

Barnabas is haunted by his past, and, more literally, by the people he loved. These people materialize throughout the story to protect others, and to protect him from himself. He becomes focused on the idea of Josette's ghost thanks to Victoria. According to her, it haunts the estate, and even acts as a protector to little David.

Then Sarah, the eleven-year-old sister Barnabas lost as a human, appears as a spirit, playing with a ball and singing "London Bridge." She helps Maggie escape from Barnabas's brainwashing and then from the asylum, saving her but also saving Barnabas from himself by preventing him from creating a twisted version of his love, Josette. Sarah also tries several times to sway Barnabas from his course when he tries to take Victoria as his bride.

Ultimately, it's Josette's spirit who stops Barnabas from his psychotic attempts at regaining her. When he calls her back from the grave, she asks Barnabas to free her and to move on. It takes telling him she didn't love him to break his obsession, freeing him from his guilt over her death and their lost love.

Lowest Point

Although he experiences many lows with the women he loves, the lowest point in Barnabas's life occurs with his father, Joshua. Having killed or driven insane much of his family and the town, Barnabas turns to (or on) his father. When he tries to kill him, Joshua exclaims, "You would kill even me! You must have always had so much hatred in you. No one could be filled with it so quickly!" It's the breaking point he needs, and he begs his father to kill him instead.

He can't, but he does lock him away in the tower room of Collinwood Mansion. Joshua studies vampirism in the hopes of saving his son, and he eventually enlists the help of a witch, Bathia Mapes, who goes up in flames of her own magic while attempting the spell. Again Barnabas begs to die, but Joshua still can't kill him. Instead, he has a servant, Ben Stokes, lock him in a coffin wrapped in chains with a cross nailed to the inside at the family crypt in Eagle's Hill Cemetery. The departing servant tells him he wasn't a good person while he was a human, either. This, his last interaction for centuries, couldn't be a more depressing send-off.

Powers

Barnabas has standard vampiric powers as far as the dark angels are concerned. Like Dracula (see "Vlad Dracula: Darkly Original"), he possesses supernatural strength, mind-control abilities, and shape-shifting capability. His mental powers center around hypnotism, which he often uses on humans, and his shape-shifting is limited to bat transformations and the ability to materialize and dematerialize like a magician.

Much of Barnabas's work is performed through magic. He conjures spirits to haunt Julia and trap Reverend Trask, a fanatical witch hunter. Also, he brings forth the spirit of Josette to warn the Collins family. He also uses the *I Ching* to travel extensively through time. As he puts it, "For most men, time moves slowly, oh so slowly, they don't even realize it. But time has revealed itself to me in a very special way."

FACTS AND TRIVIA

- Just after the end of the *Dark Shadows* series, head writer Sam Hall revealed in a *TV Guide* article that Barnabas was intended to recognize that he truly loved Julia. The two would marry in Singapore, moving on from the Collinsport, Maine, drama and into a new life.

- Barnabas has several treasured keepsakes: a cane with a silver wolf's head handle, a signet ring, a handcrafted music box he gave Josette when he sent her to Boston, and portraits of himself and Josette.

QUOTES

"I didn't say she was dead; I said I killed her." —Dark Shadows

"It was the most tragic night I have ever experienced. It all began when my mother discovered my coffin." —Dark Shadows

"Do I frighten you, Forbes? I do not plan to kill you, at least not here, now. Later Forbes, after you've had time to think about it. Nine o'clock. When the clock strikes nine, you will die." —Dark Shadows

"I said you were my friend, and how I wish that were the truth. But I am past the point when friends are possible. I'm sorry." —Dark Shadows

"At last darkness has come. Goodbye, Maggie Evans. I might have loved you, I might have spared you, but now you must die." —Dark Shadows

SPIKE: DARK POET

Played by actor James Marsters in ninety-seven episodes of the wildly popular television series **Buffy the Vampire Slayer** *created by Joss Whedon and produced by David Greenwalt, bad-boy bloodsucker Spike has also had a vigorous afterlife in the expanded Buffy-verse of comic books and tie-in novels, and made memorable guest appearances on the* **Buffy** *spin-off series,* **Angel.**

Spike is the resident poet among the dark angels. Palling around with Angelus (aka Angel) in the Buffy-verse, he goes from being a bad romantic poet to a badass, slayer-killing vampire. For stress relief and pure entertainment, he slaughters humans, vampires, and demons. To most, he's a sociopath with a wicked sense of humor. But even centuries of pillaging haven't taken this poet's soul.

William the Bloody

Spike's entire existence revolves around poetry and romance. Born William, he was a sniveling gentleman in London. As any true mama's boy, he lived with his mother, Anne, who sang "Early One Morning" to him his entire life, which eventually became a hypnotic trigger used by The First Evil, an incorporeal, shape-shifting being composed of all evil in existence, to control him. As a young man, William becomes a romantic poet, and a horrible one considering he is given the moniker William the Bloody. Apparently even putting his soul into his writing isn't enough to keep it from being "bloody awful."

Then, that love of romance leads William to Drusilla, who sires him into vampirism after another woman breaks his heart. His remaining love for his human mother, Anne, dying of tuberculosis, leads him to change her into a vampire in an attempt to save her. Eventually, Anne becomes as twisted as the others and abusive toward William, forcing him to kill her. It is perhaps the most traumatic experience of his existence, and he writes a poem centuries later titled "The Wanton Folly of Me Mum."

Spike waiting in the shadows for his dinner, acting much tougher than William the Bloody, the human poet he once was.

Dear Drusilla

Spike's love of Drusilla dictates the remainder of his unlife. As he puts it, their love is "eternal. Literally." With her, he redesigns himself, even developing a working-class accent and a Billy Idol look similar to that of his dark angels predecessor, David of *The Lost Boys* (see "David: The Original Vampire Rebel"). William finds his inner tough guy and develops a reputation for cruelty to rival that of his grandsire and mentor, Angelus (aka Angel). As he tells Angel later, referring to Angel's previous misdeeds and mentorship as Angelus, "You were my sire, man! You were my . . . Yoda." And the lessons take well. Spike is as cruel and dangerous as his vampire family, threatened only by Angelus's relationship with Drusilla. As Angelus says once Spike starts something, "He doesn't stop until everything in his path is dead."

In spite of it all, Spike maintains the ability to remain loyal and truly loving while the others are indeed soulless. He follows his heart through time, and it's Spike's love for Dru that leads him to Sunnydale to save her, and ultimately, reunite with Angelus. It motivates Spike's turning Angelus into Angel again, just so that he can keep Dru to himself. When she breaks off with him, the lovesick vampire turns to the humans in the episode "Lovers Walk," saying: "She wouldn't even kill me. She just left. She didn't even care enough to cut off my head or set me on fire. I mean, is that too much to ask? You know, some little sign that she cared?" Spike says that Drusilla left because he had "gone soft," then adds, "I gave her everything. Beautiful jewels, beautiful dresses with beautiful girls in them, but nothing made her happy." Sadly, his poetic, romantic nature makes him seem weak to the psychotic Dru.

Spike's undead ineptitude is compounded when The Initiative (aka Demon Research Initiative), a secret US government agency designed to research demons for military use, implants him with a microchip that renders him biteless. It strips him of his vampire masculinity, rendering him essentially impotent. Ultimately, Spike is humiliated.

Buffybot

It only gets worse when he realizes he's in love with Buffy, a Sunnydale High School cheerleader chosen to be the slayer (vampire killer and all-around protector of humanity) for her generation, who also has an on-again, off-again love affair with Angel. Again caught up in emotion, Spike kidnaps her to show his love by killing Drusilla in front of her. When that doesn't work, he comes up with the Buffybot, a robot replica of Buffy programmed to love him. The idea backfires, disgusting Buffy and driving her further away.

Only when Spike almost dies to protect Buffy, her sister, and her friends does Buffy begin to appreciate him. The two eventually form a physical relationship, but Spike, unsatisfied by the lack of real love he feels coming from her, pushes until Buffy admits to using him. This heartbreak inspires him to leave Sunnydale to travel, where he encounters the Demon Trials, a set of arduous physical tests that earn the return of Spike's soul.

Spike in his vamp form with Buffy in his grasp. Or is that the Buffybot?

In the end, his love for Buffy turns him into a hero to equal the demon Drusilla's influence has created. Sacrificing himself to destroy an entrance to hell resembling an open mouth known as the Hellmouth, he dies a fiery death. There, Buffy grants him his greatest wish, saying, "I love you." Spike, always true to his feelings, replies, "No, you don't. But thanks for saying it." He dies, seeing the fight to the end, as Angel said he always did.

Love's Bitch

A brief reincarnation on the spin-off series *Angel* gives Spike the chance to return to his human love: poetry. He attends a bar's open mic night for poetry to celebrate his last day and performs a poem he'd begun composing before Dru sired him. The performance is a success, finally reconciling his move from William the Bloody to Spike the hero.

In the end, Spike puts it best when he says, "I may be love's bitch, but at least I'm man enough to admit it."

Deadly, Too . . .

Being a poetic, lovesick vampire isn't Spike's only lot in life. He's also one of the deadliest— if not the deadliest—of the Buffy world. During his appearance in Sunnydale, his attack on Buffy and a large group of people at her school is the deadliest of the series. But it's not just the humans who should fear him. Spike is well known for killing at least two slayers. The first was in China during the Boxer Rebellion, and that slayer gave him the notable scar over his left eyebrow. The second was Nikki Wood, whom he killed in a New York subway in 1977. Spike's symbolic leather jacket came from Wood's corpse.

Even Dracula (see "Vlad Dracula: Darkly Original") has had run-ins with the punk vamp. In 1898, Spike purchased a signed copy of the book *Dracula* for eleven pounds. The story outing vampires irks Spike, who thinks it's dangerous to their kind. Then, when Dracula tosses Spike's book into the fire during a confrontation, he sparks an eternal rivalry that the two vampires revisit over the ages.

And Oh-So Funny

Despite Spike's danger and violence, he's always funny. It often seems the more dangerous the situation, the funnier Spike is. This is the case from the first moment we see him cruising into Sunnydale. Spike's first victim in town becomes the "Welcome to Sunnydale" sign. He knocks it over when he arrives, cracking up anyone with a sense of humor. Then he assaults the sign again when he returns, heartbroken over Drusilla's dumping him, and finally when he closes the Hellmouth, putting his mark on the very entrance to the town.

Spike has a nickname for everyone, whether it's used for insult or endearment. Drusilla is known as "Pet," as is Buffy. He even makes a "Slutty the Vampire Slayer" remark. Buffy's red-haired friend, Willow, receives the nickname "Red." Dawn, Buffy's younger sister, gets a few epithets referring to being younger, such as "Little Bit," "Nibblet," and "Platelet." The funniest names are reserved for Angel, whom he calls "Poof," "Peaches," "Captain Forehead," and "Yoda." The nicknames are just the beginning. Spike's interactions with people are sprinkled with wit.

FACTS AND TRIVIA

- Creator Whedon has made several attempts to create a Spike movie, but to date, funding has held up attempts.

QUOTES

"If every vampire who said he was at the Crucifixion was actually there it would've been like Woodstock." —Buffy the Vampire Slayer, *"School Hard"*

"Beneath me. I'll show her. Six bloody feet beneath me. Hasn't got a death wish? Bitch won't need one." —Buffy the Vampire Slayer, *"Fool for Love"*

"Damn right, I'm impure. I'm as impure as the driven yellow snow!" —Buffy the Vampire Slayer, *"Intervention"*

"You know you take the killing for granted. And then it's gone. And you're like, I wish I'd appreciated it more. Stopped and smelled the corpses." —Buffy the Vampire Slayer, *"Where the Wild Things Are"*

"I'll find her—wherever she is—tie her up. Torture her till she likes me again. Love's a funny thing." —Buffy the Vampire Slayer, *"Lovers Walk"*

"Yeah. We're all one big happy Manson family." —Angel, *"Not Fade Away"*

MINA HARKER: DRACULA'S ANGEL

A perennial heroine of the vampire genre, who becomes a vampire herself for a time, Mina Harker (née Wilhemina Murray) was introduced by Bram Stoker in his 1897 novel Dracula. *Adaptors of Stoker's book have taken great liberties with her personality, sometimes blending or switching her identity with that of her best friend, Lucy Westenra, who becomes a vampire and is destroyed. In the novel, there is nothing romantic about her relationship with Dracula, but recent adaptations—most notably* **Bram Stoker's Dracula** *(1992), directed by Francis Ford Coppola and starring Winona Ryder as Mina—have transformed Dracula's predation into a romance of reincarnation spanning centuries. Mina Harker is also a character in the comic book series* **League of Extraordinary Gentlemen** *by Allan Moore and Kevin O'Neill, in which she encounters other classic monsters, including Dr. Jekyll and Mr. Hyde, and the Invisible Man. In Stephen Norrington's 2003 film adaptation,* **The League of Extraordinary Gentlemen,** *Mina (played by Peta Wilson) also has a relationship with Oscar Wilde's mysterious antihero, Dorian Gray.*

If Dracula is the father of the dark angels, Mina is their queen. Among the oldest female vamps, only Mina has the strength and heart to stand with the boys. Via the love of the legendary Count Dracula (see "Vlad Dracula: Darkly Original"), she undergoes a massive transformation from the sweet teacher of etiquette and decorum, Miss Wilhelmina Murray, to Mrs. Mina Harker, the nocturnal vixen.

Twisted Courtship

During a summer visit to see her friend Lucy Westenra in the seacoast town of Whitby, in North Yorkshire, England, Mina begins the journey that changes her life. She leaves and travels to Budapest to nurse her fiancée back to health after he escapes from Count Dracula's castle. Jonathan Harker had traveled to Transylvania to sell property to Dracula, only to discover his client to be a five-hundred-year-old vampire plotting to invade Britain. Back

Mina, in her feistier years, as seen in the film *The League of Extraordinary Gentlemen*. As a vampire, Dracula's love can handle even the most deadly villian.

in Whitby, Lucy dies from a mystifying illness brought on by an animal that repeatedly attacks her to drink her blood at night, resulting in severe blood loss. Dracula, of course, is the culprit, having arrived in Whitby in a ghostly shipwreck.

Joining Jonathan, vampire hunter Professor Abraham Van Helsing, and others who seek to destroy Dracula, Mina catches the monster's attention and becomes the focus of his obsession. After no less than three bites and after one instance of feeding on Dracula's blood, she becomes connected to him and in danger of becoming a vampire upon her death. A psychic link to Dracula allows her to lead the others to him, bringing about his destruction and releasing her from his curse. Mina marries Jonathan, and the two name their first son Quincey after their brave American friend Quincey Morris, who died in the final fight against Dracula in Transylvania. But is that truly the end?

In several versions of the story, Mina isn't freed by killing the Count. Instead, she becomes a vampire after his death. Furthermore, her son Quincey is rumored to actually be the child of the Count, who impregnated her when he held her captive. Also, in *From the Pages of Bram Stoker's Dracula: Harker*, novelist Tony Lee tells us that Mina is bound to Dracula's spirit, and his surviving cohorts try to bring his spirit back in the body of Quincey.

Perfectly Female

In her innocence, Mina reflects the ideal Victorian woman and the opposite of the rebellious Lucy. Stoker describes her as pure and angelic. According to John Ruskin in *Appendix G: Gender*, the Victorian woman was to be cool, submissive, virginal, and above reproach. Mina is the absolute picture of Christian virtue. Van Helsing, the leader of the "good" side in the story and Dracula's antithesis, extols her character: "She is one of God's women, fashioned by His own hand to show us men and other women that there is a heaven where we can enter, and that its light can be here on earth. So true, so sweet, so noble, so little an egoist."

But the perceived innocence is a façade, covering the hidden inner powers that are Mina's greatest asset. Inside, she isn't the fainting beauty she lets the men around her believe she is, and her actions prove it. It is Mina who does the research and acquires all the materials to fully understand Dracula and finally destroy him. Then, when Lucy dies, it is Mina who pushes on, insisting that they discuss the details of her death. Later on, Van Helsing sees this in her and compliments her the only way his sensibilities will allow: "Ah, that wonderful Madam Mina! She has man's brain—a brain that a man should have were he much gifted—and woman's heart." He praises her ability to act logically and against her emotions when necessary.

Mina, the human girl and Victorian angel depicted in the film *Bram Stoker's Dracula*, worried more about being like her sexy friend Lucy than about the sexist judgments of men, as she later does.

Dark Evolution

The men around Mina see her as pure and perfect, and fail to recognize the longing she has for a life where she can embrace a more realistic identity. She expresses this openly as she watches Lucy flirt with suitors at a party. "Lucy is a pure and virtuous girl. But, I admit that her free way of speaking shocks me sometimes. Jonathan says it is a defect of the aristocracy that they say what they please. The truth is that I admire Lucy, and I'm not surprised that men flock around her. I wish I were as pretty and as adored as she," she says. With her fiancée denouncing Lucy's behavior, Mina doesn't dare venture into that conduct.

This is of no concern to the Count. He is openly attracted to her and doesn't hesitate to come close. His respect and adoration empower Mina and win her affection in a way that Jonathan couldn't imagine. She finally succumbs, telling Dracula, "I want to be what you are, see what you see, love what you love. . . ."

He responds with another empowering statement: "Then, I give you life eternal. Everlasting love. The power of the storm. And the beasts of the earth. Walk with me to be my loving wife, forever."

It's through this acceptance and recognition of Mina as an equal, a way that most Victorian men wouldn't dream of acting, that Dracula sets in motion changes that she secretly longs for, including, perhaps, bearing Dracula's child in the form of Quincey.

A New Woman

Living independently as a vampire in *The League of Extraordinary Gentlemen*, Mina is a force, both in physical and mental strength. If anything, she becomes a wiser opposite of her younger, mortal self. She seems to almost despise her former virtues. The sensuality she expressed with Dracula also seems to be a thing of the past, as Dorian Gray, another former lover, says, "Ah. The bedroom, Mina. Does it give you memories? Or ideas?" "Ideas," she replies, and stabs him in the groin.

It is Allan Quatermain, the famous adventurer/explorer, whom she acts most in opposition to, perhaps because of his old-fashioned sensibilities. Among other things, she mocks his attempt at genteel behavior. She also challenges his assumptions about her femininity: "And I imagine you with quite the library, Mr. Quatermain. All those books you must have read merely by looking at their covers." Quatermain receives the brunt of her rebellion against the Victorian virtues she'd once embodied.

Like her maker, Mina has several preternatural gifts. First, she possesses superior strength and speed, as we see her take out several grown men, achieving near-invisibility through her speed as she moves between them. She can also shape-shift into a flurry of bats.

FACTS AND TRIVIA

- Mina is also known by other names. In some versions of the F. W. Murnau film *Nosferatu*, she is known as Ellen; in others, Nina. In *Nosferatu*, she sacrifices herself in order to keep Count Orlok (see "Count Orlok: Primo Nosferatu") in the sun to kill him. In both Mel Brooks's parody *Dracula: Dead and Loving It* and the 1931 film that is well known as "Bela Lugosi's" *Dracula*, Mina's last name is Seward due to her characterization as Dr. Seward's daughter. In John Badham's 1979 *Dracula*, she is Van Helsing's daughter and plays a Lucy-esque role.

Mina, holding her own with the legendary Dorian Grey. It is hinted that the two had a torrid affair at some point after Dracula died.

QUOTES

"But doesn't each life possess a soul? Even a fly and the sparrow? Can one take a life without being responsible for the soul?" —Great Performances: Count Dracula

"I dreamt that my life was slowly being drained away and that when I had no more blood, my soul would never find peace." —Great Performances: Count Dracula

"Take me away from all this death!" —Bram Stoker's Dracula

"You broke my heart once. This time you missed." —The League of Extraordinary Gentlemen

"Don't worry; I've had my fill of throats for this evening."
—The League of Extraordinary Gentlemen

ASHER: THE WOUNDED ANGEL

Asher is a dark angel of powerful sexual energy, physically disfigured yet physically irresistible. He loves both men and women and is a recurring character in most of Laurell K. Hamilton's best-selling Anita Blake Vampire Hunter novels, including **Burnt Offerings** *(1998),* **Blue Moon** *(1998),* **Narcissus in Chains** *(2001),* **Cerulean Sins** *(2003),* **Incubus Dreams** *(2004),* **Danse Macabre** *(2006),* **The Harlequin** *(2007), and* **Skin Trade** *(2009).*

A sher is the one dark angel who is as scarred bodily as he is emotionally. Holy water scars cover the right side of his face, sparing his nose and neck, but begin again at the shoulder and continue downward. Still, from the moment we meet this six-hundred-year-old through vampire hunter Anita Blake's eyes in *Burnt Offerings*, blowing smoke rings and laughing at the gun Anita points at him, the mix of angelic beauty and dark pain defines his essential character. Without the scars, Asher would be just another incredibly beautiful vampire.

Scars

The scars are more than just mangled flesh. They represent the rift between Asher and Jean-Claude (see "Jean-Claude: Seductive Dark Master"), his long-term best friend and lover, now the Master of the City in which Asher lives. Prior to the scars, Asher was renowned for his beauty. His only competition in appearance was Jean-Claude, whom he was initially jealous of. Soon, they became lovers and formed a love triangle with Asher's former human servant, Julianna (one exceedingly lucky human). They were blissfully happy together for twenty years.

It ended badly in the seventeenth century, when Asher and Julianna were tortured by the church while Jean-Claude was away. Helpless, Asher was forced to endure agony by zealots who hoped to "burn the devil out" of him with holy water. Jean-Claude managed to rescue Asher, but Julianna was burned at the stake.

No photos of Asher exist at this time. Above is one witness's recreation of the angelic, scarred vampire's appearance. As always, he finds a sexy way to hide his scars.

The physical scarring, though emotionally traumatizing for someone as beautiful as Asher, is not the only pain remaining from that incident. It is the beginning of the rift between himself and Jean-Claude, who becomes a scapegoat. Asher, unable to cope with so much loss, blames Jean-Claude for rescuing him when he'd have preferred that Julianna live. The last words she cried out as she died were Jean-Claude's name, not Asher's, only adding to his pain.

Returning to court, Belle Morte (Jean-Claude and Asher's master) uses the disfigured Asher to punish others, forcing them to have sex with Asher because she believes his scars are disgusting. This humiliation adds yet again to the blame he feels toward Jean-Claude. Jean-Claude, feeling guilty for the death, tries to save Asher's life again by appealing to the Vampire Council, the France-based ruling vampire body composed of the eight most power-ful vampires, the Sourdre de Sangs, or founders of vampire lines. Even Jean-Claude's agree-ment to serve the Council for a hundred years in exchange for Asher's life isn't enough to repair the damage to their relationship. Asher can't forgive him. Only the life of Anita Blake, Jean-Claude's twentieth-century love, human servant, and necromancer, could begin to repay him for the pain of his lost Julianna, and Asher is happy to collect that payment.

Healing

When Asher leaves France, where he works for the council, and arrives in St. Louis, Mis-souri, the city Jean-Claude currently rules, to kill Anita in a flamboyant act of vengeance, he is shocked by her acceptance of him. Instead of killing her, he's intrigued by her feistiness and the love she shares with Jean-Claude, which mimics the relationship Julianna had been the center of. Asher chooses to stay. Using his long, stunningly beautiful hair to hide his scars, he blends in with the humans. This camouflage mirrors the hiding of his emotional scars, allowing Asher to ease into the relationship that his former lover has forged with Anita. It also allows him to take his place as Temoin, or second-in-command, under Jean-Claude and as the manager of the Circus of the Damned.

As their relationship with Anita blooms, Asher pays less attention to the physical scars that cover his body. With each step he takes on the road to accepting his scars, his emotional scars heal. When he and Anita first become lovers in *Cerulean Sins*, another mention is made of his having scar tissue removed from his genital area in a sort of circumcision to become wholly, sexually functional. This removal of the skin goes along with the reinstatement of a love triangle, though this one is with Jean-Claude and a human woman. Asher's emotional state further improves as he accepts Anita's love and her preference for kissing and caressing his scarred skin. It is then that Asher can admit that Jean-Claude would also have been simi-larly hurt if he had been present when Asher and Julianna were captured.

Hopeful that a plastic surgeon will be able to repair his scars, Asher gains a renewed confidence. In *Skin Trade*, it seems almost certain that the scars will be removed with Anita's help, and with it will surely come a renewed confidence in his appearance and a chance at the love he'd long thought lost.

The Darker Side

Though seductive and genteel, Asher has a darker side. He makes no excuses for his cravings, be they for blood, sex, or other indulgences, and he expects the same of those around him. At times, he can be a bit too blunt and demanding, not to mention intimidating. In *Narcissus in Chains,* Asher lets that dark side show. When Jean-Claude gluts himself on Micah, one of Anita's many lovers, Asher's jealousy prompts Anita to say, "Fuck you, Asher."

Not a smart move. Asher's reaction to her words is priceless:

> He was suddenly moving forward in a blur of speed. I backed up so fast that I fell against the couch. Micah caught me, or I'd have fallen to the floor. I had time to draw a gun, or a knife, but I didn't even try. Asher wasn't trying to hurt my body, just my feelings. He bent at the waist, looming over me and Micah, though I think that part was accidental. He put a hand on either side of us and leaned into my face, so close that I had to pull back to focus on those chilling blue eyes. "Don't offer things you're not willing to do, ma cherie, because that is annoying."

Asher's little display is just a warning in response to her disrespectful display, retaliation for dismissing his feelings, but it contrasts with the other vampires, who are happy to share Anita with numerous men. Not only is Asher in love with Jean-Claude and Anita, but he also confesses in *Danse Macabre* to wanting more. He wants someone to love him and only him, to be exclusively enraptured by his beauty and soul, as a lover rightly should be. If there's any justice in his world, it will happen soon.

On the Furry Side

Thanks to the threesome he's formed in St. Louis, Asher has increased power and a new ability. As with other master vampires in the world of Anita Blake, Asher now has an "animal to call:" The hyena and werehyena physically come to him whenever he calls one with his power. This new ability suits him completely, considering that Europeans used to associate the animals with deviant sexual behavior. Even early naturalists mistakenly considered the hyena a homosexual animal. Furthermore, Asher's distinctive laugh and mottled appearance are reflected in the haunting laugh and strange physical features of the hyena.

Powers

Asher is strong. In fact, he's a Master Vampire and should be ruling his own city, even if other vampires underestimate him. Were it not for his love for Jean-Claude, he probably would, but he stays, content to be with those he loves. After all, it was roughly three hundred years that he lived with the pain of losing Julianna and Jean-Claude.

His powers reflect his being of Belle Morte's lineage and revolve around physical pleasure, in particular flat-out seduction. Appearance is the most obvious of Asher's powers. Although scarred, he is still beautiful enough to mesmerize his victims. It is, perhaps, the ability to weaken his prey's psychological defenses that gives Asher the ability to "roll" Anita when no one else seems capable of doing so.

He can also fly. According to Anita, he flies better than any other vampire she's seen. At a distance, his laugh can touch others, taking on a physical quality. Anita describes the sound as "[slithering] across my skin like the touch of fur, soft and feeling—oh, so slightly—of death." It's a talent that Jean-Claude also possesses, which indicates it may be part of Belle Morte's line because he too is one of her progeny.

When the victim is within Asher's grasp, his bite can bring sexual release in his prey. However, the same bite produces an addiction to him. The victim experiences sexual flashbacks from the experience, and in Anita's case the sexual energy created by those flashbacks can be used as a source of power for Asher. Most others of his kind lean toward being either seductive or deadly. Asher mixes both aspects of his nature to make an even more formidable power. It might not be all lightning bolts and future telling, but that certainly puts Asher on the "Dark Angels Not to Screw With" list.

FACTS AND TRIVIA

- Asher can put Anita under a hypnotic trance, which she calls "rolling." No other vampire can. This suggests that Asher is possibly the most powerful vampire that Anita knows.

- The name Asher is a Hebrew name meaning "happy" or "blessed." Asher, in the Old Testament of the Bible, was a son of Jacob and Zilpah, Leah's handmaid. Some experts believe the name was derived from Ashur, the head Assyrian deity.

QUOTES

"There are worse things than death, Jean-Claude." —Burnt Offerings

"You want to pat me down? I could rip you into pieces with my bare hands, and you're worried I have a gun. . . . That is so very cute." —Burnt Offerings

"If he would only cooperate, it could be a happy foursome." [at mention of the werewolf Richard seeking a new mate]. —Blue Moon

"To drink from you is to give you power over any of us. I do not want to be your slave any more than I already am." [to Anita when she offers blood to heal him] —Blue Moon

"I would move all of hell to reach your side, you know that." —Narcissus in Chains

"I would rather try and fail, than regret never having tried at all." —Narcissus in Chains

STEFAN SALVATORE: THE VIRTUOUS BROTHER

Stefan Salvatore and his brother, Damon, are, without question, the most popular fraternal vampires you'll find anywhere. Introduced by novelist L. J. Smith for her 1991 Vampire Diaries trilogy, The Awakening, The Struggle, *and* The Fury, *and later resurrected for* The Dark Reunion *(1998), the Salvatores are currently featured in a new trilogy,* The Vampire Diaries: The Return. *In the novels, the Salvatore brothers are turned into vampires in Renaissance Italy and later emigrate to America; in* The Vampire Diaries *television series (where Stefan is played by actor Paul Wesley), their transformation happens during the Civil War. In both incarnations of their story, they battle for the affections of high school student Elena Gilbert, the reincarnation of a lost love.*

Stefan Salvatore is the perpetual younger brother. He's handsome and well mannered, plays wide receiver on the high school football team, is an excellent dancer, and enjoys a bit of solitude as much as the next vampire. He can be naive, but that also lends a certain boyish attraction that's hard for a vampire to retain. Above all else, he defines himself by his ethics and his relationship with his brother, Damon (see "Damon Salvatore: Heartbroken Rogue").

Oh, So Guilty

Like many dark angels, Stefan spends much of his undead existence in guilt for what he is, leading to his overall brooding demeanor. Popular opinion is that he is simply repentant for his vampiric nature. He is, after all, bent on refraining from the consumption of human blood, and this voluntary restriction seems to give him a great deal of pain. Stefan makes that clear when he says, "If I just give myself over to the blood, I can make that pain stop. Every day, I fight that." This all-consuming guilt also leads to more than a few moments of Stefan being slightly self-absorbed and a bit overly dramatic.

Stefan, as portrayed by actor Paul Wesley in the *Vampire Diaries* television series, has a James Dean-ish look, as does his fellow dark angel Edward Cullen.

But, he may also feel guilt over his relationship with his brother. Damon hates him for things that he had no control over, including their mother dying as a result of his birth and his father coddling him while treating Damon so poorly. Any sibling would feel some level of empathy for a brother whose life has been so disrupted by his or her very existence.

Added to that is the guilt Stefan carries for Damon's loss of Katherine, the vampire who turned both brothers. Damon, who doesn't love easily, fell completely for Katherine who, shortly after beginning an affair with him, started seeing Stefan as well. Katherine was selfish and wanted both of them, but Damon wanted exclusivity. The ensuing struggle for her affection is what caused Katherine to fake her death and leave both men for dead after a duel over her. Stefan recovered from his grief, but Damon did not. And Stefan expresses his guilt in *The Fury* when she holds them captive: "Katherine, please listen to me! We've all hurt one another enough. Please let us go now. Or keep me, if you want, but let [him] leave. I'm the one that's to blame. Keep me, and I'll do whatever you want." Sure, they're the ramblings of a man desperate to escape being burned alive, but someone who truly felt no remorse over his more pampered life would have left Damon to burn because of all the horrible things he'd done.

Knight in Shining . . .

Whether the guilt is over Damon or simply being a vampire, it causes Stefan to retreat after Katherine convinces him she committed suicide. This insulates him from the centuries of suffering that Damon endures, leaving Stefan much more human than his brother. Unlike others, much of his existence has been sheltered, leaving him a bit naive. This naivety allows him to shine as a noble supernatural protector. In fact, he's a sweetheart, determined to protect Elena, the modern reincarnation of Katherine (minus the spoiled attitude) and keep her as innocent as she was when they arrived in Fell's Church (aka Mystic Falls). This is completely in line with his strong moral code and overall chivalrous nature that could be originally attributed to his having been born a member of nobility, his Catholic upbringing, or simply his personality.

This essential humanity disparity between the two brothers is one that neither will let go. While Damon pushes Stefan to open his sensibilities, Stefan fights back, attempting to remind him of his true (and rather human) feelings. "Katherine is dead, and you hate me because you loved her," Stefan points out. "And that, my brother, is your humanity." This very human attempt to steer Damon onto the right path also reflects the undying hope that Stefan holds for his brother, because of his love for him.

As Stefan's last name implies, he is a savior, especially to Elena.

Powers, Shmowers

To Stefan, power isn't the pinnacle of existence as it is to so many others. In fact, his refusal to drink human blood, opting instead for animal blood, severely limits his access to power. Though he does have the basic speed and strength we've come to expect among vampires, that's pretty much where it ends. He has the ability to manipulate minds, but not on Damon's level. He also doesn't have his brother's shape-shifting abilities until partaking of the forbidden drink.

Stefan needs Damon because of these decisions. If not for his brother, Stefan would need to drink blood in order to protect Elena and the others from the vampires that do. However, drinking this human blood would be crossing a line for him. His humanity is much more intact than it is in the others, and killing humans to survive would probably give him post-traumatic stress disorder. He also makes a point of refraining from using his powers because he would be using them against those weaker than him in most cases, but he often lets (and even encourages) Damon to use his. Why the double standard? Maybe it's because he feels that Damon has nothing to lose. The answer isn't given directly, but Stefan does say, "I don't hurt people. I don't do that. I'm the good brother."

⁓ FACTS AND TRIVIA ⁓

- We know that Salvatore in Italian means "savior", but what about Stefan's first name? According to behindthename.com, Stefan is the Romanian version of the English name Stephen. Stephen is from the Greek (Stephanos) meaning "crown." The saint bearing the same name in the Book of Acts in the New Testament of the Bible is considered the first Christian martyr. The name fits our Stefan perfectly.

❧❧ QUOTES ❧❧

"Do you know what the name Salvatore *means in Italian, Elena? It means "salvation, savior." I'm named that, and for St. Stephen, he was the first Christian martyr. And I damned my brother to hell."* —The Awakening *(novel)*

"When Katherine died, I thought I could never love anyone else. Even though I knew she would have wanted me to, I was sure it could never happen. But I was wrong." —The Struggle *(novel)*

Elena: "FYI: Our team sucks. They could use you."
Stefan: "Can't. I'm a loner." —"Friday Night Bites" *(television episode)*

"I thought there was hope, that somewhere deep inside, something in Damon was still human, normal. But I was wrong. There's nothing human left in Damon. No good, no kindness, no love. Only a monster . . . *who must be stopped."* —"Friday Night Bites" *(television episode)*

"Everything you know, and every belief that you have, is about to change. Are you ready for that?" —"The Lost Girls" *(television episode)*

Damon: "I could rip your heart out and not think twice about it."
Stefan: "I've heard that before." —"History Repeating" *(television episode)*

Chapter Two
Dark Rulers

Kings among kings, these dark angels are leaders. They sacrifice
a life of privacy and peace for leadership. They're servants of
their people, but they won't take crap from anybody.
Rulers command respect and demand loyalty because
when things go badly, the buck stops with them.

ERIC NORTHMAN: ANGELIC VIKING

The vampire world needs its own law enforcement, and Eric Northman, Area Five sheriff of undead Louisiana, is both good cop and (very) bad cop in Charlaine Harris's best-selling Southern Vampire Mysteries series of novels. Adapted as **True Blood** *for television, the multi-season HBO hit features charismatic Swedish actor Alexander Skarsgård interpreting Eric for a ravenously loyal audience base.*

Nomadic pirates, pillaging and plundering. Bloodthirsty warriors. Such beings have much in common with vampires. Supernatural powers and primitive human instincts combine to lethal effect in Eric Northman. But his ability to be honest with his emotions is what makes this Viking vampire the epitome of power.

Snarl in the Face of Death

Sitting atop a throne at the Shreveport vampire bar Fangtasia isn't exactly what you'd expect of an ancient warrior, but modern times don't allow for the old-fashioned bloodbaths Eric loves so much. Even in the face of death, Eric is always eager to fight. It is this extraordinary warrior spirit that initially caught the attention of Godric, Eric's maker in *True Blood* (as opposed to the Roman vampire Appius Livius Ocella in the books) and proves at times to be a weakness.

In the *True Blood* episode "Never Let Me Go," he clings to his combative nature before and after his change. One of his fallen comrades, dying with him on a pyre, tells him, "All will be well. Don't be afraid." Eric replies, "I'm not afraid. I'm pissed off." Eric's warrior companions are soon slaughtered while he lies helpless. Rid of the intrusive humans, Godric tells the dying Eric of his admiration for his fighting ability. "I would fight you now if I could," he replies.

Death, and centuries of immortal life, does nothing to change his attitude. In *Definitely Dead*, the carnage of vampire battles reenergizes him. As recounted by Sookie Stackhouse, telepathic human waitress and his newest lover, the scene defines him:

Alexander Skarsgård as Eric in *True Blood*, an original Viking demonstrating his willingness to fight.

Carried away on a wave of excitement, Eric kissed me long and hard and then scooped up Wybert's head. "Bowling for vampires," he said happily, and flung the disgusting object at the black vampire with an accuracy and force that knocked the sword out of the vampire's hand. Eric was on it with a great leap, and the sword swung on its owner with deadly force. With a war cry that had not been heard in a thousand years, Eric attacked . . . with savagery and abandon that was almost beautiful in its way.

"Thou Shall Not Crave Thy Neighbor"

From the first time Eric meets rival vampire Bill Compton's love, Sookie Stackhouse, he makes his interest clear. We know that Bill Compton (see "Bill Compton: Southern Gentleman") regards Eric as the superior vampire and lover. Sookie describes him as "handsome, in fact, radiant; blond and blue-eyed, tall and broad shouldered. He was wearing boots, jeans, and a vest. Period. Kind of like the guys on the cover of romance books."

She intrigues him, too. But because of Bill, she rejects him, though he doesn't seem to take it seriously. Throughout their interactions, he makes several purposeful slips of the tongue, stating his claim on her. In *Dead as a Doornail* he says, "What can I do for you, my Sookie?" The emphasis, of course, is on "my." More obviously, in *Club Dead* he slaps a man for describing Sookie in a demeaning manner, then says, "You are speaking of my future lover. Be more respectful."

This pursuit continues despite Bill's many protests and threats. As Alexander Skarsgård states in his interview at ericnorthman.net, "He's not gonna be stopped because a little baby vampire like Bill Compton is in his way." He isn't swayed in the slightest by even the most open threat from Bill. He has an abundant age advantage, and is always ready for a fight.

Although the debate over who is the most suitable man for Sookie goes on for several books, there is a turning point in *Club Dead* that clarifies which vampire best understands and accepts her. Describing Sookie hiding a body, Eric seems to think it's cute but Bill is appalled. "My Sookie hid a corpse?" Eric, better than Bill, knows and appreciates who Sookie really is and of what she is truly capable, and is, arguably, the best man for her.

Strength in Feelings

All through Eric's pursuit of Sookie, we see his enduring emotional depth and strength. Unlike many vampires, he remains true to his human emotions even in the context of undeath. Because Vikings are already deadly and ruthless as humans, perhaps as vampires they have a special need to connect with their softer sides? In any case, Eric can appear cold and calculating, doing whatever it takes to survive. Then, in private, he can be shockingly warm and honest in his love and devotion.

Is anything lurking in the Louisiana swamps more dangerous than Eric Northman? Perhaps only his maker, Godric, and Queen Sophie-Anne.

We see Eric's devotion to his maker, Godric, indirectly acknowledged in the *True Blood* episode "Time Bomb." Attempting to rescue Godric, Eric risks everything—including Sookie. When he explains that he is following Godric's orders to save her, Sookie intuitively asks, "He's your maker, isn't he?" Eric replies, "Don't use words you don't understand." It's a quick reminder of Sookie's status outside their world and outside his relationship with Godric. Sookie says, "You have a lot of love for him." Eric's response—"Don't use words I don't understand"—reinforces the idea of his being a tough old vampire. Being ancient, of course, he understands love, but he has no intention of letting anyone think he's weak.

During the rescue, Eric allows himself to be captured by Steve Newlin, leader of the Fellowship of the Sun, a group of Christian fundamentalist anti-vampire zealots. In pain, he utters, "I . . . I offer myself in exchange for Godric's freedom . . . and the girl's as well." The standoff ends when Godric embarrasses Newlin by being more tolerant and peaceful than a human, but Eric's sacrifice is no less important.

Following the rescue from the Fellowship, Godric commits suicide by sunrise in "I Will Rise Up." Eric's emotions overflow.

> *Godric:* "*Two thousand years is enough.*"
> *Eric:* [Emotional] "*I can't accept this. . . . It's insanity.*"
> *Godric:* "*Our existence is insanity. . . . We don't belong here.*"
> *Eric:* "*But we are here!*"
> *Godric:* "*It's not right. We're not right.*"
> *Eric:* "*You taught me there was no right or wrong. Only survival or death.*"
> *Godric:* "*I told a lie, as it turns out.*"
> *Eric:* [Approaches him, angry] "*I will keep you alive by force!*"
> *Godric:* "*Even if you could, why would you be so cruel?*"
> *Eric:* [in Swedish] "*Godric, don't do it.*"
> *Godric:* [in Swedish] "*There are centuries of faith and love between us.*"
> *Eric:* [Begins crying blood tears. Begs in Swedish.] "*Please. Please. Please. Godric.*"
> *Godric:* [in Swedish] "*father . . . brother . . . child.*" [in English] "*Let me go.*"
> *Eric:* [Stops crying. Stoic.] "*I won't let you die alone.*"
> *Godric:* "*Yes, you will.*" [Eric breaks down again. Godric puts his hand on back of Eric's head, then neck. Eric looks up. Godric emotional.] "*As your maker, I command you.*"
> [Eric climbs to his feet and walks to the stairs, passing Sookie as he leaves.]

This heart-wrenching scene shows a relationship several centuries in development. Eric knows Sookie is watching. Still, he doesn't flinch at showing his true emotions. The capacity for such depth of feeling isn't universal among vampires, and some would question Bill Compton's capacity for such emotion and honesty. These feelings are Eric's most redeeming qualities, allowing him to survive for centuries without losing his humanity.

Fangtastic Skills

As with all the vampires in Eric's world, supernatural speed, strength, and senses are basic. Eric is also particularly skilled at flying, which isn't so standard. Furthermore, his abilities as a lover are another heightened skill that may or may not have to do with his vampire blood.

FACTS AND TRIVIA

- As a young Viking, Eric married his brother's widow, Aude, when he was sixteen. Together they had six children, only three of whom lived until he was changed.

- Eric uses his native language at times in *True Blood*, and there's no translation given, leaving some viewers baffled. In "Escape from Dragon House," Eric says (in Swedish) when he meets Sookie Stackhouse, "Our little zoo is starting to grow." Then, in "You'll Be the Death of Me," while leaving Bill Compton's house, he says, "Oh, sweet freedom!"

QUOTES

"The bottle will be fine. . . . I may need it to smash some skulls." —From Dead to Worse *(Southern Vampire Mysteries)*

"I may not tell you everything I know, but what I tell you . . . it's true." —Dead and Gone *(Southern Vampire Mysteries)*

"I was never a Christian. But I can't imagine a belief system that would tell you to sit still and get slaughtered." —Dead to the World *(Southern Vampire Mysteries)*

"TruBlood, it keeps you alive, but it will bore you to death." —True Blood, *"Plaisir d'Amour"*

"The bond between a vampire and his maker is stronger than you can imagine. Perhaps one day you'll find out." —True Blood, *"Time Bomb"*

"They're funny. They're like humans, but miniature. Teacup humans." [on the subject of children] —True Blood, *"Frenzy"*

JULIAN LUNA: DARK PRINCE

A role created by actor Mark Frankel for the short-lived Fox television series **Kindred: The Embraced** *(1996), Julian Luna is a Mafia-style vampire don of San Francisco in a fictional world loosely based on the 1991 role-playing game* **Vampire: The Masquerade.** *While Aaron Spelling Productions was attempting to negotiate a new life for the series on the Showtime network, Frankel was tragically killed in a motorcycle accident, and plans for a second season were dropped. The surviving eight episodes, available on DVD, now have a dedicated cult following.*

As perhaps the most well-known character to emerge from the role-playing world of *Vampire: The Masquerade*, Julian Luna serves as the Ventrue vampire clan's ruler of San Francisco. He's the Prince, President, King, and essentially the Law. But he's also a master politician in a political world where only the craftiest survive. He walks a line of good and evil, most of the time simultaneously.

Prince of the City

To understand Julian, we have to understand his complicated world. Within his world, there are several clans of vampires. Each one created progeny with specific traits inborn like vampiric genetics that both curse and empower them. The Brujah are fallen royalty who become little more than modern brawlers and mobsters (think *Scarface*). The Gangrel are furrier cousins who live in the wilderness and parks, communing with animals, almost were-wolf-like. Toreadors are sexually charged artists and performers, and the Nosferatu are hideous monsters as depicted in the silent black-and-white film of the same name. The Ventrue, Julian's clan, are Wall Street business types. All these clans who obey the old laws and try to enforce them are known collectively as the Camarilla. There are also other clans who do not bow to this authority, such as the Assimites and the Tremere, as well as the Anarchs and Sabbat believers of all clans. All vampires in Julian's world are referred to as Kindred.

As the Prince, appearance is everything. From the tailored suit to Julian's manor, it all has to exude control and confidence. For a Ventrue, that façade is second nature.

In a mob-style vampire government, the head honcho of each Camarilla clan, also known as the Primogen, meets with the Prince over matters of Kindred importance. The group of Primogens is known as the Conclave; they are the official mouthpieces for politics and are the only ones who can speak for the whole clan, though they generally take their titles through manipulation and the death of the former Primogen, which they often have a part in helping along. Julian, as the Prince, has to keep peace among these bickering groups. He also has to defend his city against the Sabbat and Anarchs who would turn the city to their rule, which is much more violent and less human-friendly. If that's not enough, he has to worry about assassination attempts and attacks by other supernatural creatures such as the Garou (werewolves) and Wraiths (ghosts).

The Prince's job is never done.

The Masquerade

The law of the Masquerade is the one truly unbreakable law in Julian's world. As he says, "The Masquerade—that is, passing as human—is the only protection we have from humans." If you break the code—and get caught—you will be subject to a Blood Hunt, which means you're free game for the other vampires, who, on this special occasion, may kill others of their kind. The reasons why are simple: No vampire wants the kine (humans) to find out they exist and start another Inquisition. However, like most of the others, Julian breaks the Masquerade to save others and himself, such as the reporter Caitlin Byrne. No one knows about these violations, and if they do, they don't live to tell about it.

Julian keeps a protective masquerade of his own. He doesn't let anyone get too close, except Caitlin. As far as the clans are concerned, he is cold and powerfully ruthless. But it's a necessary mask. Any weakness is cause for revolt, and there's always a revolt brewing in his world.

A True Ventrue

Born in 1830 in New Orleans, Julian is an ambitious human who marries his love, Evelyn, in 1856. Just after giving birth to their son, John, Evelyn dies. Archon Raine, the Ventrue Primogen and Prince before Julian, Embraces (that is, drains and transforms) the grieving Julian. He sires him into the Ventrue clan and makes him into a natural ruler, boosting his talents with aristocratic vampire genetic enhancement.

As a newborn vampire, Julian positions himself as trusted advisor and bodyguard to Archon. He describes that life, saying, "The Brujah wanted power, so I had to fight. . . . They kept coming at me, and I kept killing until I realized I was becoming one of them. Nothing more than a monster that had to be stopped. When it was done and I burned

Julian with his former love Lillie Langtry during better nights—before she tried to kill him.

the building and the bodies, I knew I couldn't kill for Archon anymore. And I never did." That is his breaking point, the moment Julian realizes that he is as much a bloodthirsty savage as any Brujah. Luckily, his more elevated sensibilities pull him out of the darkness. For a Ventrue, behaving like a Brujah is a pretty macabre place to be.

The Ventrue, after all, are the noblest of bloodlines. Its vampires are brought up to maintain an outstanding reputation for authoritative refinement. More than that, it's in their blood and their instincts. They can't fight it. Like an older brother, clan Ventrue generally knows what's best for everyone—namely, maintaining order and power—and it's willing to force everyone to follow its plans. Because of this, Archon values Julian's loyalty, honor, and intelligence. Julian is loyal to his sire and friends, always keeping his word. His dealings are honorable, which endears many of his followers from other clans as true friends. Those characteristics, combined with noble Ventrue blood, become his greatest strengths. And, on the rare occasion that this type of primal charisma fails him, his intelligence and super-natural abilities make up the difference.

Live Hard, Die Young . . .

Julian's weakness is love. His love of family and of Caitlin leaves him open to attacks by his enemies. Because of his love for his son, John, and the family he barely knew, Julian keeps watch on John's heirs, who settled in the Napa Valley. Sasha Luna, Julian's eighteen-year-old sole surviving descendant, is perhaps his greatest love. Having taken care of his heirs through-out the years, he helps Sasha, too. Then the Brujah sire her in an attempt to start a clan war and dethrone the Prince. It almost works and most definitely causes added stress with the Gangrel, to whom Sasha's love, Cash, belongs.

Caitlin, the reporter, proves a crack in Julian's carefully polished armor when she begins to get too close. Not only does her influence force him to break the Masquerade, but he also risks his life for hers. He is then forced to wipe her memories and risk her again getting too close to the truth, always a danger given her public platform. Julian's relationship with Caitlin creates emotional turmoil as he endeavors to protect her and his throne from knowledge of his Ventrue nature.

His love for other women is equally dangerous. With Alexandra, Julian's progeny and former lover, he allows her to break the rules and gives her a head start against the Blood Hunt he is forced to call on her. Then, his relationship with Lillie Langtry, the Toreador Primogen and rumored to be a famous Victorian actress, proves to be poisonous. Her jealousy skyrockets and she turns against him, opting for attempted homicide instead of moving on.

Julian Luna, Ventrue Prince of San Francisco, was scheduled for new episodes of *Kindred* before actor Mark Frankel died.

The Old and the Powerful

The Kindred have the typical abilities and weaknesses of vampires. They're faster and stronger, and they heal quicker than humans do. They drink blood and live forever. Their eyes become luminous when their emotions run high, and they can create new vampires by drinking, then replacing, human blood with a bit of the vampire kind. Kindred are also unable, in most cases, to heal sunlight and fire damage. This means that wounds from phosphorous rounds can kill them. Each vampire can have any number of personal quirks, from aversions to water to invisibility in mirrors. Julian, however, seems to have no particular quirks outside of shape-shifting and becoming part of the earth, as he does in "The Embraced" when he merges with his grave for a day's sleep.

Each clan has its own abilities and flaws. As a Ventrue, Julian has the typical powers of his family. According to *Vampire: The Masquerade*, those powers are Domination, Fortitude, and Presence. Domination is, as it sounds, the ability to overpower another's will. Fortitude is a defensive ability that allows vampires to take unimaginable injuries in stride and survive all dethroning attempts. And Presence is a sort of supernatural charisma. In other clans, it can be used to hypnotize victims, but the Ventrue use Presence to keep other Kindred obedient and to keep the Prince secure and happy.

FACTS AND TRIVIA

- The vampires of Julian's world don't call themselves vampires. As he explains: "We call ourselves Kindred. *Vampire* is a word humans invented. They needed a name for their fears in the night."

- The Ventrue clan motto is *Regere sanguine, regere in veritatem est*, which means "To rule through blood is to rule in truth."

- According to Lillie in "Live Hard, Die Young, and Leave a Good-looking Corpse," Julian saw Elvis perform in Memphis in 1955.

QUOTES

"We have Kindred in every walk of life. . . . We're all around you."
—Kindred, *"Prince of the City"*

"I'm alone. The only thing that eases the pain of loneliness is family. The irony of my kind."
—Kindred, *"Prince of the City"*

"If you want to know what I really am, I can only tell you this: I'm not what you think."
—Kindred, *"Romeo and Juliet"*

JEAN-CLAUDE: SEDUCTIVE DARK MASTER

An incubus as well as a vampire, drawing sustenance from sex in addition to blood, Jean-Claude of the Anita Blake: Vampire Hunter series appears in fifteen of Laurell K. Hamilton's best-selling novels, most recently **Bullet** *(2010).*

Among the dark angels, Jean-Claude is the master of seductive power. Born poor, he uses supernatural sex to protect and advance himself over the centuries in his rise to power. Now the Master of the City of St. Louis, Jean-Claude is one of the most threatening forces to the power and control of the ruling vampires, the Vampire Council.

Always the Whipping Boy

Born to a poor French family, Jean-Claude is sold at a young age as the literal whipping boy for the son of an aristocratic family. The position affords him the life of an aristocrat, including tutors and a proper education, but it is also a life of abuse. As the job title implies, he receives the punishments, or whippings, for the crimes of the true son. A common practice at the time, it protects the family's child from injury or death from the whippings. Abuse becomes a theme in Jean-Claude's life.

After his wife and child die in childbirth, Jean-Claude is turned by Lissette, a follower of a beautiful, two-thousand-year-old vampire queen named Belle Morte, who gives him the *ardeur*, a nearly insatiable sex hunger that is an uncommon but defining characteristic of Belle Morte's line. Soon after, Julian, the Master of the City, uses Jean-Claude's *ardeur* for his own entertainment, giving him strange people to feed on.

In roughly five years, he ends up with Belle Morte and Asher (see "Asher: The Wounded Angel"), a bisexual member of her court who is jealous of Jean-Claude's beauty. There, Belle Morte uses him, along with Asher, to seduce others and feed her own desires. Again the tool for someone's punishment and pleasure, he endures and forms a close relationship with Asher that eventually becomes a ménage à trois with a vampire witch, Julianna.

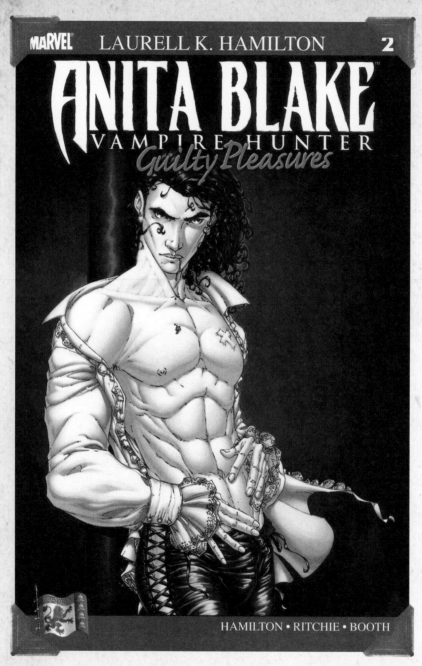

Jean-Claude bares the cross-shaped scar he was given before killing the person who put it there.

After Julianna is burned at the stake and Asher is scarred with holy water by church zealots, Jean-Claude takes on the whipping boy role voluntarily. Blamed by Asher for his inability to save Julianna, he returns to the Council and begs for Asher's life in exchange for a century of servitude. Belle Morte accepts the deal, using the opportunity to punish him for having dared leave her.

New World, New Love

After leaving Belle Morte a second time, Jean-Claude comes to America, where he meets paranormal investigator and necromancer Anita Blake and forms the legendary triumvirate, or power triangle, with her then-boyfriend and werewolf, Richard Zeeman, the *ulfric*, or leader of the local werewolf pack. It is Anita's influence through the triumvirate and Jean-Claude's love for her that reminds him of the better side of life, his lost loves, and almost humanizes his behavior. Although he can appear indifferent at times, it is obviously the result of centuries spent among cruel and savage vampires who place no value on life and have even less respect for feelings.

Before Anita, Jean-Claude lived in a dark world. Like Asher, Jean-Claude is haunted by past loves. With Anita, Jean-Claude has a new appreciation for life and love. But it's not all hearts and roses. The other Masters of the City—and those looking for their own seat of power—see this human influence as a beacon of weakness and an opportunity to challenge his power.

Too Powerful to Fall?

Jean-Claude is not easily challenged. As Anita puts it in *Killing Dance*, "You could always trust Jean-Claude to survive. It was one of his talents." Survival seems at times to almost be another power, though it's never named as one. Still, centuries of life boost his regular powers beyond those of most Masters of the City. In addition, survival skills are spread across several abilities, including his seductive powers.

The most human of these abilities is Jean-Claude's business sense. In addition to Guilty Pleasures, a male strip club in St. Louis, he owns the Circus of the Damned, a haven for vampires and a literal circus of supernatural beings. The Danse Macabre is his dance hall, which likens to old-school dance halls with the exception that instead of paying to dance with women, humans pay to dance with vampires and shape-shifters. Then, there is the mysterious J. C. Corporation, and the Laughing Corpse, which may make Jean-Claude the only vampire known to own a comedy club.

His ability to feed off something other than blood is perhaps the handiest ability. The *ardeur* allows Jean-Claude to feed off the lust and sex around him like a psychic vampire. As the owner of Guilty Pleasures, he has his pick of victims from which to feed and often feeds on the audience's lust, fueled by the sexy shows put on by Asher and the other vampires and shape-shifters who work for Jean-Claude.

To complement the *ardeur*, Jean-Claude has the ability to hypnotize his victims with a simple gaze. His voice and aura can stoke emotions or calm them in those of lesser strength, such as humans, lesser vampires, and lycanthropes. Anita describes this manipulating voice as feeling like silk or fur against skin.

As a defensive ability, Jean-Claude can make himself appear younger or older than he truly is to those who can psychically sense age. To Anita, for example, he first appears to be around two centuries old. Then, she believes him to be about four centuries. It isn't until *Danse Macabre* (book fourteen of the series) that Jean-Claude states that he is more than six hundred years old.

Advanced age bestows a competitive advantage with other master vampires. Although enhanced with age, his other powers are somewhat more typical. Of course, he possesses the standard mental powers, enhanced senses, agility, endurance, strength, and speed. He can also fly like other vampires in the Anita Blake world.

Jean-Claude's most obvious gift is his physical irresistibility to both men and women. From the double rows of eyelashes to his exceptionally graceful movements, he is breathtaking and can easily persuade the most resistant female, or male.

Don't Hate Me Because I'm . . .

Jean-Claude's hottie status can be a little overwhelming at times. Even Anita feels it in *Incubus Dreams*, asking, "Is there anything your bloodline does that doesn't involve getting naked?" This supercharged sexiness is something of a curse around males. For many heterosexual men, any homosexual feeling is cause for alarm. Rather than recognizing Jean-Claude's unique erotic power, they grow uncomfortable and resist, becoming angry and judgmental.

Such is the case with Richard Zeeman, the third in the triumvirate and the *ulfric* of the local wolf pack, which happens to be Jean-Claude's particular "animal to call." The triumvirate strengthens Jean-Claude's power base enough that he becomes a *sourdre de sang*, or head of his own bloodline, and breaks him free of Belle Morte's power and her ability to draw energy from him using the *ardeur*. However, it also pushes the three too close for someone so much in denial of his true self as Richard.

Jean-Claude can use the *ardeur* to feed off Richard and Anita's sex and enter their minds telepathically, sharing his past memories—including those of loving Asher. Feeding on Richard and Anita empowers Jean-Claude to a far greater extent than some random person's lust, but it also makes him an invisible third in their most intimate moments. Centuries have made bisexuality as natural as breathing for Jean-Claude, but it triggers Richard's jealousy and homophobia, weakening their relationship and ultimately causing a breakup between Anita and Richard. It's only thanks to Jean-Claude's personal charm and his ability to call wolves that, even when Richard hates him, the vampire is spared the *ulfric*'s rage, manages to manipulate Richard's power, and at times calls him and his pack for aid.

FACTS AND TRIVIA

Jean-Claude has a cross-shaped scar from a religious believer pressing a cross to his skin. According to what he tells Anita Blake in *Guilty Pleasures*, he killed the person who did it.

QUOTES

"I am sincere, ma petite, even when I lie."—Killing Dance

"I feel like a child in the dark who knows the monsters are under the bed. I want to be told it will be alright, but I am far too old to believe such comforting lies."—Cerulean Sins

"You take insult where none is intended, but if you will find insult where none is meant, then perhaps I should try harder to insult on purpose."—The Harlequin

"You ask yourself, What is love? Am I in love? When what you should be asking is, What is not love?"—Incubus Dreams

"True power comes when others offer it to you and you merely accept it as a gift, not as the spoils of some personal war."—Narcissus in Chains

ACHERON: ATLANTEAN ANGEL

A popular ongoing character in Sherrilyn Kenyon's best-selling Dark-Hunter series of novels, Acheron Parthenopaeus is the only Atlantean god among the dark angels. Born around 9548 BCE, he's been alive for more than eleven thousand years, which also makes him the oldest dark angel. Ash, as he is also called, is the first Dark-Hunter appointed by the goddess Artemis. He is also known as Apostolos, Akri, and occasionally T-Rex, and his own story is told in full in the novel Acheron *(2009).*

Dark-Hunters are a mysterious group. They describe themselves on sherrilynkenyon.com: "We are Darkness. We are Shadow. / We are the Rulers of the Night. / We, alone, stand between mankind and those who would see mankind destroyed." Each member is an immortal, resurrected to protect humanity against vampires ("Daimons" in Kenyon's world) and other evil beings. Their leader, the oldest of them all and the one these tough guys are afraid of, is Acheron.

As the first appointed Dark-Hunter and the youngest at the time of his death, Ash fought Daimons alone for thousands of years. He wrote the Dark-Hunter Creed and Code, which all Dark-Hunters abide by. His position makes him the head honcho of his kind, but it's a lonely position.

Apostolos

Acheron has never been like others. His mother was Apollymi, queen of the Atlantean gods and goddess of life, death, and wisdom. She is also known as the Great Destroyer because, as Ash puts it, "the other gods feared Apollymi's wrath, and in the end she killed them all." Archon, his father, was king of the Atlanteans.

Acheron's real name was to be Apostolos. He has three half-sisters, all Greek Fates who are the result of Archon's affair with Themis, the Greek goddess of law, order, and good counsel. The sisters are jealous of the coming baby and, before Ash is born, go to Archon

The cover of Sherrilyn Kenyon's *Acheron* features Ash's lightening bolt and sun symbol (center) and the double bow symbol (bottom), which is the brand of the Dark Hunters.

to deliver a prediction that Apostolos (Ash) Parthenopaeus will be the end of the Atlantean pantheon, which would spell the end of their world and power. The other gods are frightened and demand the baby's death.

Apollymi does the only thing she knows to do: she returns to her home in Kalosis, the Atlantean hell realm, where no other god will venture. To protect Apostolos further, she cuts him from her womb with an Atlantean dagger, extracts his soul, binds his powers, and has her niece place him in the womb of Queen Aara of Didymos, merging his "life force" with the human child inside Aara so that she cannot harm Apostolos without also harming her human child. The date is May 9, 9548 BCE.

On June 23 of the same year, Apostolos is born, along with a human twin, Styxx. When Queen Aara sees the swirling silver in his eyes, like his true mother Apollymi's, she becomes concerned. His father begins to suspect her of being unfaithful, and an oracle gives a horrible prophecy. "None will be safe from his wrath," she says, and then tells them that the twins are connected supernaturally. Both Queen Aara and her king refuse to accept Apostolos as their child, and Styxx becomes the official heir.

A River of Woes

The oracle, recognizing both his pitiful situation and his potential to spread sorrow through the world, names him Acheron after the river of woes in the Underworld. Her reasoning for the name choice is that "like the river of the Underworld, his journey will be long, dark, and enduring. He will be able to give life . . . and to take it away. He will travel through life alone and abandoned, ever seeking kindness and ever finding cruelty. May the gods have mercy on you, little one. Because no one else ever will." The statement is prophetic.

When Acheron is seven, he is stolen from his sister, Princess Ryssa, and taken to Atlantis. There, his uncle Estes becomes his guardian, though he fails miserably in that capacity. Because he has been blessed (or cursed) at birth by a goddess aunt who wishes him to be sexually irresistible to all adults, Ash is trained from that point on to be a *tsoulus* (sex slave). He is abused sexually, castrated, starved, and beaten regularly. Nine years later, one of Acheron's aides writes a letter to his long-lost sister who, upon hearing of their uncle's prostituting Ash, ushers him away to her summer palace. He is so traumatized that it takes months in hiding for him to trust Ryssa enough to relax.

As soon as he does, Acheron is found by his father and sent back to live with Estes, who begins the abuses again. After a few years, the uncle dies. Because Ash has lost his home along with his uncle, he survives by prostituting himself in Didymos. Again, Ryssa finds him, but Ash refuses to go with her and risk opening himself to further pain. He continues to work, sleeping with senators who come to him to take out the anger they feel at Styxx, his twin. The embarrassment of having his twin working in such a demeaning job triggers Styxx to put Ash in the palace dungeon.

Over the months that Acheron lives in the dungeon, he nears death from starvation. With Styxx dying too, thanks to the connection Apollymi created, he is taken from the dungeon and isolated in a room, where he is kept alive, just to make sure that his brother survives.

Artemis

Later in Acheron's life, he falls for the goddess Artemis, the twin sister of Apollo (god of music, prophecy, and light), daughter of Zeus (the supreme god), and goddess of the forest and the hunt who is often depicted with a bow and arrow. Artemis continues to claim her love for him until she finds out who he is. She drugs him with the plan to kill him so that their affair is kept secret. The next day, Ash discovers that Ryssa, who had been in an affair with Apollo, was assassinated during the night along with the son born of her relationship with the god. Apollo, grieving and furious that Ash did nothing to save Ryssa and his son, guts Ash. Artemis watches silently, protecting herself and her secret.

Afraid that Apollymi will come after her, Artemis tricks Acheron into drinking her blood, bringing him back from death. Drinking starts a process that keeps him returning to her for survival. Then, two thousand years later, Artemis drinks Ash's blood. Through blood, she steals his power of creation and resurrection, allowing her to create the Dark-Hunters and bind Ash to her forever. In public, she refuses to acknowledge him, just the way the senators had when he worked as a human prostitute. Still, Artemis's blood betrayals keep him returning to her, long after he realizes how selfish and shallow she is, just to drink her blood and barter for the souls of his Dark-Hunters.

Becoming Immortal

Like Acheron, the Dark-Hunters were once mortal. They are souls who screamed for vengeance after wrongful deaths, those who wanted their revenge more than all others and were loud enough to be heard in Olympus, the home of the twelve Greek gods, where Artemis answers their pleas. The deal she makes is to allow them twenty-four hours to take their revenge in exchange for their soul. Those who accept are touched by Artemis, marking them with a double bow and arrow that is the brand of the Dark-Hunters. Once their day is up, she sends them to Acheron for training.

Acheron teaches them the Dark-Hunter Code, to which they must abide: "Honor Artemis. Drink no blood. Harm no human or Apollite. Never touch a Squire. Speak with no family or friends who knew you before you died. Let no Daimon escape alive. Never speak of what you are. You walk alone. Keep your bow mark hidden." Then, after they are fully trained, the new Dark-Hunter is given a squire (human helper) and assigned to a location, where he will spend eternity fighting to protect the innocents (humans) from evil.

There is one way to escape this eternity in service: If the Dark-Hunter finds someone who loves him enough to hold the medallion that holds the Dark-Hunter's soul to his double bow mark, even when it becomes molten hot, then his soul will be returned to his body. He begins life again at the age of his death. However, if the medallion is dropped, the Dark-Hunter's soul is lost.

This medallion is acquired by Acheron through sex or beatings, whichever Artemis wants. Generally, she prefers the beatings because they make her feel powerful over Ash, whom she can't control. Artemis says of Acheron in the book bearing his name, "He held no fear of anything or anyone. Like a powerful, untamed beast, he was defiant and bold." It's a trait she loathes. So, Artemis takes the power struggle a step further with Katra, the daughter Artemis hid from him to keep Acheron from receiving any of their daughter's love.

Mystery Man

Ash also has a reputation for mystery. He understandably refuses to answer personal questions. Even questions that he does respond to have such vague answers that the listener is often left with more questions.

Because he isn't well received, Acheron only interacts with the other hunters if the urge strikes him, which isn't often. Given his limited public appearances, the information on him ranges from fact to legend. Some say that no mortal who ever lived is as physically perfect as Ash. More descriptive reports from those who have seen him state that he's muscular and tall, about six foot eight. His voice is sexy and deep, and his walk is almost primal. Because Ash has a flair for the dramatic, his hair could be any color on any given day. It's been golden, black, silver, metallic purple, red striped black, brown, and dark green. He can change it easily with his god power. Sometimes it's flowing in the wind and other times it's braided, but he always wears it long. This unique appearance, combined with Acheron's age and reputation, makes it hard (if not impossible) to fit in with other hunters and be normal . . . not that he ever was.

Even though Ash is generally seen as a gorgeous man, this physical persona is a façade. His natural form, the one given to him by his real parents, is very different. Ash has fangs, claws, ebony horns, black hair, blood red eyes, and blue skin. There is a handprint on his neck where Apollo choked him and a line from Acheron's throat to his navel where he was gutted. It's a far cry from the cover model look.

Lonely Hero

Artemis once asks Acheron if he has friends, and he responds that he does not. His reasoning for that lack of friendship is: "I suppose I'm not worthy of any." Friendship is, for him, "an elusive dream he dare not allow himself." Although he commands an army of Dark-Hunters, the rest of his life has been a lonely one. Gods think him beneath them and his own hunters don't accept him. He has no double bow mark from Artemis, as they do, so he has one added, but they still don't accept him.

For a companion, Ash has Simi. A gift from Apollymi on Acheron's twenty-first birthday, Simi is a nine-millennia-old Charonte (demon). She is a daughter and friend who, when not hiding on his body as a dragonlike tattoo, looks like a roughly nineteen-year-old girl. This relationship becomes even stranger when Ash's one friend, Nick Gautier, sleeps with Simi. In his anger, Ash curses Nick to commit suicide. Artemis brings him back as one of the Dark-Hunters, and Ash barters for his soul, setting right the wrong he's done Nick.

His greatest companion comes to him in modern times. The first being to treat him like any other regular person, Soteria "Tory" Kafieri is Acheron's first true love. Their story is told in *Acheron*. Although Ash still hates to have his hair pulled or to have someone breathe on his neck, reminding him of his days as a whore, Tory makes him believe in love and the nicer things in life that he's never experienced before her.

Powers

Being a god has its powers and privileges. Essentially, Ash is omnipotent, omnilingual, and omniscient. He can toss some lightning bolts, and is immortal. He can read and alter the memories and thoughts of others. He also has the astonishing ability to create life, destroy it, and alter the future with a single word. Likewise, he can see the fates of everyone except those to whom he is closest. He can kill gods and make women swoon with his supernatural sexuality. Although it's more of a curse, his powers of Ultimate Destruction, it is said, will bring about the end of the world. Ash sums up his abilities best in *Acheron* when he says, "I am the god Apostolos. The Harbinger of Telikos. The Final Fate of all. Beloved son of Apollymi the Great Destroyer. My will makes the will of the universe."

FACTS AND TRIVIA

Akri, which is the name Simi uses for Acheron, means "lord and master" in Greek.

Ash's personal emblem is a sun pierced by three silver lightning bolts.

Acheron has very defined tastes. In art, he prefers manga and anime. His favorite song is "Salvation" by Five Finger Death Punch. He loves guitars and has a large collection. He refuses to use cell phones and doesn't like guns.

QUOTES

"Life is a tapestry woven by the decisions we make." —Kiss of the Night

"I'm the top of the food chain and well . . . you're the food." —Dance with the Devil

"My ego's had enough time to recover a modicum of dignity. Let's make sure we crush it again before I mistake myself for a god." —Acheron

"He who lets fear rule him, has fear for a master." —Night Embrace

"Forgiveness is the best part of valor. . . . Discretion is easy. It's finding the courage to forgive yourself and others that is hard." —Dance with the Devil

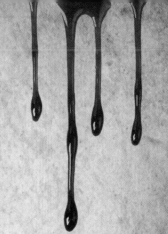

AKASHA: DARK QUEEN

As the Queen of the Damned, and the title character of the third novel (1988) of Anne Rice's Vampire Chronicles, Akasha is the first vampire ever created, according to her legend. She's described as "too pretty to be truly beautiful, for her prettiness overcame any sense of majesty or deep mystery." She hails from Uruk, or modern-day Iraq, and rose to power in Kemet. Once an Egyptian queen, she's accustomed to being worshiped, and she demands no less of the vampires of current times. In the 2002 film adaptation of Queen of the Damned, Akasha was played by R&B singer Aaliyah, who tragically joined the immortals herself in a fatal plane crash shortly before the movie's release.

Originally human around 5000 BCE, Queen Akasha is the mother of all vampires in the same world as Louis and Lestat of the Vampire Chronicles (see "Louis de Pointe du Lac: Dark Bohemian" and "Lestat de Lioncourt: Dark Rock Star"). With an ego the size of the Nile, Akasha has existed through time, quietly ruling all the vampires using nothing but fear of their own demise to keep them from killing her. She is vain, selfish, and ruthless. Although she exists mostly as a psychopathic killer, she sees herself as responsible and merciful to those who follow her, a true dark angel.

Curiosity Killed the . . . Vampire?

An ego isn't the only thing that gives Queen Akasha a bit of trouble. Her curiosity is another weakness. To satisfy her metaphysical curiosity during the time of her rule, Akasha summons redheaded twins Maharet and Mekare to her palace to help her communicate with the spirits. As witches, they are already in contact with the spirit world. It backfires and the spirits shun her; one particularly bloodthirsty spirit named Amel attacks her. Taking the rejection and attack as a personal insult, Akasha looks for someone to punish and has Khayman, her servant, rape the twins in public for "witchcraft." Then Akasha exiles Maharet and Mekare from Kemet.

Akasha, as portrayed by Aaliyah in *Queen of the Damned*, is the queen mother and psychotic leader of the immortals.

Later, after the followers of Akasha and her king, Enkil, revolt and kill them, Amel merges with Akasha's rising spirit and reenters her body through a wound. It fuses with her blood and flesh and reanimates her, turning her into the first vampire. Akasha then goes to Enkil, drains him of blood, and feeds him hers to make him a vampire, too.

But like a frightened, spoiled child, Akasha panics and has the twins brought back to the city to answer her questions. Khayman, now a vampire himself, changes them after cutting out Maharet's eyes and Mekare's tongue, damning them to an eternity of undeath.

It's also curiosity that brings her around, out of the centuries-long petrified stupor that has earned her and Enkil the title of "Those Who Must Be Kept," to meet the vampire Lestat, whose music wakes her. Lestat intrigues her and makes her spirit burn again as it did when she was young—and human. When she rises to follow him, she kills Enkil, her one true protector. Then she follows Lestat, who is uninterested in the life she craves but is too afraid to contradict her wishes. This eventually leads to a fatal confrontation.

Family and Self

The blood that ties the master to the progeny in her world also links the king and queen to all vampires. If they die, so do their children. When they are placed in the sun to die, the younger vampires around the world are incinerated by proxy.

When Akasha rises at the sound of Lestat's music, she kills every vampire she meets except those who are "family" to Lestat. Marius, who has dedicated his life to protecting her and her king for so long, is treated with disdain because Akasha's world revolves around Akasha. She's spoiled. Modern psychologists would describe her as narcissistic and sociopathic. And she doesn't see anything wrong with it. She is in her own eyes, after all, the "Queen of Heaven."

Centuries of Female Strength

Akasha is absolutely lethal. She views the world in black-and-white terms. Humans are useless. Vampires are either for her or against her, and being "for" her may be as simple as her liking them. Being female is a definite plus.

With Lestat tagging along like the nice boy toy he is, Akasha orders women to step in to control and kill most male vampires. She doesn't want much, only a new Eden, where about ninety percent of the world's vampire males are dead, females reign, and she is their goddess. "The world is our garden," she says, and fully intends to trim out any weeds of dissent. Events proceed nicely until Maharet and Mekare, her early enemies, behead her and eat her organs, making themselves the new mothers of all vampires.

The Dark Queen definitely has a style all her own. From unique clothes that reflect her Egyptian home to her desire for a female dominated vampire utopia, she is unmatched in flair among the undead.

Powers

The vampires of Akasha's world have a number of powers, most of which are standard dark angel abilities, such as enhanced senses, speed, and strength. She is the most powerful of all, possessing a higher level of these. She can destroy most all vampires in a ball of flame with only a thought, and she can survive sun exposure. In suspended animation, she is as hard as stone and her blood is so powerful that she can make others stronger by allowing them to feed from her.

FACTS AND TRIVIA

• Akasha is awakened by Lestat's playing a violin, then comes to him after the concert. She is arguably the greatest fan of his music.

• *Akasha* means "aether" (or ether), which in Paganism, Hinduism, and other beliefs is the center or soul of everything. The upward point of the pentagram represents Akasha, and without Akasha there is no spirit, soul, or magic.

QUOTES

"You think you can change my will? I've had enough of this discussion. Join me or die!"
—Queen of the Damned *(film)*

"Humans are animals. Brute creatures. Their destruction can only make sense."
—Queen of the Damned *(film)*

"My children. Warms my blood to see you all gathered plotting against me."
—Queen of the Damned *(film)*

LESTAT DE LIONCOURT: DARK ROCK STAR

A main supporting character in Anne Rice's novel Interview with the Vampire *(1976), Lestat de Lioncourt took center stage in Rice's 1985 sequel,* The Vampire Lestat, *and became the focal character of her ongoing Vampire Chronicles series. In Neil Jordan's 1994 film adaptation of* Interview, *Lestat was played by Tom Cruise (a controversial casting choice first denounced by the author, then lavishly praised by her upon the project's completion). In the 2002 film* Queen of the Damned, *Lestat was played by Stuart Townsend. In the 2006 Broadway production* Lestat: The Musical, *with music by Elton John and Bernie Taupin, the role was played (and sung) by Hugh Panaro. As of this writing, a film adaptation of* The Vampire Lestat *is in the planning stages, with Robert Downey Jr. mentioned as a possibility for the title role.*

Among the dark angels, Lestat de Lioncourt is the preeminent rock star. Both literally and figuratively, he commands the stage. In *The Vampire Lestat*, we see him as a human actor in Paris whom a critic describes as a "blond-haired rogue who steals the hearts of the ladies in the third and fourth acts." Although he died centuries ago, he's far from being withered. Instead, he relishes his vampire death style and lives his unlife to the max.

Lestat was born in Auvergne, France, in 1760, and reborn into vampirism in 1781 at the age of twenty-one. In his human family, he is the youngest of the sons of the blind Marquis de Lioncourt, which means he has no prospects as far as land is concerned, unless his other siblings all die young. So, he moves to Paris, where a vampire recognizes his brilliant charisma and gives him the Dark Gift (vampirism).

Lestat, beautifully portrayed by Tom Cruise, became the boy-toy of Akasha, almost bringing about the vampire apocalypse.

Survivor

Lestat's greatest strength is the ability to always survive—and even thrive—in circumstances that would drag others down. He was forced into the vampire life, but he learns to shine as one of its brightest personalities. To survive, he befriends those who can protect and teach him. He keeps in mind the little practicalities of vampirism, such as choosing prey carefully and keeping authorities in the dark. It's not so much a learned trait as a natural skill.

These traits serve him well through the centuries, where most others, unable to adapt, die or commit suicide. Lestat, however, learns to latch on to others, making friends with those who can help him learn and conquer the new ways and attitudes of the latest century.

Along with his fighting, survivor spirit, Lestat has a penchant for indulging himself. Perhaps he believes in playing as hard as he works, or perhaps it's simply his own aristocratic nature? Either way, it grates on those around him at times. We see this in the early days when his companion Louis (see "Louis de Pointe du Lac: Dark Bohemian") says, "Lestat killed two, sometimes three a night. A fresh young girl; that was his favorite for the first of the evening. For seconds, he preferred a gilded beautiful youth. But the snob in him loved to hunt in society, and the blood of the aristocrat thrilled him best of all." He sees how Lestat enjoys the game of hunting and drinking simply for pleasure.

Lestat equally resents Louis's less-than-elegant lifestyle, once saying to their child-vampire companion Claudia, "*Mon dieu*, what melancholy nonsense. I swear you grow more like Louis each day. Soon you'll be eating rats!" This difference in their personalities causes numerous rifts, especially in regard to Claudia. Her love for Louis and jealousy of his attachment to Lestat accentuates the fact that the two men, though both vampires, are as different as night and day.

The Moon to Louis's Sun

Just as Louis represents day and humanity, Lestat is the moon and death. He is night embodied, with all its energy and dark beauty. "Have you said your good-byes to the light?" Lestat asks before taking Louis into the world of darkness. He reiterates his literal and metaphorical reference by twisting a quote from Shakespeare's *Othello* to suit his giving Louis the Dark Gift of vampirism: "But once [I] put out thy light, I cannot give it vital breath again. It needs must wither."

Lestat's beauty is astounding. He is described as a luminous creature, physically comparable to the moon's beauty. He's tall, approximately six feet, looming above the others of his time. His hair is thick, blond as moonlight, and curly. Under fluorescent lights, it appears white. His eyes are gray, absorbing and reflecting colors as the moon does, appearing blue or violet at times. His mouth is sensual and a little too big for his face, which is extremely white and reflective, just as the rest of his skin is. Starved, he is the picture of horror, but well fed, the only giveaways are his glasslike fingernails.

Balance

A handsome devil, Lestat rules the night he loves, walking the Earth as possibly the most dangerous creature alive due to his beauty and charisma. Lestat knows this and isn't beyond reminding others, especially his beloved Louis, who doesn't enjoy the undead life as much as Lestat does. So, he tries to spice things up. Laughing, he says, "But just remember, life without me would be even more unbearable." And he's right.

Without Lestat, Louis's life would have been unbearable. He would have grieved his brother indefinitely and probably died. Lestat brought him into the first real life he ever had, introducing him to worlds he would have otherwise never known. He added excitement and tried more than once to show Louis how to embrace it all, only to be repeatedly frustrated. More than once he said, "Oh, shut up, Louis! *Mon dieu!*" And when they meet again in modern times, it's still a point of contention. "Oh Louis, Louis. Still whining Louis. Have you heard enough? I've had to listen to that for centuries," he says, making it plain to anyone who'll listen. But just as Louis needs Lestat, so too does Lestat need whining Louis to bring some semblance of human feeling into his life. Without Louis for balance, Lestat would wander off into darkness, unable to find his way back.

Dark Gift

For all of Lestat's posturing, he truly does understand Louis. He, too, regrets receiving the Dark Gift. At twelve, Lestat entered the monastery, indicating that his devotion to God was strong. Louis's claim that they are both damned strikes straight to the heart of Lestat's original belief system.

Also, although he does chastise Louis for his religious guilt, Lestat feels it as well. He is a tortured soul and sees his nagging desire to be human again as a weakness. So, he pushes it away, careful not to feel it too much or too often. Detachment becomes his defensive strength, enabling him to live without the guilt that Louis has. When he says, "Merciful death. How you love your precious guilt," to Louis, he reveals this. While Louis basks in his guilt, feeling it thoroughly, Lestat runs from it most of his life. Only at a point when he is sick and destitute (like a dying and forsaken mortal) does Lestat decide that he doesn't want to be human after all. He realizes that his nostalgia for humanity has been an empty yearning, that the reality is much less glamorous than he remembered.

Lestat hovers over a victim like a true predator in *Interview with the Vampire*. As much as he pretends to be cold-hearted, he, like Louis, despises his parasitic life.

Egomaniac

Lestat has one major flaw: his ego. He sees himself as something of a god, and admits it when he tells Louis, "God kills indiscriminately and so shall we. For no creatures under God are as we are, none so like him as ourselves." Such self-aggrandizement leaves him open to making several major mistakes. Arrogantly freeing Akasha, the mother of all vampires (see "Akasha: Dark Queen"), thereby nearly destroying all the undead is only one example.

Lestat does back down when his ego gets the best of him. If Lestat were truly the ruthless character so many believe him to be, he would have had no problem killing in lockstep with Akasha. Instead, he is reluctant to kill at first, and then refuses completely as she continues her rampage. He tries to stop her repeatedly and ultimately allows the others to kill her. Despite his insistence that he is more godlike than human, there is humanity left in him yet. But the other vampires always find a way to fix his mistakes, enabling Lestat to break the rules over and over again.

A New Life

Lestat learns at an early age to question and resist authority. His father and brothers want to keep him at home, subject to their control and approval. When he joins a monastery at the age of twelve, they quickly drag him home, depriving him of an education. They drag him back again at sixteen when he joins a troupe of traveling Italian actors. Lacking experience and learning, even at twenty, Lestat can only read and write his name and a few remembered prayers. This life of cruel bondage leads his mother, Gabrielle, to sell family heirlooms to pay for Lestat's hunting and give him something to enjoy. When this fails, she encourages a more decisive rebellion, urging him to flee to Paris so that she can die knowing that he has found freedom.

That dying wish gives Lestat a new life, complete with all the opportunities that passed him over while he was human. He becomes a great actor and attracts the attention of a great vampire. His maker, Magnus, also bestows him wealth and power. Lestat buys the theater where he performs. He is also able to repay his mother's gift by providing her with a new vampire life just before her natural human death. Then Lestat gives a new life to a rival vampire, Armand, after his disciples try to kill Lestat. He gives Armand's coven the theater and makes Armand master of the Théâtre des Vampires. Despite all the lives that he assists and renews, the recipients all betray him. First his mother, then Armand, and so on. They little appreciate what he has done for them, and do little to ease his loneliness.

Lestat with this third progeny, Claudia (Kirsten Dunst), before her betrayal. His attempt to hang onto Louis by making a child vampire almost killed him.

Powers

Lestat possesses the standard vampire powers of enhanced speed, stamina, and strength. He can mentally sense other vampires and read the minds of humans. Like Anne Rice's other vampires, he is immune to the stake and classic anti-vampire weapons. Fire and sunlight will work, if the vampire is young enough. It is fire that kills Lestat's maker, Magnus, and sunlight that takes out Claudia.

The Children of the Millennia, those over a thousand years old, are often spared death by fire and sunlight. Lestat joins this category with Akasha's ancient blood. For example, a suicide attempt in the desert leaves him only with a tan. Like the Children of the Millennia, he receives other gifts: Fire (the ability to set something ablaze with a glance), Killing (the power to rupture the cardiovascular system), and Cloud (the ability to fly). These powers mark Lestat as a danger to the other vampires.

FACTS AND TRIVIA

- Lestat's birthday is November 7, the same date as Stan Rice, the husband of author Anne Rice, who is said to be her inspiration for the character.

- The list of his progeny grows, but includes Gabrielle, Louis, Claudia, Nicolas, David, and Mona.

QUOTES

"I'd like to meet the devil some night. I'd chase him from here to the wilds of the Pacific. I am the devil." —Interview with the Vampire *(novel)*

[To Louis] *"You whining coward of a vampire who prowls the night killing alley cats and rats and staring for hours at candles as if they were people and standing in the rain like a zombie until your clothes are drenched and you smell like old wardrobe trunks in attics and have the look of a baffled idiot at the zoo."* —Interview with the Vampire *(novel)*

"Don't be a fool for the devil, darling! Unless he treats you a damn sight better than the Almighty!" —The Vampire Lestat *(novel)*

"I can't help being a gorgeous fiend. It's just the card I drew." —Queen of the Damned *(novel)*

"I've always been my own teacher. And I must confess I've always been my favorite pupil as well." —Queen of the Damned *(novel)*

"Lord, what I wouldn't give for a drop of good old-fashioned Creole blood." —Interview with the Vampire *(film)*

Chapter Three
Dark Rogues

rogue (n): A vicious and solitary animal that has separated itself from its herd.

These dark angels aren't like the rest. They make a conscious effort every moment to be something different from those around them. It's generally a struggle to be better than them. Whether it's refusing human blood, seeing demons for what they truly are, or coming back to life to avenge others, they risk everything to stand up for what they believe or to just be who they are.

THE CULLEN FAMILY: DARK CLAN

There have been many vampire families in fiction, but none so richly chronicled as the Cullens, introduced by author Stephenie Meyer in her best-selling novels Twilight *(2005),* New Moon *(2006),* Eclipse *(2007), and* Breaking Dawn *(2008). In the wildly successful screen adaptations of Meyer's books, the family members are played by Peter Facinelli (Carlisle), Robert Pattinson (Edward), Elizabeth Reaser (Esme), Nikki Reed (Rosalie), Kellan Lutz (Emmett), Ashley Greene (Alice), Jackson Rathbone (Jasper), and Kristen Stewart (Bella).*

The Cullen family is the only true family of dark angels. Even the tightly knit Black Dagger Brothers don't function in the true sixties sitcom–family fashion of the Cullens. They live together in the Pacific Northwest, have family meetings and family votes, throw parties, travel to visit extended family, and eat dinner together, albeit one consisting of a free-range diet of deer and grizzly bear. A father with exceptional wisdom and compassion and a mother full of love lead a group of talented vampires in the pursuit of a life more honorable than common vampires could imagine. This determination to rise above their circumstances is their saving grace and the one trait that most qualifies them as dark angels.

Slightly Flawed

As a group, the Cullens have one major weakness: their number, which makes it harder for them to assimilate into human society. One exceptionally alluring person is easy to overlook, but a family with seven of them is more than unusual. The size of their group, combined with their gifts, also makes them a serious threat to the Volturi, the ruling vampire monarchs of the *Twilight* world. That threat becomes even clearer after the Cullens stand against the Volturi in *Breaking Dawn*, becoming the first real threat the ancient family has faced since they conquered the previous rulers. Like any government, they take threats to their power very seriously.

The Cullens (left to right): Emmett, Rose, Esme, Edward, Carlisle, Alice, and Jasper. In *Twilight*, they mostly share the Cullen name, though it's only their latest cover story. They have been other ages and names in other places before returning to Forks.

Beauty and Power

Beauty and power abound in the Cullen home. Like a carnivorous plant, they draw humans in with their radiant, diamondlike skin, supernaturally attractive breath, intoxicating voices, and grace. The humans don't stand a chance. It is this way for all *Twilight* vampires. However, the Cullens have a greater ability to blend in. Their honey-colored eyes change, growing darker, even black, with hunger. They're well fed and appear almost human. Only the human subconscious registers the difference. Eye color is the most obvious physical difference between the Cullens and human-drinkers, who have crimson eyes.

In addition to their exceptional appearances, they possess standard dark angel powers such as heightened senses, strength, and speed. This makes them dangerous to humans, but average among vampires. But they are not unfortunate. As with human families, the Olympic Coven's strength lies in their individual differences. Each Cullen brings something unique to the combined family arsenal of gifts. Most members have special "gifts," such as Edward's mind-reading abilities (see "Edward Cullen: The Dark Romeo").

A Cullen Family Album

The following entries are detailed profiles of each Cullen family member. Their histories, human lives, and relationships are discussed here.

CARLISLE CULLEN

It's not often that a person, or even a dark angel, can overcome such a compelling instinct as eating, simply to be a better person. But that's where Carlisle Cullen, the wizened father and dedicated human physician, shines. As Edward puts it, "Carlisle has always been the most humane, the most compassionate of us. . . . I don't think you could find his equal throughout all of history." Add that compassion to the fact that he looks like a six-foot-two supermodel and you've got a doctor who'd be booked up for the next century!

Born the son of an Anglican pastor in 1640s London, Carlisle is the oldest of the Olympic Coven, named for its location in the Olympic National Forest at the time of the *Twilight* saga. Unlike many others, he became a vampire with the knowledge that his father, not a random stranger, would hunt and kill him just as the pastor and other religious zealots were killing humans believed to be witches and other damned creatures. Carlisle struggled through the painful vampiric change alone and then made several attempts to kill himself. These were among his darkest days.

Carlisle's worst time may have been his stay in Italy with the Volturi, but he hasn't spoken much about it. We do know that he was part of their inner circle for some time. Apparently, he received lavish bribes to persuade him to drink human blood. It's hard to say for sure, but given that the eccentric Volturi leader, Aro, said he never thought anyone could be stronger-willed than Carlisle, we can assume that he did not give in. Of course, he may have indulged in a bloodbath or two with the decadent vampire rulers. We simply don't know for sure. Either way, the lack of information about Carlisle's Italy years insinuates that they are the darkest of his unlife.

In contrast, several high points in Carlisle's life are clear. Taking the beautiful and sweet vampire Esme as his wife and making the decision to be a "vegetarian," as the Cullens call vampires who refrain from human blood, certainly make the list. Other great moments include Carlisle's work as a doctor. He describes his work during a historical plague in *New Moon*: "That was a hard time to pretend—there was so much work to be done, and I had no need of rest. How I hated to go back to my house, to hide in the dark and pretend to sleep while so many were dying." Another example occurs in *Eclipse* when Carlisle overcomes his instinctual aversion to werewolves in order to save Jacob Black, the reluctant wolf leader, forcing the pack to see how much humanity the vampires retain.

Even after hundreds of years of life, Dr. Carlisle Cullen enjoys baseball as much as the "kids" do. But does the good doctor still indulge his need for playing the Italian vampire superhero?

When others would walk away, Carlisle says it is compassion that drives him to do the impossible. Compassion is also generally considered his particular gift. A more likely power is that of self-control. Compassion is why he takes care of others, such as his "adoption" of the younger vampires he didn't create, but it's Carlisle's self-discipline that keeps him from ripping into every bleeding patient he treats. Aro, who certainly read Carlisle's memories and thoughts during their time together through his own gift, points this out to Edward in *New Moon* when he says, "I certainly never thought to see Carlisle bested for self-control of all things." Aro points out that self-control is another strength—the only thing that allows Carlisle to transform each of his companions without draining them dry, something virtually impossible for most vampires of the *Twilight* world. The ability gives him hope for a normal life and the motivation to follow through with his dream of caring for others as a physician.

To say that Carlisle is passionate about medicine is an understatement. As he puts it in *New Moon*, "What I enjoy the very most is when my enhanced abilities let me save someone who would otherwise have been lost. It's pleasant knowing that, thanks to what I can do, some people's lives are better because I exist. Even the sense of smell is a useful diagnostic tool at times." It's enough to make you feel warm and fuzzy when he says it like that.

It's a noble attitude, and one that seems to come from Carlisle's religious beliefs. He says that though he doesn't have his father's beliefs, he has never, in nearly four hundred years, "seen anything to make [me] doubt whether God exists in some form or the other. Not even the reflection in the mirror." And who couldn't agree with that? If ever there were a creature that looked like God had perfected His work, it's Carlisle. (Okay, maybe Edward, too.) Like anyone willing to admit the impossibility of truly knowing what the afterlife holds, Carlisle resigns himself to hoping for the best. He says he also has faith that "there is still a point to this life, even for us. It's a long shot, I'll admit. By all accounts, we're damned regardless. But I hope, maybe foolishly, that we'll get some measure of credit for trying." No doubt, if there is a God in Carlisle's world, He will welcome Carlisle as a reward simply for his remarkable ability to resist temptation.

EDWARD CULLEN

Edward was Carlisle's first progeny, turned while he lay dying from Spanish Influenza. He appears to be seventeen, though he is actually more than a hundred years old. He holds several degrees from lifetimes of attending different colleges, and medical degrees are among them. Of all the siblings, he is most like Carlisle. (See "Edward Cullen: The Dark Romeo.")

ESME CULLEN

Esme Cullen was born in Columbus, Ohio, in 1895 with the human name Esme Anne Platt. According to stepheniemeyer.com, the five-foot-six brunette beauty fell out of a tree and broke her leg at the age of sixteen (in 1911). Because her doctor was out of town at the time, she was taken to the Columbus hospital, where she was treated by a doctor—Dr. Carlisle Cullen—who moved out of town shortly after treating her.

The infatuation Esme carried for the doctor after that day shadowed her life. Other men couldn't measure up to her dreamy doctor, and she didn't marry. By the rules of her day, Esme was an old maid at twenty-two, and had no real prospects for marriage. She dreamed of moving west and working as a schoolteacher and planned to do so, but her parents wanted her to stay, marry, and live a "respectable" life. It didn't work out. So, through what amounted to an arranged marriage, she wed Mr. Charles Evenson, the well-off son of a family friend.

However, Charles began to abuse Esme soon after. Urged by her parents to work it out, Esme stayed and endured the abuse. Fortunately, Charles was drafted during World War I, giving her a break from his ill behavior. She was happy during his absence. Then, when he returned, so did the abuse. It wasn't long until Esme discovered that she was pregnant with Charles's son. Maternal instincts finally forced her to protect herself and her baby. Esme ran away to Ashland, Wisconsin, and started a new life, where she claimed to be a war widow and worked as a teacher, just as she'd always dreamed.

The dream ended in 1921 when the baby died of a lung infection days after his birth. Esme tried to commit suicide not long after that by jumping from a cliff to what she hoped was her death. Instead, it was the leap into her new life. When her body was placed in the morgue, her old friend and the physician on duty, Dr. Cullen, heard the faint heartbeat. He recognized Esme and refused to let her die.

Esme didn't fight the life she was given. Instead, she was happy to spend it with the man she'd been thinking about for so long, the standard against which she judged all men. Although there is no word on how long Carlisle and Esme were together before they married, Stephenie Meyer has said that their relationship formed "quickly and easily."

Now the mother of the Olympic Coven, Esme is perpetually twenty-six. The child she lost was replaced by her six adopted vampire "children": Edward, Rosalie, Emmett, Alice, Jasper, and Bella. Her special gift is boundless love, and it allows her to care for her adopted family just as she would a real one. They are her world. Edward describes this love in *Midnight Sun*: "If Carlisle was the soul of our family, then Esme was the heart. He gave us a leader who deserved following; she made that following into an act of love." Esme's other passion is remodeling old homes, as we see in the cottage she gives Edward and his young bride Bella as a gift in *Breaking Dawn*.

ROSALIE HALE

The third of Carlisle's progeny, Rosalie, is the unhappiest with vampire unlife despite the fact that she is considered the most beautiful of the Cullen clan. As she puts it in *Eclipse*: "If we had happy endings, we'd all be under gravestones now."

She was born Rosalie Lillian Hale in Rochester, New York, to a homemaker mother and a banker father, who maintained his wealth even during the Great Depression. Rosalie was happy. She had everything a girl could want: money, status, beauty, and constant reminders of how beautiful she was. At her mother's urging, Rosalie put on her best dress and went to her father's job to deliver his lunch. There, Royce King II, the son of the bank's owner, noticed her. The attraction was superficial and immediate. He began sending her roses and soon the two were engaged.

Then, in 1933 and at the age of eighteen, Rosalie went to visit her friend Vera. Watching Vera with her loving husband and curly-haired baby boy, Henry, saddened Rosalie. It didn't take her long to see how loveless her relationship with Royce was and that she wanted what Vera had: a real family. On the walk home, Rosalie ran into Royce and his friends, all of whom were drunk. After her fiancé bragged about her beauty to his pals, the group raped and beat her. Rosalie was left for dead.

Drawn by the scent of her blood, Carlisle found her. He changed her, even though the other Cullens at that time (Edward and Esme) didn't fully agree with the decision. Rose, as the other Cullens often call her, woke and was happy to see her beauty even more enhanced by vampirism.

Soon, Rose set out to take revenge on the men who had taken her life. Rose murdered each of the guys who took part in her assault, carefully covering her tracks. Then, having saved Royce for last to torture him psychologically, she put on her wedding dress and went after him. Rose killed two guards and went through a vault door into a windowless room to find the terrified Royce. She didn't drink their blood, though. As Rose puts it, "I was very careful not to spill their blood—I knew I wouldn't be able to resist that, and I didn't want any part of them in me, you see."

When Rose returned to the Cullens, she experienced her first real rejection. Edward, whom Carlisle had hoped would fall for Rose, loved her only as a sister. Her beauty and status as a human led to a rather shallow personality, which kept her focused on vanity, money, status, and possessions. Rose is materialistic and completely into appearances, be they her personal appearance or how others perceive her acts or possessions. Edward sought his intellectual and spiritual match. It is an insult that Rose never quite forgave.

Two years later, while in a forest close to Gatlinburg, Tennessee, Rose found young Emmett McCarty, her soul mate and future Cullen sibling. She rescued him and asked Carlisle to turn him for her. The two have been together ever since, but even her marriage is about making an impression. She and Emmett have had several weddings just for this purpose. Impressions are also the basis of her and Emmett's mostly physical relationship. Where Bella and Edward are all about intellectual connections, she and Emmett are both into simple physical qualities. She is the five-foot-nine beauty and Emmett is the strong, rough male.

Contrary to her very feminine appearance, Rosalie's hobbies are boyish. She likes to tinker and has a collection of things to work on. Cars are her favorite, and she maintains the Cullen fleet. No special power is noted for Rose.

EMMETT CULLEN

Emmett Cullen was born Emmett McCarty, the youngest in a large Scotch-Irish American family. In 1935, at age twenty, Emmett was hunting in a Smoky Mountain forest near Gatlinburg, Tennessee, when he was mauled by a bear. He was near death when Rosalie found him. Emmett reminded her so much of Vera's baby boy, with his curly hair and dimples, that she carried him more than a hundred miles back to Carlisle and asked him to change Emmett into a vampire.

The vampire table in Forks High's lunchroom (prior to Bella). Left to right: Jasper and Alice, Emmett and Rose, and Edward.

At six foot five, he's the largest of the Cullen clan. He often relies on brute strength, because that is his particular gift. As a vampire, Emmett is all about competition, whether it's arm wrestling or taking down a grizzly. None of the Cullens is able to match Emmett in strength. He is also the fun one, often pulling pranks and being as playful as Rose is intense. When it comes to mealtime, he prefers bears, as if he will someday run across the same bear that mauled him and rip it to shreds.

ALICE CULLEN

Little is known about Alice Cullen. What we do know about her is limited because the transition to vampirism wiped her memory clean of her previous human life. Through research, Alice found that she was born Mary Alice Brandon in 1901. She lived in Biloxi, Mississippi, and, even as a human, she had visions. During that time, psychic powers were considered made-up, strange, and evil. So, Alice was marked as insane and tucked away in a sanitarium.

According to the tombstone on Alice's empty grave and the file she stole from the asylum, her family pretended that she died. Though Alice survived, her human family eventually died out, with the exceptions of her younger sister, Cynthia Brandon, and a niece, who both still live in Biloxi.

One factor in her lack of human memories is that Alice was kept in an unlit cell, living much of her life in the dark. This limited her contact with the outside and other humans, but James, the vampire tracker who chased Bella Swan in *Twilight*, caught wind of Alice's exceptionally sweet blood. He decided to make a snack of her, but, from what Alice can surmise, a vampire who worked at the asylum changed her in an attempt to protect her, and her abilities, from death. She has no memory of the change, only that she woke up as a vampire. Her maker, however, must have abandoned her. It is also possible that James killed Alice's maker.

Unlike the other Cullens, whom Carlisle taught to refrain from human blood, Alice developed her own vegetarian ways. Then, through precognitive visions, she met the others. First, she found the still human-drinking Jasper at a diner in Philadelphia, where she waited day after day until he walked in. As Alice and Jasper explain in *Eclipse*, she walked right up to him and told him she'd been waiting. He was, of course, taken aback by the display and "bowed his head like a good Southern gentleman." With her usual confidence, Alice offered him her hand. It was the first sign of hope that the battle-weary Civil War veteran Jasper had seen in a very long time. He took her hand and let Alice lead him into a better life, one filled with true love and peace.

Now, they have a type of sweet, silent communication that goes beyond words. Alice is a soothing force for Jasper, especially when his bloodlust becomes unbearable. In return, Jasper would die to defend her. Like the wife in an old married couple, she just smiles and calls him an "overprotective fool." Also, Alice and Jasper's relationship is a bit more conservative than Emmett and Rose's. They refrain from public displays of passion, opting for private, intimate moments. Perhaps this is due to their Southern upbringing.

After another vision, Alice led Jasper to the Cullen family. Knowing how well they would all get along, she invited herself to join the family. And they did get along fabulously, especially where Edward is concerned. Within the Cullen clan, he is Alice's closest friend. The two relate better than most real siblings, communicating in a silent language of their own thanks to their mental powers. Alice also shares her precognitive visions with Edward whenever he's nearby, giving him an insight no one else has.

Throughout the *Twilight* saga, she is the greatest supporter of Edward's relationship with Bella Swan. Alice is immediately ready to be Bella's best friend because of a vision about Bella's future with Edward. Then, in *New Moon*, it is Alice who operates at breakneck speed and against the Volturi to save Edward from suicide. And it is Edward who is most distraught by Alice's sudden disappearance with the impending arrival of the Volturi looming over the family in *Breaking Dawn*. It is a relationship topped only by their love for their spouses.

Where looks are concerned, Alice is as beautiful as the other Cullen women. She often appears as carefree as a child, dancing rather than walking. Her doe eyes and delicate features, combined with her being physically smaller than most adults (four foot ten), causes her to be underestimated by many outsiders. But Alice's stature doesn't affect her ability to take down vampires twice her size.

Alice's power gives her the ultimate advantage. Her precognitive visions help the Cullens navigate the human world safely and help save Bella through a number of attempts on her life. They also make Alice even more deadly than other vampires. Alice is always one step ahead because she knows her enemy's next move as soon as they think of it. It makes her the most formidable in battle.

However, the visions are limited and offer only the results of decisions that are made. As minds change, so does the outcome, making the visions dispensable. Alice also cannot see the future when other monsters, such as the werewolves, are involved. She believes that is because she's never been a shape-shifter, so she cannot relate. Carlisle, using his vast medical experience, theorizes that the gaps in her visions have to do with the twenty-four chromosome pairs that the beings (whom Alice cannot see in her visions, or who block her from seeing others) share. This unusual trait makes Alice not only unique among the vampires of the *Twilight* universe but also a pretty danged exceptional dark angel. Jasper calls her "one frightening little monster," and Edward gives her the teasing nicknames of "Shorty" and "Little Freak." But Alice takes it all in stride. She jokes of her precognitive ability by trying to trick the others: "I know—I'll play you for it. Rock, paper, scissors."

JASPER HALE

Born Jasper Whitlock in 1843, he is the most experienced fighter and second oldest member of the Cullen coven. As a human, he was the youngest major in the Confederate Army. That was before January 1, 1863, when a power-hungry vampire named Maria bit the handsome, honey-blond Texan and turned him into a vampire.

His special gift, which was apparent after his transformation, is to manipulate the emotions of those around him. At first, this power was a blessing, allowing him to control the newborn army that Maria made. Because newborns are savages in the world of *Twilight*, it was a great advantage to calm them and use the neonates' exceptional strength to conquer the covens of older vampires. Jasper became Maria's general and helped her establish a newborn vampire army, which she used to conquer the Texas area.

During those dark years, he was a vicious predator, indulging his thirst regularly. In *Eclipse*, he explains: "In so many years of slaughter and carnage, I'd lost nearly all of my humanity. I was undeniably a nightmare, a monster of the grisliest kind." As time went on, the excessive killing took its toll on Jasper's psyche. He was lonely and lost until he befriended one of the vampires, a young man named Peter whom Maria had decided to keep. The pair were friends until Jasper was told to kill Charlotte, a newborn Peter loved. The two younger vampires ran away together. That was Jasper's breaking point. He disobeyed Maria's orders and let them escape. It was possibly the best decision he ever made because they returned later to tell him how the vampires of the north lived peacefully together. He left with them.

A few years later, unable to tolerate the emotions of his dying human victims any longer, Jasper struck out on his own. He still fed off humans when he had to, but that stopped when he met the love of his unlife, Alice, at the diner in Philadelphia, Pennsylvania. The six-foot-three Jasper fell immediately for the tiny, beautiful vampire, and they've been together ever since. And it is Alice, not the Cullens, who taught him how to survive on animal blood.

But it has been a struggle.

His life prior to Cullen-ization still makes it hard for him to stick to their vegetarian diet. Jasper says in *New Moon*, "After a century of instant gratification, I found self-discipline . . . challenging." That's perfectly understandable. Were it not for Jasper's love of Alice and her fondness for the Cullens, he probably wouldn't go through the trouble of pretending to be Rosalie's twin and one of the adopted Cullen kids. He's not like them, and it's obvious at times. Besides the emotional scars, he carries physical scars from so many years of fighting. They make it almost impossible for Jazz, as the Cullens call him, to forget how much more savage his life has been or that he's one of the few to survive the Southern Vampire Wars, the vampire equivalent of the American Civil War. However, those experiences also make him the vampire his allies in *Breaking Dawn* call "power and speed and death rolled into one."

BELLA SWAN-CULLEN

Isabella Marie Swan's human life and transformation is well documented in the *Twilight* saga. She was born on September 13, 1987, and is the wife of Edward, whom she met at the Forks, Washington, high school while he and his siblings were pretending to be human high school students. On September 10, 2006, during the birth of Renesmee, their hybrid vampire-human daughter, Bella's blood loss and impending death forced Edward to turn her. Because of this, she is the newest *transformed* vampire of the Cullen family.

At five foot four and possessing no significant offensive skills, Bella appears very average. However, her special "shield" abilities make this twenty-first-century addition the strongest defense the family possesses. While human, her mind was locked away, unreachable by Edward's telepathy for some unknown reason. It wasn't until other vampires met her post-transition that anyone realized it was a special ability, and the term *shield* was applied. She also learned that the force field can be stretched to cover the entire Cullen clan and several other people at once. Bella can sense anyone within her protection, but protect her mind at the same time. With great effort, she can lower her shield and allow others, such as Edward, into her mind. This power is only impermeable to mental attacks, but she is still vulnerable

Bella and Edward entering their Monte Carlo–themed prom at Forks High School in *Twilight*.

to physical assaults. Yet, Bella is one of the most powerful vampires. Aro, the Volturi leader and collector of vampires with particularly useful gifts, made this obvious when he tried repeatedly to make Bella a part of his guard.

Bella's nicknames also include "Bells," "Bell," "Vampire Girl," "Leech Lover," and "Love," which of course is Edward's title for her. Although her official married name in Forks is Isabella Cullen, it's only part of the Olympic Coven's cover, as Edward has been using Carlisle's name, Cullen, while in the National Forest area. At some point in the future, they will most likely go by the names Edward and Bella Masen, using Edward's real name.

RENESMEE CULLEN

The half-breed child of Edward Cullen and the human Bella Swan, Renesmee Carlie Cullen (or Renesmee Carlie Masen, since Edward is her dad) is the newest member of the Olympic Coven, born in *Breaking Dawn*. She is also the most gifted.

"Nessie," as the others call her, was born on September 10, 2006, a few days before Bella's nineteenth birthday. She is named for her grandparents. Her first name is a combination of her grandmothers' names, Renée Swan and Esme Cullen. Her middle name is a combination of the grandfathers' names, Carlisle Cullen and Charlie Swan. She physically resembles both families with a perfect blend of their features, including long bronze curls and chocolate brown eyes. Like her mother's human side, she has body heat, a pulse from the blood flowing through veins, and a slightly rapid but beating heart. She also has the ability to sleep.

From her father's vampiric line, Renesmee gets the craving for blood. In fact, she prefers it, but she can survive on human food as well. Her skin is strong but soft and glows in the sunlight, rather than sparkling. She lacks the venom that the other vampires have, and therefore cannot create vampires and is not dangerous when she playfully bites her family members and friends.

Renesmee also has many of the vampires' powers, such as enhanced senses, speed, and strength. Plus, she has the extraordinary ability to pierce mental shields like Bella's and can transmit thoughts by touching someone's skin, somewhat like Edward's telepathic abilities. Her gifts seem to be the same as her parents', only in reverse. Rather than being immortally unchanging, she matures at a breakneck speed. Renesmee will reach adulthood in roughly one-third the time of a normal human. At about age seven, she will look close to eighteen years old.

Jacob Black, Bella's best friend, Quileute Tribe Chief, and leader of the wolf pack, will one day be her husband. Just after she was born, he "imprinted" on her as his kind does, making it impossible for him to want anyone but Renesmee as his future bride. He is the perfect best friend and protector, and already a welcome member of the family.

❧ FACTS AND TRIVIA ❧

- Carlisle believes in God, or at least an afterlife. He says so in *New Moon*: "I look at my . . . *son*. His strength, his goodness, the brightness that shines out of him—and it only fuels that hope, that faith, more than ever. How could there not be more for one such as Edward?"

- Rosalie and Jasper go by the name Hale when the others all claim the Cullen name. According to stepheniemeyer.com, Rose and Jasper look like siblings—twins, in fact. So, their current cover story is that the two are twins, and Jasper took Rose's last name because that's the way Rose wants it. Although most of the Cullens have learned to let go of their pasts, for someone like Rose—someone who found her value in her family name, status, and beauty—it's too hard to look beyond what was her heyday. She was a socialite, and name was everything. Being Rosalie Hale was all she knew, and she still isn't ready to let that go.

- It appears that Carlisle is the legendary Italian *Stregone Benefice*. Rumors say that he started the legend of the superhero-like vampires who defended humans against the evil vampires. It's even one of Carlisle's aliases in several profiles. So, prior to finding Edward, our fair doctor was secretly roaming the moonlit Italian streets in a cape and mask, protecting humans.

- Because Esme was changed just after the birth of her son, there is a strong belief that she probably has a slender but slightly more voluptuous shape than the other women of the Cullen family due to the hormonal changes she was going through at the time. Does this also mean that she would be lactating for eternity? It's doubtful.

- Alice has a strange hobby. Like a sadistic karaoke singer, Alice enjoys using that high-pitched "bell-like voice" to sing three octaves higher than a song is. Shattered glass, anyone?

- In the April 2010 issue of *Forbes* magazine, Carlisle was named number one in the "Forbes Fictional Fifteen," a listing of the richest fictional characters, due to Alice's stock market insights and the bribes Carlisle received during his time with the Volturi. Plus, he's been a doctor for centuries. Carlisle's listing in the Fictional Fifteen reportedly cost Carlisle his medical license, led to an IRS audit, and forced him to flee Forks. His only response to the investigative team: "It took you long enough to find me." Does this add to his dark side? Maybe. But it also makes us smile.

- While cute, Alice's constant focus on what Bella wears borders on obsessive-compulsive disorder at times and leaves some readers wondering whether it is a manifestation of a problem or a sweet way for Alice to make Bella look the part of Edward's mate. Perhaps neither; stepheniemeyer.com states that Alice enjoys using Bella to live out human experiences that Alice doesn't remember. It's also possible that Alice does it purely for her own entertainment. She is, after all, the most childlike of the Cullens.

QUOTES

"It sounded like you were having Bella for lunch, and we came to see if you would share."
—*Alice,* Twilight

"There are exceptions to every rule." —*Esme,* Twilight

"I think she's having hysterics. Maybe you should slap her." —*Alice,* New Moon

"Was it right to doom the others to this life? I can't decide."—*Carlisle,* New Moon

"I'm really glad Edward didn't kill you. Everything's so much more fun with you around."
—*Emmett,* Eclipse

"I will do what I can to help him. . . . I've never been to veterinarian school." —*Carlisle,* Eclipse

"I'm not going down without a fight." —*Emmett,* Breaking Dawn

"Over my pile of ashes." —*Rosalie,* Breaking Dawn

MR. CREPSLEY: CIRCUS FREAK

Larten Crepsley is notable among modern vampires by making his home in a freak circus, where his supernatural strangeness is somewhat camouflaged by natural oddities. Crepsley is the creation of Irish writer Darren O'Shaughnessy, who, writing under the pen name Darren Shan, is responsible for the first-person Saga of Darren Shan young adult vampire novels, twelve in all, beginning with Cirque du Freak *in 2000. Crepsley doesn't make it through the entire series, but in 2010 begins a new life in Shan's* Birth of a Killer, *the first in a four-book adventure known collectively as the Saga of Larten Crepsley. The other three books will be titled* Ocean of Blood, Palace of the Damned, *and* Brothers to the Death, *according to the* Shanville Monthly *newsletter. In Paul Weitz's 2009 film* Cirque du Freak: The Vampire's Assistant, *Crepsley was memorably played by the Academy Award–nominated character actor John C. Reilly.*

Larten Crepsley is a dark angel truly like no other—and it's not just his orange hair. He has a flair for the dramatic, spending most of his time in a freak show, dating the bearded lady. Still, it's his refusal to be anything other than himself that makes him a rogue.

The Early Years

Before Darren began referring to him as Mr. Crepsley, he was simply Larten. We don't know exactly when he was changed, but we know that he worked at a young age and lived a "poverty-stricken" life. So, it had to be before child labor laws were enacted. There is a mention in *Allies of the Night*, book eight of the Saga of Darren Shan, that Vampires came to his hometown more than 150 years ago. If this is when he was blooded, he could be around 160 to 170 years old. According to the description of *The Saga of Larten Crepsley: Birth of a Killer* on darrenshan.com, as of the date of this publication, Larten's story is said to span two hundred years of his life. It is possible that he is therefore two hundred years old.

Mr. Crepsley from the *Cirque du Freak* film is very similar to the Larten of literature. But does he have nose hair?

However old Larten is, his story begins when he is still a human boy, laboring under horrid conditions in a workhouse since the age of eight. He is a hard worker, but when the boss makes an example of Larten's brother and kills him, Larten goes into a frenzy. He kills the foreman. As a result, he is forced to flee and live a sad existence of cobweb eating and crypt sleeping.

Until a man named Seba Nile finds him, sleeping in one of those crypts.

Seba Nile

Seba offers a different life to Larten. He is sophisticated and worldly, and in need of an assistant. In exchange for Larten's willingness to be the vampire's assistant, he provides the boy with protection and shelter.

Those early years with his mentor define Larten. Through their travels, he grows to respect Seba and models himself after the ancient vampire. Seba dresses in red, which inspires Larten's red wardrobe. The proper manner in which Larten speaks is also due to his sire's influence. Every contraction that Larten uses costs him a nose or an ear hair. Seba plucks them in an effort to teach the boy to use excellent grammar. It works, obviously.

The Middle Years

The years between this rocky start and his time with Darren (see below) are not yet clear. We do know that he's been known by the names Larten, Quicksilver, Vur Horston, and Mr. Crepsley. He can neither read nor write, indicating that no one took the time to teach him in all those years. Although it's unclear exactly when the height of Larten's Vampire political career was, we do know that he was a revered general and close to becoming a Prince. Staying true to himself, he walked away from that option, resigning his post to do more fascinating things.

A close friend of Larten's seems to think that he became weary of the violence in that lifestyle. He could be right, but Crepsley's disdain for politics seems to state otherwise. Either way, Crepsley could have simply become part of the Vampire hierarchy and perpetuated their agenda. Instead, he chose a life with more color and adventure.

Darren Shan

In *The Saga of Darren Shan: Cirque du Freak*, we watch as Larten meets a human boy, Darren Shan, who steals Larten's talented and deadly spider, Madam Octa. The spider then bites Darren's best friend, Steve Leonard. To save Steve, Darren goes to Larten for help. Rather than simply giving him an antidote, Larten gives the boy the choice of being his assistant or letting Steve die. Of course, Darren chooses to be an assistant. Larten bloods him (feeds him blood) almost immediately, sealing their bond. It's a mean and altogether underhanded way to gain an assistant, one that makes Darren resent him.

Darren tries to kill Larten shortly after being blooded. Then, in *Tunnels of Blood*, he tries again, allowing a killer to escape. Larten manages to control his temper and understand the boy's mistrust of him. But it's Larten's good advice, teaching in the Vampire ways, and fatherly direction that make Darren's feelings warm to him.

The two become close and Mr. Crepsley, as Darren calls him, goes with Darren through several trials on Vampire Mountain. Once there, Larten is forced to answer for his blooding a child. He has no real answer and is punished, though the Princes are creative. They force Larten to start Darren in the Trials of Death, which end in a disqualification. Darren makes Larten proud, though, by returning to inform the Princes of a plot to betray them. Together, they flush the Vampaneze (evil vampires) out of their hiding places on the mountain, and the battle ends with Darren becoming a Prince himself.

In *Hunters of the Dusk*, Larten and Darren become Vampaneze Lord Hunters. These Vampaneze are relatives of the Vampires, an offshoot marked by their purple skin and red eyes. They also differ in that they enjoy killing their victims, unlike the Vampires, who try not to kill them. The Vampaneze spend a great deal of time seeking out a "Lord" (ruler) of their own, to help them win the war against the Vampires. The Vampires, in an effort to protect themselves, have established hunters who search out this Vampaneze Lord, to destroy him. The assignment is Larten's last.

Mr. Crepsley's worst time comes in *Killers of the Dawn*. In an attempt to kill the Vampaneze Lord, Larten fights what he believes to be the lord and kills him. However, Steve (Darren's former best friend) is the true Lord, and he pushes Larten into fiery stakes, killing him. As if dying weren't enough of a low point, it's coupled with his failure to kill the true Vampaneze Lord.

Ladies' Man

Larten's life story also includes the love of a few women. During those middle years, he and Arra Sails, one of the few female Vampires, were mated. Although they broke up some time ago, he is still at least somewhat attracted to her. It comes out in his attitude toward her during Larten's stay on Vampire Mountain in the book by the same title. Also, when Darren asks about her, Mr. Crepsley avoids the topic. Then, when she dies, it is a mourning Larten whom Seba has to pull away from the body.

We also find out that the distinct scar on Larten's face, which runs from his left ear down to his mouth, is from Lady Evanna, a sorceress and half-vampire. It is revealed in *Hunters of the Dusk* that she gave it to him as a gift for an unwelcomed kiss Larten gave her when he was feeling particularly attractive and intoxicated. However, she does give him several gifts to make up for it, the last of which is a group of frogs that together form a picture of Larten's deceased love Arra.

In the film, Mr. Crepsley dates Madame Truska, the bearded lady in the freak show that he travels with. The two have a very warm relationship and act more like a married couple than a dating pair. In a classic line, he says, "Your mouth says no, but your beard says yes." In addition, there are two other loves in Larten's life. Although we're not sure, one of them may be the girl in the painting found in his quarters in *Cirque du Freak*.

Some habits are hard to break. Larten still sleeps in a coffin, uses proper grammar, and dresses in red as his former teacher Seba Nile did.

Myths and Realities

Mr. Crepsley has many standard vampire powers. His strength and senses exceed human levels, and his speed can reach heights that will fool vision because he's faster than the eyes are. Running this fast is referred to as "flitting" in his world. As with other Vampires of his world, sunlight will kill Mr. Crepsley, and he ages at one-tenth the human rate. Vampires' mouths are valuable weapons. First, their teeth, just like their fingernails, are much harder than a human's. Their saliva can heal wounds, as with many of the other dark angels, but their breath is unique. It's not sweet like the Cullens, but becomes a gas that can knock victims unconscious for a half hour or more.

Vampires in Larten's world do drink human blood, but with some major exceptions. They have to feed from humans at least once a month to live. When they do feed, it's only a small amount. In their world, if they kill a person through exsanguination, they drink in part of the victim's spirit as well, so the Vampires avoid it as much as possible. How would you like to be haunted by the spirit and memories of the person you drank?

According to Darren, some of his powers are beyond what regular Vampires have, such as playing with illusions. He can telepathically control some animals and insects, such as wolves and spiders, though wolves are drawn to Vampires anyway, making this power not specific to Larten. He is also an exceptional fighter in both hand-to-hand and melee combat, and he is stronger and faster than most Vampires, as we see in *Trials of Death*.

FACTS AND TRIVIA

- Mr. Crepsley carries bottled blood from corpses because he prefers to be prepared.

- Believing that everyone should be able to cook, Larten teaches Darren how to cook a stew. He also keeps collapsible pots and pans with him, which he received from Evanna.

QUOTES

"I hate children. What is it you want? Money? Jewels? The rights to publish my story?"
—Cirque du Freak

"Vampires are almost always saying good-bye. We never stop anywhere very long. We are forever picking up our roots and moving on to new pastures. It is our way." —Cirque du Freak

SCHUYLER VAN ALEN: BLUE-BLOODED ANGEL

If you somehow haven't noticed, high schools are among the hottest settings for modern vampire tales, but few have the exclusive class-stamp of Duchesne, an educational enclave in Manhattan with undead secrets reaching back to the Mayflower. *In a five-novel series by Melissa de la Cruz,* Blue Bloods *(2007),* Masquerade *(2007),* Revelations *(2008),* The Van Alen Legacy *(2009), and* Misguided Angel *(2010), Schuyler (or Sky) Van Alen is a student pulled deeper into the vampire world through both her classmates and her personal family history. De la Cruz has also produced a bonus novella,* Bloody Valentine *(2010) and a supernatural spin-off adventure,* Wolf Pact *(2012).*

Schuyler Van Alen is the blue blood of the dark angels. Even if she doesn't look like a snooty socialite, she belongs with the inner circle of the elite Manhattan vampires. It is in her blood. And, with a name like Schuyler Theodora Elizabeth Van Alen Chase, who would ever question her pedigree?

Aperio Oris

"Reveal Yourself." Or in this case, reveal her.

Born on September 1, 1991, Schuyler is an attractive young woman with blue eyes, otherwise described as "startlingly pretty, with a sweet, heart-shaped face; a perfectly upturned nose; and soft milky skin." Her blue-black hair flows down her back in waves, completing the supermodel good looks that this waif-thin girl was blessed with.

She has never fit in, and the changes make her feel even stranger. Unlike the other girls, Sky rebels against the norms of Duchesne, her esteemed New York private school. It's full of socialites. Gucci and Prada grace the halls more often than plain common sense. It's annoying and shallow, and not Sky's way. She prefers the real, the classic, to things and emotions that are just for show. This ability to see deeper than the shiny surface is definitely a strength for Sky. She is also shy. She keeps to herself and pays attention to what the others do and say. This "people watching" allows her to stand outside the crowd and take in the

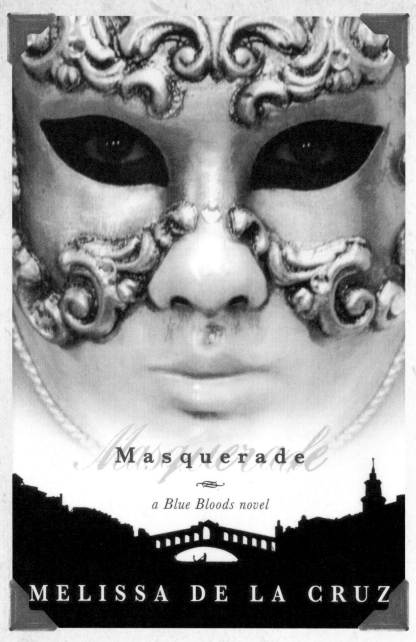

Masquerade

a Blue Bloods novel

MELISSA DE LA CRUZ

At the Four Hundred Ball, Jack revealed his true form as Abaddon.

full picture. It clues her in to things that others miss. Then, she acts in her own time. It's another of her strengths. Sky also lives with her grandmother, Cordelia Van Alen, in an old mansion and relishes her solitude.

Then, just before her fifteenth birthday, pale blue lines appear just under her skin, like tattoos. They create a lacy pattern, decorating her forearms. And then she develops a craving for raw meat. Before long, she realizes that Benjamin "Jack" Force, the most popular boy at Duchesne, is keeping his eye on her. It doesn't take long for her to discover that she belongs to an ancient race of reincarnated vampires whose powerful and wealthy members help to found America: the Blue Bloods.

In fact, she's a Dimidium Cognatus on her first cycle through life. In Sky's world, Blue Blood vampires cannot reproduce. So, they mate with Red Bloods to produce offspring called Half-Bloods, or Dimidium Cognatus. In Sky's case, the two mating vampires are Allegra Van Alen, her Blue Blood mother, and Stephen Chase, her Red Blood father and Allegra's familiar. As the story goes, Allegra is in a coma in a suite at Columbia Presbyterian Hospital because Stephen, whom she loved dearly, has died. Allegra, mourning the loss of Stephen, refused to take another familiar and the lack thereof put her into the coma.

Because of Sky's mixed blood, she is stuck in an unpredictable Transformation. Her blood is also weaker, despite the added power. It also causes her problems with status. She is the only Half-Blood known publicly. The cards are most definitely stacked against her.

Sky finds out about her true heritage just as something is killing off young Blue Bloods. She begins searching for answers, and in *Masquerade*, that search takes her to Venice, where she seeks the help of her grandfather, Lawrence Van Alen. He is the one person she believes can give her information about the fabled Silver Bloods.

When Sky rushes home, she has to attend the Four Hundred Ball and take a familiar so that she doesn't end up like Allegra. She chooses Oliver Hazard-Perry as her conduit and familiar. It's an easy fit and the two are best friends. Amid the other turmoil in the young socialite's life, she attends the ball in a dress passed down from her mother, who wore it when she was sixteen, and tries to uphold the family name.

After the ball, she attends a party where a masked boy kisses her. The party is hosted by Madeleine "Mimi" Force, another young socialite who is the twin of Jack, the boy Sky has a crush on. Because Mimi has been bound to Jack in past lives, she loves him and is jealous in ways most sisters are not. She even attempts to use dark magic to kill Sky.

In *Revelations*, Sky has to defend herself against accusations that she is a Silver Blood. She eventually wins, but it's another mark against her reputation in a place where class is everything. Also following her rebellious streak, she confronts Jack about whether he is the boy who kissed her. He admits that he is and the two begin secretly seeing each other. It's all very romantic, but the bond he shares with Mimi puts an even greater risk on their relationship. It cannot be broken. Then, when Jack and Sky spend the night together and Mimi tells Oliver about their secret relationship, Oliver's feelings are so hurt that he demands she choose between them.

Choosing Oliver, Sky joins in a battle in Rio, then ends up running for her life (along with Oliver) in Europe. In Paris, she tries to get help from the head of the European conclave. Jack goes after her in an attempt to save her from the Silver Bloods in Paris. Sky comes back to New York with Jack, where she finds that her mother is awake. Allegra reveals that the Van Alen's true legacy is to secure the gates of Hell and find the missing gatekeepers. It's no small task for a teen—even if she is a vampire.

Despite Sky's feelings for Jack, and his for her, he is to be bonded to Mimi again. Luckily for Sky, an attack by Lucifer breaks up the ceremony. While Jack is dying from an injury, he drinks Sky's blood and his bond with Mimi is broken. It pits Mimi and Jack as enemies, so Mimi leaves them to each other. Oliver, in a moment of self-sacrifice, urges Sky to be with Jack and go on to the task her mother has assigned her, to see the countess of the European coven. With Sky's true mission ahead of her, it's clear that she must choose her friends and lovers well.

Vos Vadum Reverto

"You shall return" . . . if you ever die, that is.

Like other vampires, Sky may be immortal. No one is quite sure. Her unstable Transformation leaves that a question for now. Time will tell for sure, but it's a definite possibility. And, as with other dark angels, the Blue Bloods and Sky are immune to the cross, stake, garlic, and sun exposure. They also have fangs, but not quite the way other vampires do. The Blue Bloods' wisdom teeth come in at will, sliding down into place like canines in other vampire breeds. All it takes is imaging them into place.

The vampires of Sky's world also have enhanced intelligence, speed, and strength. Some, though not all, possess shape-shifting abilities. Most have mental powers such as mind reading. Of those, the most powerful can control the minds of others. Time manipulation, specifically the ability to stop time, is also possible. Although they all would like to have this ability, only one Blue Blood has ever had it. If Sky or any of the others were to develop it, they would become heroes.

FACTS AND TRIVIA

- Sky's first word didn't come until her fourth birthday. When she did speak, she spoke in fully formed sentences.

- Sky's pet is a friendly, dark-furred bloodhound named Beauty.

- Jack was presented in his true form at the Four Hundred Ball. He is Abaddon, the angel of destruction. Not a bad boyfriend to have!

- Because she is beautiful, Sky modeled for Stitched for Civilization, a hot jeans company. Her picture was on a billboard in Times Square.

QUOTES

"God, she was really pretty, *Bliss thought.* Pretty *wasn't even the word—that would be like calling Audrey Hepburn good-looking. Schuyler was* transcendent.*"*—Blue Bloods

"I love her because she has become something more to me. She has become my life."—*Jack*, Keys to the Repository *(a companion novel to the series)*

[To Oliver] *"Thank you for loving me enough to let me go."*—*Sky*, The Van Alen Legacy

SAM WINCHESTER: SATAN'S PUPPET

Now in its sixth season, first on the WB network and now on the CW, the hit series Super-natural, created by Eric Kripke, revolves around the paranormal investigations of two brothers (see "Dean Winchester: Angelic Warrior"), as they traverse the country in a viewer-addictive combination of Route 66 and The X-Files. Sam Winchester is played by actor Jared Padalecki, himself a longtime fan of shows such as The X-Files and The Twilight Zone. Sam qualifies as a dark angel because of his work protecting humans, his taste for demon blood, his supernatural powers, his return from the dead, and his status as the "vessel" of Lucifer, the original fallen angel.

On the surface, Sam Winchester is a sweet, almost naive guy. He is neither vampire nor fallen angel, but a mix of both. He's also the younger brother of Dean Winchester and the son of John Winchester, renowned demon hunter in the *Supernatural* world. Wholesome and sincere, Sam is the brains to Dean's brawn. Choosing to break family tradition, Sam refused to be a hunter and went instead to college. He had a girlfriend, a future as an attorney, and a normal life. That is, until his past caught up with him.

Beginnings

Sam didn't choose this life of demon hunting. It chose him. Born as the second child to John and Mary Winchester on May 2, 1983, Sam was named after his maternal grandfather and fellow hunter, Samuel Campbell. When he was six months old, his mother went into his room to investigate a noise. A shadowy figure with bright yellow eyes (later known as the yellow-eyed demon, Azazel) stood next to Sam's crib. Unseen hands thrust Mary up against the ceiling and ripped into her abdomen. Then, flames engulfed her while the demon fed Sam a bit of his blood. John and little Dean rushed into the nursery, and Dean was given baby Sam to rush him outside for protection. It was Sam's first in a lifetime of battles to escape from evil.

Sam as portrayed by Jared Padalecki

Growing up without a mom wasn't easy. Sam and Dean bounced from school to school as John moved them around the country, chasing the demon that killed Mary. Family holidays and a home were replaced with motels and broken promises from their dad. Although Sam didn't know what happened to his mom or what John was doing, he knew they weren't living a normal life. Not the life he wanted. Still, he tried to be like the other kids.

One Christmas, Sam read John's journal and discovered that "monsters are real." From that evening forward, Sam trained as a demon hunter out of a need for self-protection. Accustomed to their life, he even packed a butterfly knife in his backpack. He was a natural, easily memorizing spells and remembering details of monsters and protective measures.

Rebellion

But Hell is working against Sam. Azazel's mark on him means that Sam is the subject of several attempts to compromise his moral boundaries. He grows rebellious as evil works to bring Sam into hunting, introduce him to the darker side of the supernatural, and then bring him slowly over to Hell's side.

And it works.

The first temptation to compromise comes from a teacher who pushes Sam to take a different career path after listening to Sam's story of how his family killed a werewolf. The teacher gives Sam the permission he needs to rebel against the family business.

This gentle nudge is the beginning of many tiny pushes that allows Sam to deceive himself, ditch his responsibilities, and indulge his own selfish will. It tests his disobedience in the simplest of ways.

Lies

Sam continues to deceive himself and seek a "normal" life. He shirks his duties as the son of a family of demon hunters and thinks his own way is the best way while looking down his nose at his father's wishes. He goes to college, distancing himself from his family, and makes it to his senior year at Stanford, with a promising career in law. He dates the perfect blond, girl-next-door type, Jessica Moore, whom he plans to marry. Sam does everything a person can to avoid trouble. Although he feels in control and hopes to live a civilian life in the suburbs, it is a lie.

Azazel, and most of the underworld, has set Sam up. After helping him achieve the life he wants, one he believes belongs to people who don't hunt, the demon begins to take it all away. First, his father goes missing on a hunt, and Dean seeks Sam's help. Sam goes, and they find John, but when Sam returns to finish college, Azazel kills Jessica in the same manner Sam's mother died. The loss of his love crushes his hopes.

This final act in a carefully laid plan makes Sam angry and vengeful. He leaves college and becomes a hunter with Dean, but he grows reckless and headstrong. Even though his stubborn disobedience cost him everything, he blames his family's hunting for the problems in his life. It's another self-deception because if little Sammy, as Dean calls him, had accepted his fate and become a hunter, there would have been no Jessica to kill.

Sam's inability to draw a hard line between good and evil, choosing to see the good in all those he meets, including the demons, is reckless. Sam becomes the conscience of the duo. He scolds Dean for wanting to kill a female werewolf, as well as other dangerous beings, and even trusts a possessed girl working for Azazel. Dean is his steadying force.

Sam (right) with Dean and his Impala, preparing for another case shortly after Jessica's death.

When they, along with John, almost have Azazel trapped, he turns on them and possesses their father. Sam has to choose between doing what he wants and obeying his father's wishes, shooting him with a gun capable of killing the demon (and John). He resists again, letting Azazel escape to almost kill them later. As a result, Dean is on the brink of death and John makes a deal with Azazel to take his soul in exchange for Dean's life. The results send John to Hell when Sam's obedience would have killed John and probably sent him to Heaven and ended the ongoing battle.

In addition, Sam's reluctance to kill ultimately leads to his own death when Azazel pits him against other people he marked as children in the same way he did Sam. In an abandoned town, he forces them to battle to the death. Sam knocks down his last opponent but doesn't kill him. The man literally stabs him in the back and kills him in front of Dean. Dean strikes a deal similar to his dad's, agreeing to go to Hell in twelve months to bring Sam back to life. Sam's return to life is filled with increasingly coldhearted acts that slowly rob him of his humanity. He becomes more evil as he tries to save Dean from his contract, killing in cold blood several times. These acts slowly make Sam unfeeling and hungry for an end to it all. It's the result that the evil forces had hoped for.

Then, when Sam's view of good and evil is sufficiently twisted by his experiences hunting, a demon named Ruby gains Sam's trust by claiming to be on his side. When asked about her motivations in the episode "The Kids Are Alright," she tells Sam, "I have my reasons. Not all demons are the same, Sam. Not all of us want the same thing. Me? I wanna help you from time to time. That's all. . . . If you let me, there's something in it for you." Then she promises him she can help him save Dean from his contract. Slowly, she seduces Sam and proves her loyalty by killing other demons and bringing him a knife capable of killing demons. Then she begins to feed Sam her blood, which introduces him to new demonic powers.

During season four, when Dean is in Hell, Sam falls off the grid. Without his brother to hold him back, he begins to drink and make foolish decisions. Ruby uses the opportunity to seize control of him, working her way into his life through his bed and his heart. She confuses him and coaxes him into developing significant powers and even attempts to get him to possess someone. It's a poison Popsicle meant to lure Sam to the dark side, and it works. Sam becomes addicted to demon blood, which is a total betrayal of John's wishes and the life he wanted for Sam. It resembles the story of rebellion against the Father's wishes and wisdom that leads to Lucifer's damnation, which makes Sam the perfect vessel for Lucifer.

Hope

But Dean's rescue from Hell brings Heaven to Earth and hope back to Sam. Upon his return to life, Dean and his friend Bobby have to perform a supernatural-style intervention on Sam. It's not an easy task. As Sam says when Dean confronts him about his blood use, "You were gone. I was here. I had to keep on fighting without you. And what I'm doing, it works." And it did work, even though it cost Sam even more of his moral ground. Although he is unable to stop drinking Ruby's blood as quickly as he'd committed to doing, the commitment alone is a sign of Sam's continued intention to do good. He is, even after his involvement with Ruby, naive to the truths about good and evil.

That doesn't last much longer. When Sam's belief in God and the angels is confirmed in the episode "It's the Great Pumpkin, Sam Winchester," he is also disheartened and disillusioned by their true nature. They are judgmental creatures who refer to humans with such condescending terms as "mud monkeys." Sam is confronted with the angels' disgust of his affiliation with Ruby and the demon powers that lie within him.

Later, in the episode "It's a Terrible Life," the angel Zachariah tries to force Sam and Dean to see their destinies by having them wake in a fantasy where they were never hunters and lead civilian lives. It is then, living as a corporate flunky and working for a business called Sandover Bridge & Iron Company, that Sam says, "I just can't shake this feeling like I . . . like I don't belong here. You know what I mean? Like I should do something more than sit in a cubicle." It's his first realization of how imperfect his dream life might have been, and he ends up hunting a ghost in that episode and breaking the spell.

It isn't until the world is on the brink of destruction and Sam is possessed, that Sam sees his life and his true involvement with evil. It is revealed that Azazel's minion Brady was the one who introduced Sam and Jessica in college. Plus, most of the people who led Sam toward the civilian life, into the illusion of normality, and away from the truths of the supernatural were demons, including his prom date. Seeing the ultimate truth gives Sam the clarity and strength to rouse himself into control of his body to save Dean.

Sam then sacrifices himself to pull Lucifer and the archangel Michael, who had taken part in the plot to bring down the Winchesters and the world, into Hell, damning himself right along with them. It's one last effort to right all the wrongs.

Demon Magic

Because Sam was human, he started with no real powers to speak of. As he gains more power, he embraces his darker side, which in turn inspires him to develop more power. It's a vicious cycle that begins with his first precognitive vision, sparked by another of Azazel's marked children locking Dean in a closet. The visions eventually go from manifesting only during his dream state to coming during his waking hours.

Sam also develops telekinetic powers. He learns to perform exorcisms with the motion of his hand rather than a rite or ritual. He becomes immune to the powers of demons and even learns to kill them with his. But the power use comes with a price. Sam's eyes turn completely black at times, just like a demon's. He is immune to the demon-created Croatoan virus that turns humans into psychotic, rage-filled killers. Plus, his senses increase until he can feel spirits.

The enhanced senses go away with Azazel's death, having come when he was fed the demon's blood as a baby, but they return with more force than ever once he adds Ruby's blood to his diet. Ruby suspects that Sam's powers were dormant all the time and not tied to Azazel. The "Lucifer Rising" episode reveals that he chose the powers each time he chose to follow the demon path over the more heavenly one Dean had chosen. Through everything, it is Sam's overzealous attempts at good that bring him down the path to evil. The road to Hell is, after all, very well paved.

FACTS AND TRIVIA

• In the episode "It's a Terrible Life," Sam says that he just broke up with his fiancée, Madison. Because all the family members Dean names are characters from the second season, there's a good chance that the Madison he refers to is the werewolf he fell in love with in the episode "Heart."

QUOTES

"I had a crappy guidance counselor." —*"Asylum"*

"Wait, there's no such thing as unicorns?" —*"Houses of the Holy"*

"If you know evil's out there, how can you not believe good's out there too?" —*"Faith"*

"There's something in me that . . . scares the hell out of me, Dean." —*"Good God, Ya'll"*

DEAN WINCHESTER: ANGELIC WARRIOR

*The other half of **Supernatural**'s fraternal team of frightmeisters, Dean Winchester, is played by actor Jensen Ackles, previously a regular on the WB series **Smallville**. Dean is an undead warrior, a human charged with the job of saving the world. He's been to Hell and back—literally. He is surrounded by angels, even taking one named Anna as a lover, and vows to work for Heaven. His willingness to work as a hand of God and status as the "vessel" of Michael makes him an angel. Dean's womanizing, crude ways are definitely in stark contrast to this title. This darkness makes him a dark angel.*

The ultimate dark rogue, Dean Winchester is a human born to John and Mary Winchester on January 24, 1979. As a kid, he wasn't the average boy. When Dean was four, his mother died, attacked by a demon in his brother Sam's (see "Sam Winchester: Satan's Puppet") room. His father took up demon hunting, the occupation that Mary's father had, to get his revenge and protect his sons. The guys went on the road, investigating hauntings and tracking the yellow-eyed demon (Azazel) that killed Mary.

At a young age, Dean was forced to stay with Sam in motel rooms, to keep him safe and fed. He acted as the caretaker, fully aware of their father's work. He tried to keep Sam innocent and young, protecting him from the knowledge of the supernatural.

Because he is well aware of the family's business as demon hunters throughout his life, Dean becomes a hunter at a young age. As they reach high school, Dean follows closer to his father's path while Sam tries to escape the gypsy lifestyle of the hunters. Dean learns from the older hunters and goes on hunts instead of going to college.

As an adult, Dean is a roughneck kind of guy, chasing women and guzzling beer when he's not tracking ghosts and other supernatural creatures. But when his father doesn't come back from a hunt, he goes to Sam. They form what is intended to be a temporary partnership to find their dad. But when Sam's fiancée is killed by the same demon, they go back on the road in their black Impala to bring down the demon and find John before he dies, too. It's a life-changing hunt that brings them closer to the yellow-eyed demon and their father with every suspicious happening they investigate.

Dean (right) with his younger brother Sam (left), standing in front of the Impala, salt, shotgun, and demon-killing blade ready. Angelic warriors in wolf's clothing.

The brothers find John and Azazel, who possesses John. Dean is helpless to do anything other than watch as Sam fails to kill the demon. When Azazel escapes, the brothers and John leave in the Impala, which is quickly smashed by a diesel driven by a man possessed by Azazel. The crash puts Dean into a coma where, at the hospital, he has an out-of-body experience and hunts a reaper, as in the Grim Reaper, who comes to take Dean to the after-life. It's then that John, in an effort to save Dean, makes a deal with a demon to go to Hell in exchange for Dean's life. This deal is something that haunts Dean his entire life.

Last Boy Scout

Always prepared. Always obedient.

Dean always follows his father's lead, generally doing exactly as he is told because he trusts his father's experience to guide them all to safety. A glance at Dean's gear shows that he also takes the demon-hunting job as seriously as John does. He wears an MTM–Special Ops watch to keep militarily precise time (and probably navigation with a compass attachment). On his upper left chest is a tattoo in the shape of a pentagram with rays of light around it, a symbol of protection from demonic possession. But the necklace around Dean's neck is for something other than protection.

It's a present Sam gave him when they were children, on Christmas Day in 1991, as seen in the episode "A Very Supernatural Christmas." The simple black band with a metal amulet was a present little Sammy got from Bobby, another hunter. Sam had intended to give it to John, who, once again, didn't show for Christmas. Dean, twelve at the time, tried to hide that fact by stealing presents from a nearby home while Sam was asleep and saying that John had gone back out, but the gifts were for a girl. So, Sam gave the necklace to Dean as thanks for the attempt at a real Christmas that they'd never had.

Still, the necklace is more than just a sentimental gift. Later in the series, when Sam and Dean are caught up in the oncoming Armageddon and God is not in Heaven and the angels can't find Him, the angel Castiel reveals to Dean that the necklace is capable of tracking God. Castiel then borrows it in an attempt to find God and ask for help in their fight against Lucifer. When Castiel returns with news that God has refused, Dean trashes the necklace. Mirroring how Sam's present to his dad was given away when John was absent, Dean gives the necklace away in another manner when God, the Father, is absent. The necklace is a sign of the ultimate disappointment for both boys: Sam's letdown at their dad, John, and Dean's frustration at God. This disenchantment goes on for both guys throughout their lives.

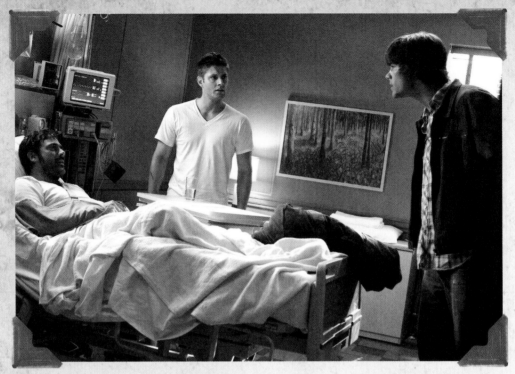

After a crash with Alistair leaves Dean comatose, he has an out-of-body experience and hunts his first reaper. Meanwhile John, his dad, trades his soul to save Dean's life.

Vessel of Michael

As it was with hunting, Dean was dragged into the battle between Heaven and Hell and nominated as the poster boy for the good side. This is confusing to some because of Dean's overall willingness to ignore the Ten Commandments. So why is this beer-drinking, cheeseburger-bingeing, crude, womanizing hunter chosen to be the vessel for the archangel Michael during his return to Earth and battle with Lucifer?

It comes down to core beliefs. Dean doesn't subscribe to religion the way many people do. Rather than being trapped in the carnal sin mentality that most religions preach, Dean looks to the heart of people. The superficial masks people put on mean nothing to him. Drinking and fornication don't equate to a bad person for Dean. And the sweet little lady next door may be a Satan-worshiping psychopath. He recognizes that appearances are of little consequence. It's a lesson he's learned through years of being a hunter, and a simple concept, but one lost on many. Perhaps that's why Dean develops the ability to see past the human mask to the demon underneath?

Despite it all, Dean has a skeptical faith in God, who seems to know this all along. Late in the Winchesters' journey, in the episode "Changing Channels," they meet the angel Gabriel, who is also known as The Trickster because he works as a trickster demon during much of the time they chase him. Gabriel tells them that the angels were told of the relationship between Dean and Sam, and how it reflected the brotherhood of the angels Michael and Lucifer before Lucifer was cast down out of Heaven. Sam and Dean's roads to greater evil and good reflect the angel and fallen angel's ancient decisions. The brothers' journey also sheds light on the natures of Satan and Michael. Sam is the disobedient, self-aggrandizing one, and Dean is the humble and obedient son, which leads to their becoming the natural vessels for the earthly battle between the two angels of light and darkness.

Dean's father's word meant everything to him. That's why John's instruction that he would have to kill Sam if he couldn't save him from Azazel's attempts to turn him to evil are so haunting. Dean would, by his estimation, have no choice but do what his father asks. Azazel dies, but not until he has orchestrated Sam's decline into demonic activity and power. Has Dean failed in the last assignment his father gave him? That remains to be seen.

Saving the World

Dean's role as Michael's vessel is only one part of the overall plan. By refusing to allow Michael to inhabit his body, thereby rejecting the rebellious archangel's plan to bring about Armageddon, Dean puts himself in position to be the ultimate hunter, overthrowing both Heaven and Hell to stop the end of the world, but it costs him everything: his family, his loves, his Impala, and his brother.

Sam has never been strong enough to do this. He seeks approval and falls for the tricks Hell plays to make him do evil by disguising it as good. Dean, however, sticks to what he knows is true and right. It's this ability that allows Dean to stand alone against the tide of betrayal and thwart Michael and Lucifer's plan. When Dean sacrifices his soul by making a deal with the demon to bring Sam back to life, Sam spends much of the year Dean has before he has to go to Hell trying to make him talk about it. It's not Dean's way; he just takes care of business. Dean says to him in the episode "Fresh Blood," "What do you want me to do, Sam, huh? Sit around all day writing sad poems about how I'm going to die? You know what, I've got one. Let's see, what rhymes with 'Shut up, Sam'?" He deals with his problems but manages to keep himself focused. However, when Dean goes to Hell, fulfilling the contract he made to bring Sam back to life, Sam wallows in self-pity and falls further from grace. It's all a matter of perspective.

It's a good thing Dean is so tough. Before he overthrows Michael and Lucifer's plot, he ends up losing everyone, right down to Castiel and his friend Bobby. The rift between him and the increasingly demon blood–addicted Sam is almost irreparable, but he keeps pushing forward. Dean's a fighter—a survivor—and that's what it takes to overcome the impossible.

Believe in the Impala

Dean's a sentimental guy, but that's not what leads him to keep his black, four-door hardtop 1967 Chevy Impala, even after it's been totaled. As a kid, his dad told him it was a good car. John took care of it and taught Dean to do the same. Always obedient, Dean follows through and tries to teach a reluctant Sam how to keep it running while Dean is planning his trip to Hell. This appreciation for what his father said has been instilled in him over a lifetime. And this obedience to his father's wishes ultimately saves them all. It is the Impala that Dean drives into the fight between Michael and Lucifer (in Sam's body) in the final moments before the world's end.

Dean stalls the fight. Then, a toy soldier that Sam had placed in the car's ashtray as a child gives Sam the strength he needs to fend off Lucifer's control and stop himself from killing Dean. It is just enough to inspire Sam to drag Michael to Hell, thus saving Dean and the world in one final good act.

Dungeon Master

The trip into the pit is a turning point for Dean. He is broken during his forty years (four months on Earth, but time flowed differently in Hell) with the dungeon master–like demon, Alastair. Dean is skinned and tortured every day, then offered his freedom if he will torture others. He's held on for thirty years of Hell-time, but being ripped apart over and over every day is too much. He cracks and goes from tortured to torturer. Caving is the first step that brings on the Apocalypse. Dean is the first "seal" because, as the prophecy states in Revelations, "The first seal shall be broken when a righteous man sheds blood in Hell. As he breaks, so shall it break." But it isn't the first time Dean has set things in motion. During the episode "In the Beginning," Dean makes Azazel first aware of the Winchester family by trying to kill him preemptively to keep Sam from being marked and to keep their mother alive. These mistakes also make Dean the only one who can stop Armageddon, according to the angels.

Angels

One angel does try to help Dean. In the "Lazarus Rising" episode, Castiel snatches Dean from the pit of Hell when it seems he can never escape, then resurrects him. Castiel's grip leaves a permanent handprint on Dean's shoulder. Castiel is then a constant fixture, often advising Dean for or against certain actions. Dean even swears an oath to serve God because of his work with Castiel. After Sam sacrifices himself, Castiel warns Dean against seeking revenge on God because it was Dean who wanted no change on Earth.

All I Ever Wanted

For all Dean's Hugh Hefner–like ways, he could have had a family and a normal life. When he meets Ben, Lisa Braeden's son, whom Dean believes might be his, it's shocking at first. Then he welcomes the idea that he might have some heir of his own. Of course, the boy turns out not to be Dean's, but it's a life he has never stopped thinking about. In the end, it's with the Braedens that he makes a new life after the showdown between Michael and Lucifer, when there's no Sam and no more hunting.

FACTS AND TRIVIA

- Dean is named after his maternal grandmother, Deanna Campbell, or so it seems. There is a good chance that he is also named after himself because he traveled through time to meet his mom in 1974 and attempted to stop the yellow-eyed demon before he had a chance to mark Sammy.

- Always a fan of classic rock and heavy metal, Dean says his favorite song is a tie between Led Zeppelin's "Traveling Riverside Blues" and their "Ramble On."

- In the series, Dean dies on Sam's birthday, May 2. He is resurrected on September 18 of the same year, 2008.

- It is revealed in the episode "Sympathy for the Devil" that Dean has a GED.

Dean's combat zone lifestyle affords him no luxuries, including love. The single exception is Lisa Braeden.

QUOTES

"Driver picks the music, shotgun shuts his cake hole." —*"Pilot"*

"It must be hard with your sense of direction, never being able to find your way to a decent pickup line." —*"Dead in the Water"*

"I'm not gonna die in a hospital where the nurses aren't even hot." —*"Faith"*

"That fabric softener teddy bear . . . oh, I'm 'a hunt that little bitch down." —*"Faith"*

"God save us from half the people who think they're doing God's work." —*"Faith"*

"You wanna kill me, get in the line, bitch!" —*"Malleus Maleficarum"*

ERIC DRAVEN: AVENGING ANGEL

*The original Gothic antihero of James O'Barr's comic book series **The Crow** (1989), Eric Draven is a revenant avenger called from his grave by a supernatural bird to mete out justice for his own murder as well as the killing of his fiancée. Many other reborn characters have assumed the dark-feathered mantle of the Crow, but Eric is the first and most memorable. In Alex Proyas's 1994 film version, Eric was played by the late Brandon Lee, who was accidently shot on the set of the movie and died three weeks before his wedding. He was then portrayed by Marc Dacascos in the 1998 television series* **The Crow: Stairway to Heaven.** *With a dark, goth look and a determination to work as the avenging angel for the humans he knew when he was alive, Eric is a dark angel.*

One of the taglines of the 1994 film *The Crow* challenges viewers to "Believe in Angels." Eric Draven is that angel, and he's a dark one. But he's like no other dark angel because of his status as a literal Revenant. Although vampires can be considered revenants because they fit the definition by being corpses returned from the grave to bully the living, the term here refers more to a ghost. Eric is neither vampire nor angel. His face is white with a black smile and darkened eyes. He wears nothing but black. The twisted nature of the image reflects the damage to his soul. He isn't even human anymore. But he does share many of the immortals' qualities and works alongside them to protect the human race—while reaping a little vengeance of his own.

Explaining the legends of the Crow, Eric says: "People once believed that when someone dies, a crow carries their soul to the land of the dead, but sometimes something so bad happens that a terrible sadness is carried with it and the soul can't rest. Then sometimes, just sometimes, the crow can bring the soul back and put the wrong things right." This is Eric's mission, his job. It's the reason he leaps, after he's crossed over, from the bridge that joins the Land of the Dead with our realm and traps himself here, in our world, until he can right the injustices.

Eric Draven as portrayed by Brandon Lee in *The Crow*. This revolutionary character started a goth hero trend followed even by a wrestling superstar, "Sting," who wore an almost identical costume.

Lost Love

Life was good for Eric. He was happy. His music filled the Detroit loft he shared with his fiancée, Shelly Webster, when he wasn't playing in the band Hangman's Joke. All of that came crashing down when on Devil's Night, otherwise known as Halloween Eve, a gang bursts into his apartment (or finds them stranded on a dark road, if you read the books). They shoot Eric, paralyzing him so that he is forced to watch helplessly as they rape and kill Shelly before he dies himself.

Because the two are bonded so tightly in love, Eric's soul is restless. He wants revenge for what was done to her, even though they are together in the afterlife. The Crow brings him back from the afterlife a year later to avenge her murder on the littered, rain-slick streets of their old neighborhood. The loss of Eric's true love is the driving force behind his mission, and, despite the pain it causes him, his greatest strength. He is fighting for something noble.

Killing the murderers doesn't give him the relief he seeks, but it is his mission. When he's not acting like an angel of vengeance, he haunts the house he and Shelly shared. The memories overwhelm him, but he is unable to find a moment's peace without her. Sometimes he loses himself in memories, but other times he tries cutting, a form of self-mutilation, to ease the pain. Those wounds don't heal.

The grief of his lost love tortures him.

Crows

Eric Draven is guided by a crow on his comic book and film journey (and called a crow himself on the television series). The Crow pushes him along the road to reunite with Shelly and guides him with information. When he lets himself get too wrapped up in Shelly's memory, the bird nudges him toward the goal again. Eric also has two other figurative "crows," in the form of Skull Cowboy and Detective Albrecht. Skull Cowboy comes to him in visions, telling him why he's back in the land of the living, and how to get back to Shelly. Albrecht helps him dodge the cops while reaping his vengeance and looking out for Sarah, a neighborhood child.

Revenants

Unlike the other dark angels, Eric can see through the eyes of a spirit guide, namely the Crow. He can also feel sensations such as pain when they come from him touching an object that connects him to a past experience, an ability known as psychometrics.

His physical powers include enhanced speed and agility. As an ethereal being, Eric feels no physical pain when he is attacked. It's a handy advantage to have when Top Dollar, a local crime boss in charge of the crew who killed Eric and Shelly, and the others are so fond of filling him full of lead. His wounds heal in seconds, as long as they are acquired while he is performing his mission. When he does other things, the bullet holes don't automatically heal.

FACTS AND TRIVIA

- In the television show, Eric Draven has a stepbrother named Chris, who is not mentioned in the movie.

- The Eric Draven persona is based on three musicians: Joy Division's lead singer, Ian Curtis; Bauhaus lead Peter Murphy; and Iggy Pop.

- James O'Barr, the author of the comic books the film is based on, plays a looter in the film who distracts Albrecht from pointing his gun at Eric on the sidewalk.

- The scar seen on Eric's face, under the eye and across the nose, was placed there as a nod to the comics, where Eric was shot in the head, cracking the bone under his eye.

QUOTES

"He was already dead. He died a year ago, the moment he touched her. They're all dead. They just don't know it yet." —The Crow *(film)*

"Little things used to mean so much to Shelly. I used to think they were kind of . . . trivial. Believe me, nothing is trivial." —The Crow *(film)*

"Suddenly, I heard a tapping, as of someone gently rapping, rapping at my chamber door. . . . You heard me rapping, right?" —The Crow *(film)*

"'Mother' is the name for God on the lips and hearts of children." —The Crow *(film)*

"It can't rain all the time." —The Crow *(film)*

Chapter Four
Dark Guardians

*Literally or figuratively, these dark angels guard others.
They protect the weaker ones, putting their lives on the line every
night. Humans can laugh off ideas of wraiths, reapers, and demons
because they fight in the background to protect our sensibilities.
Often, their job is thankless and they go home bruised and bloody.*

We owe them everything.

DARREN SHAN: FREAK'S ASSISTANT

Darren Shan's fascination with spiders and the chance to visit a mysterious traveling freak circus isn't the typical way to become a vampire, but it works well enough for Darren to earn him the starring role in twelve of his own Cirque du Freak novels, written with the help of author Darren O'Shaughnessy. Onscreen, Darren is played by Chris Massoglia in Paul Weitz's 2009 film **Cirque du Freak: The Vampire's Assistant.**

O f the dark angels, Darren Shan is the kid of the group, an actual sixteen-year-old ("going on immortal") who just happens to run into the wrong group of freaks. Literally. As a human, Darren starts out as a people pleaser. He follows the rules, is a loyal friend, and is a committed individual. He's a good kid with a healthy respect for human life and morality, which makes the beginning of his vampire life a shocking turn.

Stealing a talented spider from a freak show, Darren grabs the attention of Larten Crepsley (see "Mr. Crepsley: Circus Freak"), an orange-haired, red-suited vampire. Soon, the spider bites Darren's best friend, Steve Leopard, and puts him in the hospital. To save him, Darren goes to Mr. Crepsley, who offers him an exchange: He will provide the cure for Steve if Darren will become his assistant and a half-vampire. Darren agrees and is quickly brought into the vampire fold by being blooded, a process by which Crepsley's vampire blood is introduced into Darren's bloodstream through wounds in his fingertips. After a quick funeral to cover up Darren's conversion to unlife, the two head out on adventures within the vampire world.

Living with freaks wasn't what Darren had in mind for his life, but it's how things worked out. As he sums it up in *The Vampire's Assistant* 2009 film, "Sometimes life does seem all planned out, like there's no choice in the matter. But that's just an illusion." It's a wonderful way of looking at things. Even though he didn't ask for life as a vampire, he's making the most of it. He goes on to admit to Mr. Crepsley, "It's weird; I spent so much time wishing that none of this would have happened, that we never would have gone to the Cirque in the first place. But now I really can't imagine my life happening in any other way."

Darren, as a human in *The Vampire's Assistant*, was never comfortable with the blandness of his life. Being a vampire, however, was not on his list of possible remedies…unlike his BFF Steve.

The Trials

Time and disillusionment begin to wear away his positive traits. Darren becomes angry and his decision-making skills suffer. His humanity starts to slip away. But that doesn't mean he's giving up easily. As he tells a friend in the freak show, explaining his ability to hang on to his human side after becoming undead, "No, just because I'm a vampire doesn't mean that I'm bloodthirsty. It's not about what you are; it's about who you are." It's a noble idea. He is a noble soul. Any moral taint of vampirism, Darren will sort out in time. His greatest strength is the ability to come out on top.

Combating Darren's strength is his weakness for stumbling blindly into situations that he could have avoided with a little self-control and well-placed trust. First, it's his lack of self-control that allows his curiosity to push him into staying behind after the show at the circus. Then, greed gets the best of him when he decides to keep Madam Octa, Mr. Crepsley's unique spider. The theft costs Darren his human life and his best friend when he has to bargain his life to save Steve from the spider bite, as he heads off to be a vampire's assistant. In *Tunnels of Blood*, Darren and Mr. Crepsley head to Crepsley's hometown to investigate a string of murders by what they believe to be a Vampaneze, one of the evil, savage vampires in Darren's world. Before they find the killer, Darren loses control of his imagination and

A coffin just for the young vampire Darren.

emotions again. He overreacts, blaming Crepsley for the murders, and attacks him. Darren's lack of self-control is a recurring problem, and one that usually pits him against those he loves. However, his misplaced trust leads to several problems with Steve, who finally kills Mr. Crepsley and reveals that he is the Lord of the Vampaneze.

Flying High

The high points in Darren's life stem from his ability to overcome his faults. One example is in *Trials of Death*. On Vampire Mountain, the location of the vampire clan meeting that happens once in twelve years, he and Crepsley are confronted with the ruling of the Vampire Princes (leaders), who want Darren to prove his worth as a half-vampire through the Trials of Initiation (aka Trials of Death), where Darren faces a series of deadly physical tests. It's also a punishment for Crepsley's turning Darren at such a young age. Although Darren technically fails the trials, they are one of his high points. Having little training in the use of his powers, he manages to complete three of the tests and almost win the fourth. When a friend helps, saving Darren's life, he is disqualified, despite his doing so well in the rest of the trials.

Another high point is when he is made a Vampire Prince by the Princes of Vampire Mountain. When Darren is disqualified from the trials and flees Vampire Mountain, he learns of a plot against the vampires by a soon-to-be prince, Kurda Smahlt, and the Vampaneze. Although he is hunted, Darren chooses to return to the Princes and warn them of Kurda Smahlt's plotting to overthrow them with the Vampaneze. It is a decision that Darren knows will probably get him killed, but he does it anyway. Once there, the Vampaneze are flushed out and Darren is rewarded by fighting alongside Mr. Crepsley and Seba Nile, Crepsley's mentor. It is a fear-filled journey, but Darren's effort to go against his instincts to run and instead control his emotions makes all the difference.

The greatest pinnacle, though, is reached when Darren dies in *Sons of Destiny*. Having lived through the Vampire-Vampaneze plots and seen his friend Steve rise to Lord of the Vampaneze, Darren has written everything in his journal. He and Steve finally face off, learning that they're actually half-brothers, caught in someone else's plot to destroy the human race. Darren provokes Steve, who stabs him in the heart, and Darren pulls them both into the river, drowning Steve as he dies. Although it's a bitter end, it's also a wonderful last act as he makes a deal in the afterlife to return to the time when he first visited the cirque, handing his diaries over to the freaks there to stop everything from happening. Taking the information back to the past ends his unlife as a vampire and keeps Steve from becoming the Vampaneze Lord; then he lies down and dies his final death. The sacrifice of his life is a truly noble act.

A Freak

Compared to other dark angels, Darren's powers aren't that impressive. He doesn't share the usual undead enhancements such as mind reading. Still, Darren's strength and senses exceed human levels. His speed can reach heights that will fool vision because he's faster than the eyes are. Running this fast is referred to as "flitting" in his world.

As with other vampires of his world, sunlight will kill him. While vampires age at one-tenth the human rate, half-vampires such as Darren age at about one-fifth the human rate. Their fingernails become so strong that they can climb walls like Spider-Man.

In Darren's world, vampires are created by blood-to-blood contact because ingestion of vampire blood creates a fatal effect similar to rabies within the drinker. To turn humans, vampires simply introduce their blood into the human's bloodstream, "blooding" them. Vampires of Darren's kind do drink human blood. The new vampires have to feed at least once a month to live. When they do feed, the meal is limited. If they kill a person through exsanguination, they drink in part of the victim's spirit as well.

Their mouths are a valuable weapon. While their teeth aren't sharp enough to cut through the skin to feed, their saliva can heal wounds, just as many of the other dark angels. But their breath is unique. It's not like the sweet exhalation of the Cullens (see "The Cullen Family: Dark Clan"), but instead becomes a gas that can knock victims unconscious for a half hour or more.

FACTS AND TRIVIA

- The author has stated several times publicly that *Tunnels of Blood* is his favorite book.

- Darren Shan states in the first book that his story is absolutely true and that only the names have been changed, and that the places aren't named at all. Despite vague terms for settings such as Vampire Mountain, there is no true location named in the saga.

QUOTES

"I don't just live with a bunch of freaks, I'm one, too." —The Vampire's Assistant *(film)*

"Spending this much time in a coffin was never part of my plan. I guess I'm just lucky." —The Vampire's Assistant *(film)*

"Even a minute of dying is better than an eternity of nothingness." —Sons of Destiny

ZOEY REDBIRD: CHOSEN ANGEL

"Just when I thought my day couldn't get any worse, I saw the dead guy standing next to my locker." So begins the novel Marked, *the first book in the House of Night teen vampyre series begun by the mother-daughter writing team of P. C. Cast and Kristin Cast in 2007 and now including eight best-selling books.*

At sixteen, Zoey Redbird Montgomery is facing a future she never expected. She'd hoped for a career as a veterinarian after attending Oklahoma State University. Maybe she'd buy a nice house in the suburbs, but becoming a vampyre wasn't on the agenda. As a fledgling, she must leave her human life behind and learn the vampyre ways. It's not exactly the same as getting bitten and flying off into the night with Dracula (see "Vlad Dracula: Darkly Original"). Zoey's life is a little more complicated than that. She's part reincarnated A-ya, part vampyre, and all teenage girl!

Chosen One

Zoey is much like any other high school girl. She drives a robin's-egg blue 1966 Volkswagen Bug, likes to shop, and hangs out at Starbucks. She loves Count Chocula breakfast cereal. Her entertainment revolves around *Gossip Girls* books, *Dracula*, Dr. Phil, *The Phantom of the Opera, Finding Nemo*, and the bands Paramore and Three Days Grace. She loves her grandma and her cat, Nala, named after the *Lion King* character. She's also a little boy crazy. But in other ways she's a bit beyond normal. She is an exotic beauty with Cherokee features. Her nose is strong, and her cheekbones are high. She has round hazel eyes, olive skin, and long, straight black hair. Then, she hears the words that change her life forever in *Marked*: "Night has chosen thee; thy death will be thy birth. Night calls to thee; hearken to Her sweet voice. Your destiny awaits you at the House of Night!"

Zoey, the heroine of the House of Night series, carries vampyre DNA triggered by puberty, but there's much more than genetics at work for her.

Ink Marked

In a world where vampyres are out in the open, she's one of the chosen ones, marked to attend the House of Night vampyre school in Tulsa when puberty triggers her vampyre DNA. A tracker comes, points at her, and tells her she was chosen, just as he does with the others, and she wakes with the tattoos that magically appear on her skin, but the marks aren't the same as other vampyres'. Zoey's tattoos are unique and include a solid sapphire-blue crescent moon and other markings. Most fledglings wake with an empty crescent, waiting until full transition for the rest. As her journey through vampyre life progresses, new tattoos appear. Right now, she has lacelike tattoos that radiate across her forehead and appear on her neck and shoulders, on upper and lower sections of her back, across her chest, around her waist, and even on the palms of her hands. She's also "marked" with different abilities from other vampyres, thanks to Nyx, the main goddess of the vampyres at the House of Night.

Her parents aren't exactly thrilled when it happens, but Grandma Redbird, a Native American, is supportive as always. She's also the only one who cares for Zoey, since her stepfather, John Heffer, came into the picture, distracting her mother's attention. More than chosen, Zoey is picked as the agent of Nyx. "Believe in yourself, Zoey Redbird. I have marked you as my own. You will be my first true u-we-tsi-a-ge-ya v-hna-i Sv-no-yi . . . Daughter of Night . . . in this age. You are special. . . . There is true power in your uniqueness," Nyx says to her.

Tempted Again

Her mother isn't the only one who gets distracted by the occasional guy. Zoey has a habit of trying to manage too many guys at one time. At first, her interest in Erik Night pushes another vampyre student named Aphrodite over the edge, making an enemy of her. She also imprints accidentally on Heath by drinking directly from him, thereby creating a supernatural link between them and breaking one of the rules of the school. As if those two weren't enough, she sleeps with Professor Loren Blake, breaking Erik's heart and hurting Heath. Their imprint is broken by her forming a new one with the professor. She has a crush on James Stark, a transfer student who is also the world's best archer. At one point in *Betrayed*, Zoey says, "What the hell was I supposed to do about (1) Erik, (2) Loren, (3) the fact that drinking Heath's blood was totally against the House of Night rules, and (4) [that] I was definitely going to drink more of his blood." She later says, "Well, at least my friends didn't know what a bloodlust-filled, horny freak I was turning into." Even Nyx couldn't straighten out the mess that is Zoey's love life.

Life's Untamed

Her time at the House of Night has been a mix of good and bad experiences, just as any other high school journey. One of the high points is when Aphrodite botches the Samhain ritual, releasing evil spirits and injuring Heath. Although it is at her expense, it works out well for Zoey because she is awarded the honorable titles of Leader of the Dark Daughters and High Priestess in Training, titles that Aphrodite held before her slipup.

Zoey's lowest moment is Heath's death. She has some memories of a previous incarnation, A-ya, who was created by the Cherokee to trap the fallen angel Kalona underground. It's an ongoing struggle to keep him out of her mind. Then, when she sees Kalona break Heath's neck, it shatters her soul. Literally. She has seven days to put the pieces together again. If she doesn't, Neferet, high priestess of the House of Night, will make slaves of them all.

Vampyre Sociology 101

Within Zoey's world, religion plays an important role. Through Nyx and the vampyre religion, she begins to mature in understanding. This understanding goes beyond worldly things and to the heart of understanding others, to having compassion. Zoey says, "We *all* have bad things inside us, and we *all* choose either to give in to those bad things or to fight them." Everything we do is a matter of choice. Those who choose to do evil are evil, not those who have evil impulses that they resist, because we all have those urges at some point. It's an understanding that reflects her growing resistance to judging others. Many adults never understand this concept and continue to judge others by appearance, gossip, or other superficial things, as do the People of Faith, a religious group that opposes vampyres.

Don't Get Burned

The gods shine on Zoey. She's blessed by the goddess Nyx with a talent for all five elements: air, fire, water, earth, and spirit. Her friends are all granted one, two at most. No doubt, she will develop more as time goes on because Nyx herself said, "Within you is combined the magic blood of ancient Wise Women and Elders, as well as insight into and understanding of the modern world."

She's powerful, but with a few weaknesses. She isn't torched in the sunlight, but she is light sensitive. Zoey has bloodlust. This is strange because, in Zoey's world, most of the older fledglings and adult vampyres crave blood, but the young vampyres do not. However, the feeding is more sensual than painful for their victims and leads to imprinting, which makes the humans infatuated with their vampyre. Zoey also has the physical inability to be away from adult vampyres, like young vampyres of her world. If she's not close to one at all times, she will die. She can't leave the school without a chaperone, which is limited considering the number of teachers versus students at the House of Night. What teenager wants to be bound to the school day in, night out?

❧❧ FACTS AND TRIVIA ❧❧

- Zoey shares her birthday, December 24, with *Twilight* author Stephenie Meyer (1973).

- Most of the rituals, mythology, and religion are mixed between Pagan, Wiccan, and Native American. The Raven Mockers (children of Kalona) and Tsi Sgili (Neferet), for example, are actual Cherokee figures.

❧❧ QUOTES ❧❧

"If I died, would it get me out of my geometry test tomorrow? One could only hope." —Marked

"I'm going to heaven. Well, that'll shock some people." —Marked

"Help me know the right thing to do and then give me the courage to do it." —Marked

"I'd sacrificed true love and a popped cherry to the god of deception and hormones." —Chosen

ROSE HATHAWAY: GUARDIAN DHAMPIR

Rose Hathaway is the narrator of Richelle Mead's six-novel Vampire Academy series (2007–2010), including the books Vampire Academy, Frostbite, Shadow Kiss, Blood Promise, Spirit Bound, *and* Last Sacrifice. *Nearly all the books have been* New York Times *best sellers, and a spin-off series of six more books is forthcoming. The Vampire Academy series reaches back to the Slavic tradition of vampire legends, with numerous characters from Russia and Eastern Europe.*

Rosemarie Hathaway isn't just another teen vampire. Simply put, Rose is beautiful. She's on the taller side, five foot seven, with an athletically feminine build. She has dark eyes, dark hair, and tanned skin thanks to her Turkish Moroi dad. The other side of her genetic pool is the prominent Guardian Janine Hathaway, her mother. As for her life, Rose sums it up best in *Frostbite*, saying, "By the way, my name's Rose Hathaway. I'm seventeen years old, training to protect *and* kill vampires, in love with a completely unsuitable guy, and have a best friend whose weird magic could drive her crazy." Within her world, there are three types of vampires. The Moroi are mortal vampires who have elemental magic abilities. Strigoi are bloodthirsty, murderous immortals like some of the dark angels, who want to bring the Moroi into their ranks by turning them into Strigoi. Rose, however, is a seventeen-year-old Dhampir, half Moroi vampire and half human, who can walk in the sunlight and has vampiric strength. She's destined to be the bodyguard of her best friend, Vasilisa "Lissa" Dragomir, a Moroi vampire. She's forced to choose her duty over everything else—even her love. It's a tough road for anyone, especially a young dark angel.

Shadow Kissed

After an accident kills Lissa's parents and Rose, Lissa unintentionally brings her back, and the two run away. The experience turns Rose into a Shadow Kissed Dhampir, a Dhampir who has seen the other side. This also creates a bond between the two girls that cannot be broken. Rose can hear Lissa's thoughts, feel her feelings, and even see what Lissa sees, adding a bit to the learning curve of being a Guardian.

Vampire ACADEMY

THE INTERNATIONAL #1 BESTSELLING SERIES BY

RICHELLE MEAD

Rose, the heroine of the Vampire Academy series, lives up to her promise to kill the man (or vampire) she loves.

A Guardian vampire named Dimitri sends a team to retrieve them. When they return, Dimitri volunteers to be Rose's mentor and is assigned as Lissa's Guardian. As they spend time together at the St. Vladimir's Academy deep in the forests of Montana, Rose trains with Dimitri and falls for him. She and Lissa also grow closer as the two learn their skills at the school, preparing for lives of defending themselves (and Lissa too, in Rose's case) against the Strigoi. Through the ups and downs of a teen vampire's life, Rose maintains a modicum of teen normality.

Bitten by Truth

Rose's sarcasm and quick wit are liabilities at times, but generally fall into the strength category. Another strength is her ability to be honest with herself. One of the best examples of this comes in *Frostbite*, when she says, "You can't force love, I realized. It's there or it isn't. If it's not there, you've got to be able to admit it. If it is there, you've got to do whatever it takes to protect the ones you love." She follows her own advice. In a moment of clarity, she encourages Dimitri, the man she loves, to have children with Tasha because he is also a Dhampir and they can only breed with Moroi vampires. Pushing him to do so is an unselfish act that would have truly hurt her if he'd taken the advice.

Another of her fabulous truthful moments occurs in *Blood Promise*, when she's praying for help and says, "Okay, God, I thought. Get me out of this and I'll stop my half-assed churchgoing ways. . . . Let me get out of here, and I'll . . . I don't know. Donate . . . money to the poor. Get baptized. Join a convent. Well, no. Not that last one." It's hilariously Rose and oh, so honest.

Dimitri

Rose's greatest weakness is Dimitri Belikov. She's supposed to be training as a Guardian for Lissa, but she can't focus completely with her mind running in circles around the idea of Dimitri. Then, she gets the whole forbidden mentor-trainee romance going, further complicating the process of learning to kill the Strigoi (aka the bad vampires). Dimitri points out the problems in the relationship by saying, "If I let myself love you, I won't throw myself in front of her. I'll throw myself in front of you." In other words, he'd choose to save her instead of his charge, Lissa, whom he protects while he trains Rose to protect her. Rose knows the danger in that possibility, but she jokes about their relationship in *Frostbite*: "The other problem in my life is Dimitri . . . he's a total badass. He's also pretty good-looking. Okay—more than good-looking. He's hot—like, the kind of hot that makes you stop walking on the street and get hit by traffic." He's the world to Rose.

Spirit Bindings

The moments of Rose's journey work to free or bind her. The freeing ones are generally high points, as when she falls for Dimitri. He makes her happy and lightens her life. Even daydreaming is better because, as she says in *Vampire Academy*, "The only thing better than imagining Dimitri carrying me in his arms was imagining him shirtless while carrying me in his arms." Though he is her weakness, he nonetheless makes her happy, raises her up through training, and strengthens her self-opinion.

The binding moments are those that damage her soul and drag her down. Dimitri is also the source of the lowest point in her life. When Dimitri turns evil, becoming a Strigoi, Rose is forced to kill him to keep the promise she made him: "We'd both agreed that we'd rather be dead—truly dead—than walk the world as Strigoi." Rose describes the pain in *Blood Promise*: "My heart shattered. My world shattered. You will lose what you value most. . . . It wasn't my life . . . it wasn't even Dimitri's life. . . . It was his soul." She goes through with the promise and tries to kill him, but fails, which extends the low point as she realizes that he is coming after her, to reap revenge as a bloodthirsty Strigoi.

❧ FACTS AND TRIVIA ❧

- According to richellemead.com, Rose is pictured on the covers of *Vampire Academy*, *Frostbite*, *Blood Promise*, and *Spirit Bound*. Some copies of *Shadow Kiss* also feature her likeness.

❧ QUOTES ❧

"You will lose what you value most, so treasure it while you can." —Shadow Kiss

"I set off, off to kill the man I love." —Shadow Kiss

BLADE: DARK AVENGER

Wesley Snipes's portrayal in three highly successful horror/action films, Blade *(1998), directed by Stephen Norrington;* Blade II *(2002), directed by Guillermo del Toro; and* Blade: Trinity *(2004), directed by David S. Goyer, made this vampire a Hollywood icon, but Blade's pop-culture history began as a rather different character in Marvel Comics's 1972–1979 series* Tomb of Dracula, *created by comic veterans Marv Wolfman and Gene Colan. Blade appeared in several other comic books before the debut of his own title,* Blade: The Vampire Hunter *(1994–95).* Blade: The Series *manifested on Spike TV in 2006 with Kirk "Sticky Fingaz" Jones in the title role.*

There are several avenging dark angels, but only one struggles so thoroughly to fight his own nature. Though he isn't quite human, Blade protects the weaker race by hunting down and slaughtering vampires, but it isn't just humans that Blade is avenging. His entire life revolves around avenging his mother.

Mommy Complex

According to Blade, "I have spent my entire life searching for that thing that killed my mother and made me what I am. And every time I take one of those monsters out, I get a little piece of that life back."

Blade's entrance into the world was tainted when his mother was bitten by Deacon Frost while she was giving birth to him, turning her into a vampire. Although it did give him a physical advantage that we'll get to later, it put him at a psychological disadvantage. He could focus on nothing other than avenging her death, and it cost all of those around him.

Blade, portrayed by Wesley Snipes, is always ready for the fight. As Eric Brooks, he probably would have had a much safer life.

Losses

Before Blade can vote, he is training to kill vampires. Jamal Afari, a friend and hunter, trains him to hunt. His first big kill, the oldest and most powerful vampire he's met at that point, Lamia, boosts his confidence and costs him Glory, his girlfriend. That first death doesn't sway his mind. After hunting on his own for a while, he hooks up with a group of hunters to slay Dracula (see "Vlad Dracula: Darkly Original"). However, his success in killing the vampire lord leads to an insurrection in which Dracula retaliates by slaying the group, save Blade.

Then, in a battle with Varnae, the supposed first vampire, more of Blade's friends pay for his bloodlust. Frank Drake and Hannibal King, friends who have been helping him hunt Frost, die. Rather than realizing his growing obsession, Blade becomes even more determined. This arrogant disregard for the human lives that his obsession requires continues throughout the comic series.

Making Peace

Blade's affinity for killing vampires also expresses a certain self-loathing. While a large part of him is human, there is an element of vampirism in his nature. It isn't something that comes from a later bite, as it is with many dark angels. His vampire side comes from birth. Still, Blade can make no peace with that side.

It haunts Blade, forcing him to have things in common with a race that he wants annihilated. He hints at this when he says, "There are worse things out there than vampires . . . like me." Blade almost seems to think he's worse than a regular vampire, a freak like the feuding vampires who see their own differences among born and created vampires. However, Blade fights his difference. In the movies, he takes painful injections of garlic and silver to keep down this side of him. It isn't until he is almost killed by his own mother, then a vampire, that he finds some peace with who he is. He drinks blood from the doctor, and then slays the woman that is his mom and the vampire who bit her, Frost, effectively avenging the death of his human mother, his own infection, and the loss of his human life.

Powers

Unlike many vampires, Blade is somewhat human. His strength comes from an intensive exercise regimen. His masterful use of bladed weapons and hand-to-hand combat skills are human based as well. Even the ninjalike use of his favorite teakwood knives is within human capacity.

The only real supernatural ability that Blade possesses is his immunity to the vampire's bite. Where other humans become vampires after being bitten in Blade's world, he only suffers teeth wounds. This is perhaps the only benefit of his mother having been bitten while she was giving birth to him. The enzyme in his bloodstream from the vampire's blood is what makes him partially vampire and immune.

It must be noted that the Blade portrayed on screen has all of the vampires' strengths and none of their weaknesses—except for a growing need for blood, and he uses injections to keep that in check. He has superhuman agility, reflexes, senses, speed, stamina, and strength, as well as rapid healing. However, he is not immortal and ages as any other human does.

Because he is partially human, he doesn't have adverse reactions to sunlight, which is why he's called the "Daywalker." This aids in hunting because normal vampires don't have it. This quality is exclusive to Blade in his world.

A Broken Mirror

The other differences between the movie and comic book representations of Blade are just as extreme. In the comics, Blade is from England, not Detroit. He is arrogant and pigheaded rather than stoic. Even his weapons are different.

The comic book version relies on teakwood knives and mahogany stakes. He upgrades to include bladed weapons and firearms, but the most striking is a weapon appendage he acquires after losing his hand. In the movies, he favors a double-edged sword with a titanium blade that includes a security feature to chop off the hands of anyone who tries to use it without knowing how to disarm it. The more creative of the movie weapons includes anticoagulant injectables and silver spikes.

❧ FACTS AND TRIVIA ☙

- The Book of Erebus is another name for the Vampire Bible in the Blade universe. In Greek mythology, Erebus is a god of dark night.

- Blade's real name is Eric Brooks, but the name Eric is only mentioned once in the film. His mother's Florida driver's license is shown, featuring the name Vanessa Brooks.

- Blade's car in the film is a 1968 Dodge Charger.

Kickin' ass and not really caring about names. Unlike the Blade of the comics, the movie Blade has both hands.

QUOTES

"We have a good arrangement. He makes the weapons. I use them." —Blade *(film)*

"Some motherfuckers are always trying to ice-skate uphill." —Blade *(film)*

"The world you live in is just a sugar-coated topping. There is another world beneath it. The real world." —Blade *(film)*

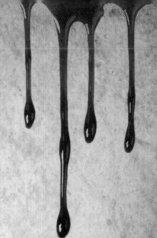

ANGEL: SOULFUL DEFENDER

One of television's most popular spin-off characters ever, Angel (aka Angelus) began his undying career as a major character on **Buffy the Vampire Slayer** *but earned his own series,* **Angel,** *in 1999, which ran for five seasons. Buffy creator Joss Whedon was also responsible for the new show, with collaborator David Greenwalt. David Boreanaz played Angel in both series.*

Angel is more than just a vampiric defender of the human race, more than a private investigator, and certainly more than just Buffy's past love interest. He's a vampire with a soul. Living in a world of soulless vamps, Angel is on a lighter path, struggling to make up for the deeds committed during one very long crime spree in his past life as Angelus.

Angel vs. Angelus

As Angel says on *Buffy,* "For a hundred years I offered ugly death to everyone I met, and I did it with a song in my heart."

Before we get into Angel's details, one thing should be made clear. Angelus—not Angel—did all those things that brought about the 1898 Romanian gypsy curse. The man born as Liam was turned by Darla, his lover, and then named Angelus. It wasn't until the soul reentered the body that he became Angel. Because there are essentially two identities in one body, it has to be said that Angelus is, in a way, a separate dark angel. However, for our purposes, we'll focus on Angel, who is most angelic in his fight for humanity. Angelus is more of an evil angel or soulless monster, which is a whole different book.

Cursed Gypsies

As for the curse, well, it has to be torture for Angelus, trapped in a body that denies all those guilty pleasures he basked in for so long.

Angelus in his younger years, played by David Boreanaz (above), kills even the family who knew him as the human Liam.

But is it a fair curse? Not quite. When the gypsies punished Angelus, they condemn Angel to an eternity of torture, too. The Kalderash gypsy elder says, "The face of everyone you have killed—our daughter's face—they will haunt you and you will know what true suffering is." This means that even though he's a soft-hearted hero, he has to live with the memories of what Angelus did. All the death, blood, and torture of innocents. Plus, one of the aspects of the curse provides that a moment of true happiness, such as the occasion when he and Buffy make love, forces him to lose his soul again and revert to Angelus. So, not only is he burdened with Angelus's deeds, but he also can't have even one moment of true happiness.

Good vs. Evil

Those duel identities, one good and one evil, are the motivating forces behind Angel's existence. With the assistance of his detective team at Angel Investigations, he helps "the helpless," a vampire superhero. He keeps up this struggle, always fighting back the bad (and Angelus) in hopes of atoning for the past and generally becoming a victim of circumstances, or of Wolfram & Hart, a demonic law firm.

At least until Darla reenters the picture.

As his sire and past love, Darla tips the balance in his internal struggle, pushing him toward Angelus by simply blurring the line that separates good from evil. First, she does this through her being human with a solid determination to become a vampire again. No matter how Darla beckons to his inner Angelus, Angel is also drawn to her because of their shared past, his feelings for her, and his envy of her new mortality. He even says to her, "It's a gift . . . to feel that heartbeat. To know, really and for once, that you're alive. You're human again, Darla. Do you know what that means?" For Angel, who wants his humanity back more than anything else, her seeking vampirism again is the ultimate wrong. The closer she gets to her goal, the more confused and lonely Angel becomes. It opens the door to more confusion from his enemies, as when Holland points out, "You see, if there wasn't evil in every single one of them out there—why, they wouldn't be people. They'd all be angels." The resulting frustration and discouragement for Angel ends in his firing his entire staff and going to bed with Darla to lose his soul again.

Then, she pushes Angel's perspective further toward moral ambiguity by bringing him Connor, the child the two miraculously conceive. He loves Connor and commits to protecting him. However, good works for evil and evil works for good after Connor enters the picture. Connor is the reason for him losing both loves: Darla through death and Cordelia through her relationship with his son. It is also Connor who puts Angel at the bottom of the ocean and in a way leads the others to invoke Angelus. After their attempt to use Angel's evil side for good fails, Angel makes a deal to run Wolfram & Hart, the ultimate symbol of evil in his world. He sells out in exchange for rewriting Connor's life so that he grows up with a "normal" family. In the end, Angel dies to save Connor's life.

All the lines he's clearly drawn between good and evil from the beginning are crossed to protect his son. For Angel, this miraculous baby is the end of Angel's world and the ultimate blur of good and evil. It is only because of his friends, particularly Wes and Cordelia, who cheer him on, that he finds hope when there is none. This is particularly true in the comic book *Angel: After the Fall*, when the two push him to keep fighting when the city has literally gone to hell and Gunn kills Connor in the alley. So, while Darla and ultimately Connor are his major weaknesses, Angel's soul and his friends are his strengths.

Powers That Be

Angel's powers are pretty standard as far as vampires and dark angels are concerned. Supernatural speed, agility, stamina, and strength are common enough. Rapid healing and immortality are as well. However, Angel surrounds himself with others who make up for any shortage of preternatural ability. Cordelia's visions and Wesley's knowledge are just two aids in Angel's journey. Furthermore, as the character Twilight in the *Buffy* Season Eight series, he gains real superhero powers, including flight, to rival those of Superman. Still, for all his agility, one thing Angel is not blessed with is the ability to sing or dance!

FACTS AND TRIVIA

- Because the curse on Angel means that he loses his soul if he experiences a moment of true happiness, sex seems to equal the loss of his soul. However, Angel can have sex without losing his soul. Not every time Angel hooks up with someone will be pure happiness, as we see when he is with Darla. So, even if killing a particular demon gives him pure happiness, he will revert to Angelus. But sex alone won't do it.

- Angel has a tattoo, on his right shoulder blade, of a gryphon holding an "A."

- The fictitious address for Angel Investigations at the old Hyperion Hotel is 1481 Hyperion Avenue, Los Angeles, CA 90026. The phone number is (213) 555-0162 and the fax number is (213) 555-0163.

- Angel is a fan of Barry Manilow's song "Mandy." He sings the song twice in the series (in "Judgment" and "The Magic Bullet"), and he plays the song on a jukebox in "Orpheus."

- Angelus wastes no time killing. His first kill is the cemetery groundskeeper where he is buried. Then, he kills his (Liam's) family.

Angel, hard at work on the next case at the Hyperion Hotel in Los Angeles, California.

QUOTES

"Not to go all schoolyard on you, but you hit me first." — *"Sanctuary"*

"My parents were great. Tasted like a lot chicken." — *"Sense and Sensitivity"*

"I've got two modes with people: bite or avoid." — *"She"*

"You guys go on. I think I'll stay here and not burst into flames." — *"Fall to Pieces"*

"I've seen some horrors, scary behavior . . . and a couple of fashion trends I constantly pray to forget." — *"Untouched"*

"It's been a long time since I've opened a vein, but I'll do it if you pull any more of this Van Helsing Jr. crap with me." — *"Are You Now or Have You Ever Been"*

"The more you piss me off, the longer I'll keep you alive. Ooh, there's something tells me she's a screamer." — *"Soulless"*

NICK KNIGHT: ORIGINAL DARK KNIGHT

Canada's major media vampire, Nick Knight achieved worldwide fame as the starring character of the series Forever Knight, *created by Barney Cohen and James D. Parriott, in seventy episodes between 1992 and 1996. The character had already been introduced in a 1989 television movie,* Nick Knight, *with Rick Springfield in the title role. Geraint Wyn Davies assumed the part for the series. The popular program also inspired three novels:* Forever Knight: A Stirring of Dust *(1997) by Susan Sizemore,* Forever Knight: Intimations of Mortality *(1997) by Susan M. Garrett, and* Forever Knight: These Our Revels *(1997) by Anne Hathaway-Nayne.*

Before we met Angel (see "Angel: Soulful Defender"), there was Detective Nick Knight. He's the original vampire who sought redemption for his centuries of killing and evil by helping others, in the hopes of becoming human again. Nick is one of the few medieval knights among the dark angels.

Nicolas de Brabant

Roughly eight hundred years old, Nick has seen his share of evil. Maybe that's why he needs the aliases of Chevalier, Parker, Girard, Thomas, Corrigan, Hammond, and Forrester.

He's perpetrated much of it, but it hasn't always been that way. He started as a medieval knight in Brabant, known as Sieur Nicolas de Brabant. He followed Sir Raymond DeLabarre loyally and went to Wales when he was ordered to investigate a brewing revolt. It wasn't in his nature to question nobles at that time—but he learned from the experience.

Sin

The lowest points in Nick's life have included women. In Wales he finds Gwyneth, a Welsh noblewoman, who leads the resistance to the Normal ruler, and he falls for her. His lord kills Gwyneth and blames Nick for her death. Then he sends Nick to take part in the Crusades rather than allowing him a trial. When he returns, he isn't the naive guy he'd been before.

Nick, vampire and detective, has historically taken on protector roles such as detective, soldier, and knight.

"I don't think Betty Ford takes vampires." The need for blood is often overshadowed by the lust for it.

In 1228, back from the Crusades and traveling through Paris, Nick meets Janette Du-Charme. He is seduced and allows himself to become enthralled by her. It is another mistake because she soon introduces him to Lucien LaCroix, her master. LaCroix offers vampirism to Nick, who doesn't fully understand the offer and follows the woman into a life of darkness.

His next great fall comes because of his sister, Fleur. After her son Andre is put in Nick's care, he tries to raise the boy as a nobleman. Then, LaCroix prompts the nephew to discover his uncle while he is feeding, driving a permanent wedge between them. Nick truly feels like a monster because of it.

This psychological battering comes again when he meets up with Joan of Arc in 1429. Her refusal to allow him to make her a vampire and save her life challenges his own beliefs and ultimately makes him examine his own mistake. Then, in 1528, he accidentally kills his new bride, Alyssa von Linz, while attempting to turn her. And finally, he hits perhaps his lowest point since Gwyneth when he kills a young woman because of LaCroix's lies.

The ultimate low point comes with the near death of Dr. Natalie Lambert. When she attempts to help Nick become mortal, he drains her out of lack of self-control from so many years of refraining from human blood. He is despondent and begs LaCroix to stake him, to put him out of his misery. We don't know whether he actually does, or whether he brings Natalie over after the many times he swore he never would.

Redemption

For much of his existence after the transition, Nick kills to sustain his own life. He's obviously begun to question his decision after meeting Joan of Arc and hearing her surprising refusal. Then, around 1890, his life takes an upward swing after killing an innocent girl. He realizes then that he's become a monster.

Nick turns away from the lifestyle and vows to find a way to be human again. LaCroix describes this decision: "He was brought across in 1228. Preyed on humans for their blood. Now he wants to be mortal again. To repay society for his sins. To emerge from his world of darkness. From his endless Forever Knight." Repayment means repaying in lives. If he can save lives, they might offset the ones he has taken, so he becomes a homicide detective in Toronto. And he does save lives, although he can't save his original partner, Don Schanke, from dying in a plane crash.

His new life also brings about a friendship with Janette that leads her to protect both Schanke, before he dies, and Natalie at the club The Raven. This relationship brings him the answers he craves. Janette returns after moving away, and she is human. But before Nick can discover how to become human too, she dies.

Powers

Similar to most of the dark angels, Nick is immune to gunshots and injury from blades or beatings. He's also immortal in the sense that he does not age. Like the others, he has the standard enhanced speed, strength, and senses. He also has a bit of mind-control ability, though it's a subtle form that can easily be circumvented with physical proof that Nick is lying.

The process for becoming a vampire is different in Nick's world, too. He is drained by LaCroix, but while near death he has a vision. He is offered the opportunity to pass through a doorway or go back to the human world. He decides to return, which sparks his body to drink LaCroix's offered blood, and he wakes as a vampire.

FACTS AND TRIVIA

• Nick and Janette are a couple for ninety-seven years.

• Nick has several aliases, which include Nicholas (Nichola) de Brabant, Nicholas Girard, Nicholas "Nick" Thomas, Nicholas "Nick" Hammond, Nicholas "Nick" Parker, Nicholas "Nick" Forrester, and Nicholas "Nick" or "Nichola" Knight.

QUOTES

"I am what I am, and I don't think Betty Ford takes vampires." —"Pilot"

"Word to the wise—immortality is no excuse not to floss." —"For I Have Sinned"

"I learned that I have to live with the choice I made eight hundred years ago. And forgiveness is not something you ask for. It's something that you earn. . . . Here. Among the living." —"Near Death"

"Science won't help you to understand what I am, or the hell of an existence I've locked myself into." —"Last Knight"

SELENE: DEATH ANGEL

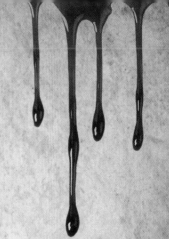

The only female assassin among the dark angels, Selene is known as a Death Dealer. She appears in the movies Underworld *(2003) and* Underworld: Evolution *(2006), and briefly in* Underworld: Rise of the Lycans *(2009). She is portrayed by actress Kate Beckinsale, for whom the role was written.*

There's no dark angel warrior quite like Selene. Beautiful and deadly, she fights against the Lycans (lycanthropes or werewolves), reaping centuries of revenge for the family she lost. At least, until she knows the truth. Selene sums up her unlife by saying, "For six centuries I was a loyal soldier to the vampire clan. But I was betrayed. The war was not as it had seemed. In one night, the lies that had united our kind had been exposed." The path between those two sentiments has been rocky.

History

While a child in Hungary, around the beginning of the fifteenth century, Selene witnesses her father working for Viktor, a vampire elder, to build what would be a place to lock away William, the first Lycan. Then, on a stormy night when she is a young woman, werewolves attack her home and kill her family. In the barn, she meets Viktor, a distinguished older gentleman who turns her into a vampire.

In modern times, Selene has done well for herself. She has the admiration of Kraven, the coven's leader, and she's a renowned Death Dealer, but she's more loyal than the other vampires. Naive, even. Then, while killing Lycans, she meets a human named Michael Corvin. After a lot of fighting and vampire politics, Selene discovers a conspiracy between Kraven and the werewolf leader, Lucian, who are supposed to be enemies.

Selene with Michael as both journey to become the first of their own breed, more powerful than all others in their world.

Michael

As a normal, modern human, Michael Corvin is unaware of the supernatural world Selene is part of. Then Lucian, the werewolf leader, bites him, infecting him with the Lycan virus. Unknown to Michael, Lucian does this because Michael is the only descendant of Alexander Corvinus and has a genetic quirk passed down from the original Alexander, allowing him to carry both vampire and Lycan viruses.

After the entire plot between Lucian and Kraven is uncovered, Selene attempts to wake Viktor, whom she believes to be the original vampire as well as her protector. When he rises, he learns all that he needs to know, but he doesn't act as she'd hoped. Instead, she learns of Viktor's original role as the one who killed Selene's human family. "How could you bare my trust knowing that you killed my family?" she says, unable to understand his betrayal. Even for a killer centuries old, Selene has a pure heart. The corruption in Viktor's soul isn't something she can relate to. The deaths she's dealt have been straightforward.

Disillusioned, Selene joins completely with Michael as they both fight for their survival. She falls in love with him, and when Kraven discovers this, he shoots Michael. In one last attempt to save him, Selene bites Michael, doubly infecting him. This starts the hybrid process. Where most characters are vampire or werewolf, Michael becomes a vampire/Lycan hybrid.

After he and Selene kill Viktor, they are forced to flee because both races want Michael, whom they consider a threat to their species and the murderer of their leaders. It's one of Selene's lowest moments. She has had to side against her vampire family, and Viktor, the only family she's had since her human one was slaughtered. Plus, learning that "Viktor was not the savior [she] had been led to believe" leads to a period of disillusionment and sadness. Selene feels truly alone, and almost is. As she says, "I have but one ally left: Michael, the human descendent of Corvinus. Neither vampire nor Lycan, but a hybrid. It's only a matter of time before we're found."

During their time on the run, Selene spends much of her energy trying to force Michael into his new role. "There's never been a hybrid before," she says. "However ambivalent you might feel about it, the truth is, your powers could be limitless." For a while he refuses to drink blood and experience his true power.

After Michael gives in and feeds, his powers are certainly stronger than those of the others, both Lycan and vampire. Together they find Alexander. Marcus, the true oldest vampire, catches up to them and impales Michael. It's another major low point for Selene. Not only does losing him leave her without allies, but she is also without her new love.

Selene escapes, but only after Marcus tastes her blood and sees where his brother William, the original Lycan and a mindless beast, is kept. After Marcus leaves, she takes blood from the dying Alexander, the only other hybrid and father to the first vampire and Lycan. The blood changes her, making her the strongest vampire alive. Determined to keep Marcus from releasing William, she goes after him. But Selene refuses to leave Michael and loads his body into a body bag and places him in the helicopter so that she can mourn him later.

From there, she and a small crew head to the remains of the chamber her human father built to contain William. There, she is outnumbered by werewolves. She survives only because Michael comes back from what appears to be death. Then, as Michael kills William in *Evolution*, Selene kills the original vampire, Marcus. It's the symbolic end of the old ways and old races. The two start their new life as the sun rises, and Selene stands in the light of the sun for the first time in centuries.

Selene's eyes in that awesome shade of bite-me blue. It's a color driven by emotion and bloodlust.

The Men

Selene's betrayals come from her reliance on men to rescue her. Throughout her unlife, she trusts several people who don't deserve it because she's always the damsel in distress—the victim. When she wakes Viktor in *Underworld*, she addresses him by admitting to this weakness, saying, "I've been lost without you, my Lord." Her dependence on Viktor leaves her vulnerable. He uses her, after slaughtering her entire family and blaming it on werewolves. Betraying her also allows Viktor to keep her as a map to find William's chamber, since she was too young to know what information she's carried with her into her undead life. Then, he uses Selene's anger to make her into a killing machine. His disloyalties trigger the events that ruin her family, her coven, and take down the hierarchy of both races. Perhaps this reliance stems from the lingering fifteenth-century gender roles she was raised with.

Blood Power

Selene possesses several superhuman powers. She has enhanced strength and speed, as many of the other dark angels do, except hers are on the level with an elder vampire. She absorbs gun blasts, tosses heavy items around like they are weightless, and kills werewolves with a few punches. The most astounding demonstrations of her abilities come as leaps from tall buildings. After she drinks from the dying Alexander Corvinus, her current abilities increase and she develops the new capability of going into the sunlight unharmed.

FACTS AND TRIVIA

• Lily Mo Sheen, who portrays the child version of Selene in the films, is the real-life daughter of Kate Beckinsale, who plays Selene, and Michael Sheen, who plays Lucian. They were no longer together during the filming of the movies.

QUOTES

"I am a Death Dealer, sworn to destroy those known as the Lycans. Our war has waged for centuries, unseen by human eyes."—Underworld

HELLBOY: DEMON SPAWN

When it came time to cast Hellboy for the movies, there was really no other choice than that perennial beast-boy actor, Ron Perlman. But prior to his Hollywood appearances in Guillermo del Toro's Hellboy *(2004) and* Hellboy II: The Golden Army *(2008), the character had a long history (1993–1999) as the creation of Dark Horse Comics artist/writer Mike Mignola. The character has also appeared in two animated DVD films,* Hellboy: Sword of Storms *(2006) and* Hellboy: Blood and Iron *(2007), and has inspired a series of novels and video games. Despite his being a demon, Hellboy is a dark angel. Like his vampire companions, he is a creature returned to Earth from the afterlife. He is as good as he can be bad, but he chooses to protect the human race. He has supernatural powers and is forced to live a life in secret, much like the vampires. He only lacks a few of the vampiric weaknesses.*

Unlike the vampires and other creatures among the dark angel ranks, Hellboy is a demon. Although his real name is Anung Un Rama, or the Beast of the Apocalypse, he generally goes by the nickname Hellboy, a title given him by his adoptive father, Professor Trevor "Broom" Bruttenholm. He looks like no other dark angel, but tries to fit in. He is huge and red, and has two large horns growing out of his forehead that he keeps sanded short. These flattened horns are the trademark of his appearance. When they grow out, the Crown of the Apocalypse appears over them. His right hand is very large compared to the rest of his body, and it's made of stone. Some say he smells like dry-roasted peanuts, and those who've seen him unclothed note a long red tail. To blend into the human world, Hellboy wears a trench coat and pants. Rather than being known for his demonic heritage, he is noted as the "World's Greatest Paranormal Investigator."

His story is even more unusual than his appearance. It is documented in the comic book series *Seed of Destruction* that a ritual is performed on December 23, 1944, by the resurrected Russian mystic Grigori Rasputin, which summons Hellboy to the ruins of a church just outside the fictional English village of East Bromwich. The act is a success for

The "World's Greatest Paranormal Investigator" is Anung Un Rama, or the Beast of the Apocalypse…better known as Hellboy.

the Nazi occultists who are behind it all. Allied forces discover him shortly after, and take him to an Air Force base in New Mexico, where he is raised by the military and the US government's paranormal bureau.

He eats pancakes for the first time in New Mexico in 1947. Then, in 1952, Hellboy is declared an honorary human by the United Nations. He is also given the status as a field agent with the Bureau for Paranormal Research and Defense (BPRD). In 1954, he takes an assignment to kill an alligator-type monster in Britain. In an interesting turn, lilies grow where he sheds blood. During the rest of the '50s, Hellboy helps people in Norway, India, Malaysia, Ireland, Brazil, New Guinea, and Virginia. He kills such creatures as werewolves, a vampirelike monster, and a mad scientist. In the '60s, he helps perform an exorcism in Connecticut, traps a demon in Ireland, meets a witch in Norway, faces a hydra in Alaska, takes out a militia in Tennessee, and takes care of some floating heads (*nukekubihr*) in Japan. The '70s are a little slower. Between 1979 and 1981, he goes on hiatus to travel with an archaeologist.

Then, Hellboy returns and seems to go on a vampire spree. In1982, he beats the famous Vampire of Prague, who is a devout gambler, at poker. Then, he wraps up his seven-year search for Countess Ilona Kakosky by killing her in Britain. He also squeezes an Indian werewolf case into the year. The rest of the '80s are slow, too. Then, in 1990, Hellboy and Abe Sapien, his aquatic sidekick, track down a Wendigo (a cannibalistic phantom entity) in Canada.

The year 1991 brings more strangeness when, on a haunted house case, Hellboy time travels to 1902. His blood is used then by a satanic brotherhood to transform a chimpanzee into a psychopathic demon. Once back in the present, he spends 1992 tracking down a flesh-eating ghoul and a sea serpent, which injures Abe.

The remainder of the '90s sees Hellboy coming to terms with his own identity. In 1993, he is invited into an exclusive club. The members have a mummy who wakes to tell of Makoma, the hammer-handed beast who kills a demon at the world's end. That mummy disintegrates when he finishes, and the members disinvite Hellboy. In 1994, he meets Rasputin, the man who summoned him. Then, in 1995, he visits the church where he was born to this world. He dreams of his mother, which allows him to see that she was a young witch, Sarah Hughes, who conceived him with a demon on Walpurgisnacht (a holy night for witches). The unborn Hellboy stayed dormant inside the woman until, near the woman's death, the demon came to claim him and her. In 1998, on a trip to Spain, he and Adrian Frost discover that Hellboy's oversized hand is the trigger for the Apocalypse. And in 1999, during a scuffle with a demon in Scotland, his Crown of the Apocalypse is snatched and taken to Hell. It's 2001 before Hellboy quits BPRD so that he can investigate his own life.

A poster for one of Hellboy's animated appearances.

Hellboy saving the city and a baby in the opening scenes of *The Golden Army*. Despite his heroics in public, the people simply see him as weird.

Hellboy is, in 2004, in trouble when an undersea monster takes him captive, intent on dismembering him to prevent the Apocalypse. It isn't until 2006 that he escapes, thanks to a mermaid. Washing up on a deserted island, he learns the secret history of the universe from a mystic, then manages to escape the island. It's right back to the fight in 2007, when he is offered a position as king of witches, which he refuses. Finally, in 2008, he is called to partici-pate in "The Wild Hunt," where fighting with giants was to ensue, but he soon becomes the real target. During the hunt, Hellboy discovers that Sarah, the witch who mothered him, was the daughter of Mordred, the son of King Arthur, and the legendary sorceress Morgan le Fay. Morgan claims Hellboy as the last heir of Arthur and the real king of England. He draws the sword Excalibur, which proves his birthright.

Powers

Hellboy, like other dark angels, has superhuman strength and healing abilities. His fortitude is astounding as he survives machine gun blasts to the chest and other large amounts of damage. He can be injured by standard weapons, but his rapid healing makes it hard to kill him. Also, at ten years old, he is fully grown in the comic book *Nature of the Beast*. After reaching physical maturity, he has not aged. He also keeps a Batman-style utility belt with holy relics and other items used to battle the supernatural. Often, Hellboy brags about being a bad marksman, but he makes up for this by carrying a huge gun.

FACTS AND TRIVIA

- In the film version of Hellboy's life, he lives at BPRD headquarters with many cats. He is an urban legend, showing up in magazines such as the *National Enquirer*. However, the comic books, which feature his original story, show him interacting and living among the populace.

QUOTES

"Didn't I kill you already?" —Hellboy *(2004 film)*

"Look, Sammy, I'm not a very good shot . . . but the Samaritan here uses really big bullets." —Hellboy *(2004 film)*

"I know; I'm ugly!" —Hellboy II: The Golden Army *(2008 film)*

Chapter Five
Darkest of the Dark

What would the dark angels be without the monsters that keep them all struggling against the beasts inside them?

The following dark angels are great at being dark. They indulge their desires, bathe in blood, dress like Billy Idol, and rule the night with iron fists. Their mission is to do nothing but have what they want, when they want it. They survive, taking lives as they choose.

These are the guys who make your hair stand on end when you get that feeling that someone's watching you. In their twisted minds, they believe themselves angels, doing God's will or justice on Earth.

DAVID: THE ORIGINAL VAMPIRE REBEL

Played by Kiefer Sutherland in Joel Schumacher's cult favorite horror-comedy **The Lost Boys** *(1987), the California vampire known only as David is still a major Goth icon more than twenty-five years after the film's release.*

David, the motorcycle-riding, white-spiked-hair vampire is the original rebel of the dark angels. While Spike (see "Spike: Dark Poet") shares an almost identical look, David catches our attention first, tempting the young mortals of Santa Carla into drinking his blood in *The Lost Boys*. Even though he has few redeeming qualities, we can't help but love him.

Vicious and Delicious

Although David has chipmunk cheeks and a boyish smile, there's no denying that he is a vicious killer. The black clothes, trench coat, and earring only hint at the inner monster. Unlike most of the vampires prior to the late 1980s, David enjoys being what he is. He and his friends spend most nights hanging at the boardwalk, which is decorated with the flyers of all the "missing" people that David probably has had as a snack.

When we first meet him, David goads Michael, a teenager who moves to his grandfather's home in Santa Carla with his mom and younger brother, into a motorcycle race in an attempt to lead him over the edge of a seaside cliff. This is no random act. Michael is pursuing Star, the only female in David's small gang of vampires. She is obviously David's, and Michael is intruding on that relationship. But when Michael is too smart to fall for David's underhanded attempt to kill him, David recognizes the mortal's intelligence, respects him for it, and decides to bring him into the fold. He could have killed him and dumped him over the cliff with less effort. Or he could have allowed Star to kill him as originally intended.

It's only after Sam, Michael's younger brother, and two vampire-hunting teens called the Frog brothers go to David's haven during the day that things cross over to David attacking Michael's family. This is because the boys take Star and Laddie, a male vampire child in David's gang, and then kill one of David's friends. In many ways, their meddling forces

David, portrayed by Kiefer Sutherland, hanging out under the bridge during Michael's initiation in *The Lost Boys*. The gloves on David's hands had a more utilitarian use than just looking cool. (See Facts and Trivia.)

David's to react. What little patience he has with Michael and his human family is lost when they start attacking the vampires. Not even the sweetest dark angel would tolerate that, but David's retaliation is limited, as he and the other vampires only frighten the kids.

Illusions and Pranks

David's sense of humor hasn't suffered with his becoming a vampire. He uses his powers to entertain himself and others, even if that entertainment has a sadistic slant. Making Michael see maggots instead of rice and worms instead of noodles is a harmless joke. Horrifying Michael by having him dangle with the gang from beneath train tracks, then watch as they drop to what seems like their death is a classic rite of initiation.

Blood Benefits

As with most vampires, David survives on blood and is susceptible to a stake through the heart. Daylight torches him and mirrors don't show his reflection. In fact, most of the mythic ways to harm or kill a vampire work on David and his group, as the Frog brothers discover.

His vampire powers are relatively standard. He has the ability to manipulate humans' minds. Based on the motorcycle race, he most likely possesses supernatural agility and reflexes. His only exceptional ability is flight. Not all vampires are gifted with the ability to fly long distances, as we see David do when he flies down to snatch a couple out of their car.

Coffin Buster

Even though most of the dark angels who've come out of their crypts since we've met David have a punk or modern edge, he is the original. His predecessors are Dracula-esque European vampires with accents and romantic or straight horror leanings. They sleep in coffins and slink away at the sight of a cross.

David breaks that vampire mold. His youthful modern appearance and butt-kicking persona became the standard in the decades to follow. Even his haven, an earthquake-sunken hotel lobby with a canopy bed, Doors poster, and jeweled bottle of David's blood, is completely original. Without a doubt, David is the beginning of the modern vampire. His motto is summed up by the tagline "Sleep all day. Party all night. Never grow old. Never die. It's fun to be a vampire."

David ready to make a quick snack of Michael, possibly because the Widow Johnson wanted to take Grandpa's family for her own.

FACTS AND TRIVIA

- Santa Carla, the city where David and his gang reside, is actually Santa Cruz, California, the name of which means "Holy Cross" in Spanish.

- The cool black gloves that are part of David's trademark outfit weren't planned. As it turns out, actor Kiefer Sutherland broke his wrist during a motorcycle stunt. The black gloves were a way to hide the performer's injury.

- Not much is known about David, but he did survive the antler impaling that appeared to kill him in *The Lost Boys*. His story continues in *Lost Boys: Reign of Frogs* comic books.

- David's progeny, Shane, is the vampiric leader in the film *Lost Boys: The Tribe* (2008).

- In *The Lost Boys*, Michael's mother's boyfriend, Max, is David's maker. Most fans are left with this belief, but it is revealed later in the comic books that Michael's grandfather's love interest, the Widow Johnson, is actually David's maker.

QUOTES

"You don't have to beat me, Michael. You just have to keep up." —The Lost Boys

"What, you don't like rice? Tell me, Michael, how could a billion Chinese people be wrong?" —The Lost Boys

"Now you know what we are. Now you know what you are. You'll never grow old, Michael, and you'll never die. But you must feed!" —The Lost Boys

"Initiation's over, Michael. Time to join the club!" —The Lost Boys

DAMON SALVATORE: HEARTBROKEN ROGUE

Like his brother, Stefan (see "Stefan Salvatore: The Virtuous Brother"), Damon is the creation of novelist L. J. Smith in her 1991 Vampire Diaries trilogy: The Awakening, The Struggle, *and* The Fury. *They were later paired in* The Dark Reunion *(1998) and most recently in a new trilogy,* The Vampire Diaries: The Return *(begun in 2009). In the television series, Damon is played by actor Ian Somerhalder.*

Of all the dark angels, perhaps Damon Salvatore is the most tormented soul. He can be devious and ruthless, and a healthy share of *The Vampire Diaries* characters and fans alike despise Damon for his wicked ways. But few vampires in fiction or on television can simultaneously be so endearing and so deliciously evil. He can plot to kill his brother, seduce a naive human, and still do something heroic before midnight.

And he doesn't apologize for it.

That's Damon's most engaging quality: his inability to be anything other than himself. He enjoys his undead life thoroughly. Immortality doesn't weigh him down. Instead, he embraces what he is, revels in it, and seeks little more than to enjoy his undead life with his brother Stefan and Elena, the girl they both have their sights set on because she looks like the recreation of Damon's lost love and the woman who turned both brothers into vampires, Katherine. His actions, though somewhat twisted at times, are motivated by a heart-wrenching combination of love and loneliness. Sure, he killed a few humans and threw some wild parties, but what's an immortal bad boy supposed to do?

A Strength or a Weakness?

The torrent of hot-tempered Italian emotion that churns just beneath the cool surface of Damon's demeanor is both his greatest strength and his greatest weakness. Love is his greatest motivation, second only to survival. As an asset, it allows him to do the dirty work to save those he loves. He's willing to kill, torture, and do whatever it takes to keep him, Elena, and Stefan safe in Fells Church, Virginia (or Mystic Falls, depending on whether you watch the television show or read the books).

Damon as portrayed by Ian Somerhalder. Both character and actor are fans of fashion designer John Varvatos.

A more subtle show of his love comes in his willingness to help others. Damon wipes the mind of Elena's brother, Jeremy, free of the memory of the death of Vicki, his girlfriend turned vampire by Damon, and the events that led up to it. In doing so, he acts in mercy, saving Jeremy from the pain that Damon knows all too well, the death of the woman he loves. He also saves Elena from the pain of watching her brother suffer. He even goes so far as to inspire Jeremy to a better life with a subconscious suggestion.

However, this depth of emotion cuts both ways, driving Damon to justify his most monstrous actions. Since Katherine died, Damon has wandered the Earth lonely, miserable, and angry at his brother Stefan for his part in her death. It is this unending pain that weakens Damon and twists his thoughts. At times, he seems unable to stifle the hurt he endures from Stefan, constantly insulting and playing word games with his brother. Maybe it's because sibling rivalry continues for eternity? Or maybe it's that he can't resist getting in every single jab possible at the man who ultimately took his true love from him.

Loyalty? Ha!

Perhaps Damon does count overreaction as one of his weaknesses. And yes, he does do wicked things at times, but he always steps in at the last minute to save Stefan's rear, whether he put it in the fire or not. He also works tirelessly to convince Stefan to embrace who he really is, just as any big brother should. Because he prefers to keep his true feelings private, these actions can be mistaken as coldheartedness and arrogance by those who don't know him.

His other apparent betrayals of Stefan come from trust issues that both he and Stefan have. First, as with any adult who grew up abused or mistreated, trust doesn't come easily for Damon. When you add to it the years of living in a harsh world as a vampire and working as a mercenary, it's easy to see how Damon trusts no one.

He *is* loyal to his brother, but he doesn't trust him—and with good reason. Time after time, Damon steps out to help Stefan and Elena, only to be hurt or insulted again. In the television episode "Children of the Damned," they lie, swearing to help Damon find the book that will release his beloved Katherine from her tomb. When he doesn't trust anyone, he trusts them. And it's Damon who's hurt, finding them in the dark, holding the book that they were planning to hide from him.

Stefan: *"I'm sorry."*
Damon: *"So am I . . . for thinking for even a second that I could trust you."*
Stefan: *"You are not capable of trust. The fact that you're here means that you read the journal and you were planning on doing this yourself."*
Damon: *"Of course I was going to do it myself because the only one I can count on is me. You made sure of that many years ago, Stefan. But you . . . [to Elena] you had me fooled."*

After his last words, Damon grabs Elena. Although he tries to convince Stefan and Elena that he is going to kill her, he is too gentle and doesn't have the heart to do it. After all those years of being a killer, it would have been nothing to off her, but he doesn't—even after he has just been betrayed. Instead, he puts enough of his blood in Elena's mouth to convince Stefan that he will snap her neck and turn her into a vampire. In their world, a bit of ingested vampire blood before death is enough to start the conversion, and it sways Stefan into giving up the book. Immediately, Damon comforts Elena and helps her to his brother, careful not to let her stumble. These are not the acts of a heartless villain.

Who Would Win?

Damon is loyal to Stefan, and any question to the contrary can only be asked by someone who doesn't understand him. Still, Damon would never allow Stefan to kill him. He would, and does, fight. But he doesn't kill Stefan. It leads fans to wonder: Who is stronger? It's no secret that Damon is one tough cookie. According to Ian Somerhalder, who plays Damon on *The Vampire Diaries* show, Damon could even kick Edward Cullen's butt. That's because, in addition to the standard enhanced physical abilities, Damon has the vampiric powers to persuade and even to manipulate the mind. He erases memories, implants thoughts, and calls humans to him, using a form of mind control to have them do as he wishes. This could be a great advantage where humans are concerned. Damon could not only turn an entire town against his foe, but he could also have his enemy commit murders and be put away for life as a serial killer.

While that's all great, his most impressive powers are his elemental and shape-shifting abilities. He can turn into a crow or a wolf, which is also rare among the dark angels. Though astounding, Stefan seems only slightly moved by this power, saying, "Crow's a bit much, don't you think?" To this, Damon answers with his usual wit: "Wait till you see what I can do with the fog." He refers to his ability to manipulate the weather, which implies that Stefan doesn't have that ability. In a fight, the fog alone could be a great advantage that would spell any opposition's ultimate end, even Stefan's.

Damon at His Finest

In *The Awakening*, Damon uses that sharp tongue of his to wound Stefan. The scene is classic Damon and very telling:

> *"You always were selfish. Your one fault. Not willing to share anything, are you?" Suddenly, Damon's lips curved up in a singularly beautiful smile. "But fortunately the lovely Elena is more generous. Didn't she tell you about our little liaisons? Why, the first time we met she almost gave herself to me on the spot."*
>
> *"That's a lie!"*
>
> *"Oh, no, dear brother, I never lie about anything important. Or do I mean unimportant? Anyway, your beauteous damsel nearly swooned into my arms. I think she likes men in black." As Stefan stared at him, trying to control his breathing, Damon added, almost gently, "You're wrong about her, you know. You think she's sweet and docile, like Katherine. She isn't. She's not your type at all, my saintly brother. She has a spirit and a fire in her that you wouldn't know what to do with."*
>
> *"And you would, I suppose."*
>
> *Damon uncrossed his arms and slowly smiled again. "Oh, yes."*

It's in this scene that we see Damon's attraction to Elena and the foreshadowing of her being a little more like her predecessor than Stefan wants to believe. It also allows us to see how Damon tortures his brother a little, and then tenderly adds a truth that is sure to hurt Stefan. With or without meaning to, Damon expresses his love for the brother he feels so strongly has betrayed him, delivering the blow with care.

Not Every Vampire Recites Sonnets

Damon's sarcasm during times of emotional stress is often an attempt to avoid being vulnerable. Other times, he's simply a cynic who spouts the truth as he sees it. Through these Damon-isms, we see a vampire who is determined to make the most of what he is. And no matter the motivation, it's that wicked sense of humor that makes us love him most.

FACTS AND TRIVIA

- In the television episode "Family Ties," Stefan stabs Damon, who replies, "This is John Varvatos, dude. Dick move." Besides being humorous, it's a reference to Ian Somerhalder's favorite clothing designer.

QUOTES

"The name is Salvatore. As in savior." —The Struggle *(novel)*

"I can waken things inside you that have been sleeping all your life." —The Struggle *(novel)*

"You're right to be afraid of me; I'm the most dangerous thing you're ever likely to encounter in your life." —The Struggle *(novel)*

"Little brother, the world is full of what you call 'wrong.' Why not relax and join the winning side? It's much more fun, I assure you." —Dark Reunion *(novel)*

Damon: "It's good to be home. I think I might stay a while. This town could use a bit of a wake up call, don't you think?"
Stefan: "What are you up to, Damon?"
Damon: "That's for me to know and for you to dot dot dot." —"The Night of the Comet" *(television series)*

"It's cool not growing old. I like being the eternal stud." —"Family Ties" *(television episode)*

[On the phone with Stefan while cleaning up dead bodies in the forest—by burning them]
Stefan: "Where are you?"
Damon: "I'm at the Sizzler. At the buffet." —"The Lost Girls" *(television episode)*

COUNT ORLOK: PRIMO NOSFERATU

Unforgettably introduced in 1922 by expressionist filmmaker F. W. Murnau in **Nosferatu,** *Count Orlok remains one of the most chilling vampires ever to appear on screen. As played by Max Schreck (an actor whose name means "terror" in German), Count Orlok is definitely dark, and as an angel . . . well, he's strictly for Satanists. There is nothing suave or seductive about his ratlike teeth, bald head, and clawlike fingers.* **Nosferatu** *was remade in 1979 by director Werner Herzog, with actor Klaus Kinski wearing the same makeup, but playing the role for pathos as well as horror.*

We first learn of Count (or Graf) Orlok in the silent movie *Nosferatu, eine Symphonie de Grauens (Nosferatu: A Symphony of Horror).* Fans have compared him to Bram Stoker's Dracula (see "Vlad Dracula: Darkly Original") throughout the years—as well they should, because the film stole its basic plot from Stoker—but Count Orlok is really his own man. As writer Kim Newman reveals in his book *Anno Dracula,* Orlok was once a Carpathian guard to Dracula and the governor of the Tower of London, though he doesn't like to talk about it. It was a dark time. He prefers to focus on his coming "out of the coffin," as those young vampires Bill Compton and Eric Northman call it today. Later, he was a nobleman who lived in an old castle in the Carpathian Mountains. It was a fixer-upper, but it was home.

Bird of Death

Count Orlok has never been the handsome prince of fairy tales, and it is his biggest challenge. Dracula got all the looks and charm, but Orlok comes from the shallow end of the gene pool. He's so unattractive that the locals are afraid of him. In addition to the indignity of forcing him to live in a dilapidated castle, vampirism hasn't been kind. He is bald, with a hunched back, long gnarled fingers, elfish ears, and dark eyes set in a gaunt face. Rats follow him everywhere, probably because he looks like the granddaddy of them all. It's ridiculous: A simple trip to the market means he scares women and makes babies cry. So, he stays home and does his shopping in the dark.

Count Orlok reportedly has a bit of trouble opening doors, flipping pages, and scratching sensitive places because of his claws.

Getting Out of the House

Another downside of being an unattractive count is that Orlok's life is pretty dull. At best, the Count suffers from depression. That feeling inspires him to seek a life outside the sleepy Carpathian town. Thomas Hutter, who arrives representing real estate in Wisborg, Germany, is the first visitor he's had in years. The meeting makes Orlok sure of his decision to move, even though his condition forces him to travel in a soil-lined coffin on the ship and feed off the crew.

The people of Wisborg aren't any more welcoming than the yokels of the Carpathians. They think he's brought a few diseases with him, and so they quarantine the ship. How could he know that the soil he's brought is infected with the Black Death?

Vacation Hottie

Since he hasn't been out of the castle for so long, Orlok is smitten with the first beautiful girl he sees, easily swayed by a pretty face. Thomas Hutter's young bride, Ellen, catches his eye. He only wants a little snog session—and perhaps a little blood—but he gets caught up in her beauty. Before he realizes it, the sun peeks through the window and torches him. Or so they think . . .

Modern Celebrity

Contrary to modern belief, Orlok does not die in the sunlight. The final title card from *Nosferatu* reads: "And the stifling shadow of the vampire vanished with the morning sun." This isn't Orlok's death. Instead, he dashes away, leaving a puff of dust in his wake. All the years of being called "hideous" and "monstrous" are finally repaid when the silver screen comes calling. Posing as actor Max Schreck, Orlok plays himself in *Nosferatu*. It isn't until after the twenty-first century dawns that anyone finds out his secret, which is revealed in the 2000 film *Shadow of the Vampire*, with Willem Dafoe playing Schreck/Orlok.

There was also a television series titled *Kindred: The Embraced* (see "Julian Luna: Dark Prince"). Although Orlok saw no royalties from the series or the *Vampire: The Masquerade* role-playing game, the Nosferatu in them were modeled after him. Some of his relatives even played the parts. A similar thing happened in the *Castlevania* video game. He's a character in several places in the game, but because he gave no permission for his likeness, they called the character Orlox in the English version and Orlock in Japanese. It's still a sore point for him.

His appearance on *SpongeBob SquarePants* was, however, at his own request. Although it's only a cameo in the episode "The Graveyard Shift," flipping the light on and off was an honor. He's a huge fan of the little square guy.

Unlike the more attractive dark angels, Orlok and those of his kind prefer to drink from sleeping victims.

There is also a California band named after him. He's become a fan of Californian grindcore since discovering them. As for his possible appearances in *Are You Afraid of the Dark?* and *Angel*, he has refused to comment. He did however say that he'd heard that a certain Mr. Barlow of the movie *'Salem's Lot* resembled him greatly, but he hasn't watched it to know whether there is any truth to the rumor.

The Book of the Vampires

The Nosferatu of Orlok's world are old school. Sunlight sends them up in a cloud of smoke. They have to sleep in the dirt of their homeland, and they drink the blood of humans.

In *The Book of the Vampires*, invoked in the film *Nosferatu*, it is said that "only a woman can break his frightful spell—a woman pure in heart—who will offer her blood freely to Nosferatu and will keep the vampire by her side until after the cock has crowed." That's sure playing to his weakness, blinding him with beauty. It also states that the vampire's power comes from the soil he was buried in, which in this case is the soil inside Orlok's coffin. The Count refuses comment on whether this is a fact, as well.

FACTS AND TRIVIA

• The word *Nosferatu*, long associated with vampires and used by Bram Stoker in *Dracula*, has no known origin in any language. Its true history remains a total mystery.

QUOTES

"Blood! Your precious blood!" —Nosferatu, eine Symphonie des Gravens *(1922)*

"What a beautiful neck!" —Nosferatu, eine Symphonie des Gravens *(1922)*

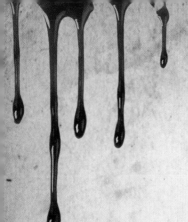

ELIZABETH BATHORY: COUNTESS DRACULA

Usually known as the Blood Countess or Countess Dracula, Elizabeth Bathory is closer to being a fairy-tale wicked stepmother than any other dark angel. And if she is indeed an angel, it is only in her own deluded mind, for she's insane by even Akasha's standards (see "Akasha: Dark Queen"). Her cruelty and depravity are unmatched among her kind. Worst of all, unlike the other dark angels, she has her origins not in fiction or folklore but in reality. Her horrific exploits were chronicled by Sabine Baring-Gould in his Book of Were-Wolves, *which brought her to Bram Stoker's attention while he was writing* Dracula. *She has appeared in a number of frightening films, including* Countess Dracula *(1970), starring Ingrid Pitt, who also played Carmilla in* The Vampire Lovers, Daughters of Darkness *(1971),* The Legend of Blood Castle *(1972),* Three Immortal Women *(1974), and* The Craving *(1980).*

Born August 7, 1560, Elizabeth Bathory, or Ecsedi Báthory Erzsébet in Hungarian, is perhaps the most prolific serial killer ever. According to official records, she killed dozens of females ranging from young women down to girls. However, she is said to have kept a list that totals more than six hundred victims between 1585 and 1610. At first, she coaxed them to her castle, offering to pay them well to work. Later, she killed the daughters of people who sent them there to learn etiquette. Some she even kidnapped or procured from people who were capturing them for her. According to reports, the girls died from various things, including severe extended beatings, starving, surgery, and freezing. Among other injuries were flesh bitten off the face or other body parts, sexual abuse, needle use, and burns or mutilation of the hands, face, or genitals.

Locked in Cachtice Castle near what is now Hungary, Elizabeth was spared an execution because of her title. She was found dead on August 21, 1614, at the age of fifty-four, although it is thought she may have been dead for days because of uneaten food. The villagers loathed and feared her so much that her body had to be buried at her home instead of the cemetery.

Elizabeth Bathory, distant cousin to the legendary Vlad Dracula, is one of history's most notable serial killers.

In 1971, she was reported to be alive and well, although preferring the company of females, in the film *Daughters of Darkness*, a good fit considering her affinity for virtuous women to rape and torture.

Lovesick

The Countess's marriage to Ferenc Nádasdy on May 8, 1575, was arranged, according to most experts. The fact that Elizabeth moved to Nádasdy Castle in Sárvár after the wedding and her husband to Vienna seems to back this up. For a wedding gift, he gave her his home in the Little Carpathians, Csejte Castle, with a country house and seventeen villages.

In 1578, Nádasdy went away to war against the Ottomans. Elizabeth was left to care for the villagers, even performing their medical care and defending the women. During the same year, she had a daughter and named her Anna. Two children died when they were still young: Ursula, daughter number two, and Andrew, her first son. She followed them up with Katherine in 1594, Paul in 1597, and Miklós, whose birth date is unknown. Her husband died of battle wounds shortly after this, in 1604. The deaths of her children and her husband's frequent absence must have left Elizabeth lonely. The grief likely drove her over the edge, perhaps into making a deal with the devil.

Or perhaps into becoming a vampire. Twisted by a need to be stronger than the men around her to maintain her power, and forced to be as violent as the Turks, Elizabeth became bloodthirsty. Literally.

Obsessed with Youth

Elizabeth's beauty was her weakness. She was Snow White–like, with pale skin and dark hair. Known for her beauty, she focused on it as her defining quality. According to some accounts, Elizabeth changed clothes up to six times a day and spent hours admiring herself in the mirror. Then, like so many modern women, her looks started going downhill when she hit twenty-five. Elizabeth longed for youthful skin and the admiration that came with it.

Legends say that after blood splattered on her skin from a maid she beat, her cleaned skin was beautiful. According to Sabine Baring-Gould's translation of a 1795 manuscript by Michael Wagener, Elizabeth's skin was "whiter and more transparent on the spots where the blood had been." It was just the thing she needed to feed her obsession and depravity. From then on, her victims were drained, and witnesses say Elizabeth would have servants fill the bath with the blood of virgins, then "bathe at the hour of four in the morning. After the bath she appeared more beautiful than before." Some reports also have her taking a blood shower beneath a cage, suspended from the ceiling, where a young girl was impaled on spikes. Still others claim that she was seen biting them to draw their blood to the skin, which she drank in vampire fashion.

The Countess loosely portrayed in *The Brothers Grimm* film.

As the real Countess feared, the lack of blood from her young victims allowed age to overtake her beauty in *The Brothers Grimm*.

FACTS AND TRIVIA

• The actual Elizabeth Bathory and the real Vlad Dracula (see "Vlad Dracula: Darkly Original") were distantly related to the aristocracy of Transylvania. Killing must have been a family thing.

QUOTES

"I feel it in my bones, the night is dying . . ." —Daughters of Darkness (*1971*)

"Love is stronger than death . . . even than life." —Daughters of Darkness (*1971*)

"From now on, you will be my faithful servant, and soon your master will be my slave." —Night of the Werewolf (*1981*)

VLAD DRACULA: DARKLY ORIGINAL

The most mediagenic vampire of all time, Count Dracula of Transylvania began his career in a Victorian novel, continued as a stage star in the West End and on Broadway, and has enjoyed an afterlife in the movies and television unparalleled by any fictional character. No book in history has been dramatically adapted more frequently than Dracula. *Among the most notable film versions are the 1922 expressionist classic* Nosferatu *(a pirated adaptation, hunted down like a vampire itself by Bram Stoker's angry widow), the 1931 classic with Bela Lugosi, the 1958 remake with Christopher Lee, television movies with Jack Palance (1974) and Louis Jourdan (1977), and two groundbreaking romantic interpretations by Frank Langella (1979) and Gary Oldman (1992). Dracula has gotten swoonier as he has gotten older, and although Bram Stoker wouldn't recognize the horrible old man he envisioned in his novel, it is the lovesick Dracula that a new generation of vampire fans loves the best.*

What is there to say about Dracula? He was the first and most original dark angel of them all. He made his entrance on the scene, starring in his own multimedia "show," before most of the others. At the very least, he was the first to become a celebrity.

His coming out in Bram Stoker's 1897 novel *Dracula* received mixed reviews in the vampire community. It made a number of other vampires angry while others were inspired. Spike of *Buffy the Vampire Slayer* (see "Spike: Dark Poet") took particular offense to it, saying, "That glory hound's done more harm to vampires than any Slayer. His story gets out and suddenly everybody knows how to kill us." Spike held a grudge for some time. Others shared their opinions, too. Hundreds of movies and novels have since been written and produced about his life or the lives of his family, but few show the whole story.

Permission British Museum

Vlad Dracula was as mysterious and cruel as the legendary Dracula.

Mixed History

Several connections are drawn between Count Dracula and the real-life Vlad III of Wallachia, and many believe they are one and the same thanks to a 1972 book by Radu Florescu and Raymond McNally titled *In Search of Dracula*. Perhaps they are; it's certainly easy to see how the authors came to the conclusion.

Vlad III, Prince of Wallachia, was born in Sighisoara, Transylvania, on November 25, 1431. The bulk of his reign was from 1456 to 1462, and he lived all his adult life in Wallachia, except for periods of imprisonment at Pest and Visegrad (in Hungary). He posed a strong resistance to the Ottoman Empire's expansion, and was best known for his cruelty. According to records, he died on December 18, 1476.

Names

His most common alias is Vlad Țepeș, meaning Vlad the Impaler, because he liked to impale people on pikes as punishment, and then display them publicly to quash rebellion and warn those considering it. It is believed he impaled somewhere between forty thousand and one hundred thousand victims.

One of the ways he is tied to Count Dracula is through his other alias, Vlad Dracula. The name comes from his father, Vlad II Dracul. *Dracul* in Romanian is *drac* for "dragon" or "devil" and *ul* as the definitive article. Likewise, Dracula can be divided into "drac" and "ula," which is understood to indicate *ulea* and mean "the son of." In essence, Dracula means "son of the dragon" or "son of the devil," either of which fits the man in this case.

The Dracul name, the dragon on Vlad II's coins, and the fact that from 1431 forward, Vlad II wore an emblem of the secret fraternal order of knights points to him having joined the Order of the Dragon around 1431. The group's mission was to protect Christianity and keep the Ottoman Turks from taking over. It is suspected that he gained membership because of his efforts against the Turks. His son was just continuing the family business.

Stoker obviously knew his Romanian history, because he mentions that Dracula "won his name against the Turks." However, he is also noted in the story to be Székely, a descendant of Attila the Hun.

After waiting centuries for his lost love to return or for death to find him, Dracula meets Mina Harker, who becomes his lover and—rumor has it—mother to his child.

Time and Age

Dracula loses his place in the world at times. Of it, he says in *Tales of the Vampires: Antique* (2004), a comic book set in the world of *Buffy the Vampire Slayer*, "The world cycles. . . . Each generation must negate the generation before it. Overstay your welcome, and you'll become a tall tale for children. Fodder for terrible films and television serials. All because you committed the one cardinal sin—you aged." It can become disheartening. By the time Dracula meets Jonathan Harker, the English solicitor he hires to buy him a house and, although unknown to Harker, bring him up to speed with the modern world, he's a shadow of his former self. Still a sorcerer and Transylvania nobleman, he's centuries old. His castle near the Borgo Pass in the Carpathian Mountains is in disrepair. Still, he keeps the aristocratic charm he's always had, speaking only slightly accented English.

Physically, he's let himself go. Before Harker arrived, there was little in life that inspired the effort to keep up appearances. He grew thin, pale, and old. His ears appear pointed, and his mustache has grown long and white. He wears only black.

Assets and Faults

For all the Count's powers, there are weaknesses in his armor. First is the hair on his palms, a true giveaway for vampires. Another is his reflection. Unlike some of the more modern, weaker-blooded vampires, Dracula has no reflection. Harker notices this too and realizes it indicates his ethereal nature.

His eyes are the final clue. Try as he might to keep down the hints, Dracula's eyes always betray him. His emotions control their color. When he's happy or calm, his eyes are a gentle blue. However, when he's angry, the Devil shows through. Harker notes this in his journal, stating: "I saw . . . Count Dracula . . . with red light of triumph in his eyes, and with a smile that Judas in hell might be proud of." It's a frightening visage that can work both for and against him.

There are other mixed blessings in Dracula's life that he, recognizing his weaknesses, utilizes as his strengths. When people figure him out, he doesn't hesitate to kill them or bring them onto his side of things. He embraces his darkness and uses it to his benefit. It's a killer's instinct forged through years of battling the Turks. He employs it on the Russian ship, *Demeter*, when, during the voyage across the sea to Whitby, England, he is forced to feed on the crew. He manages to dispose of all the bodies except for the captain, who is left tied to the ship's helm. It isn't exactly an impaling, but certainly a clear nod to his former hobby.

His upbringing as an aristocrat is another strength. When Harker first meets Dracula, his manners, education, and grammar earn the English solicitor's respect. Remembering his impressive background, Dracula also brags to Harker about his warrior lineage.

Blind Ambition

Both a strength and a weakness, ambition drives Dracula throughout his life. He has something to prove. Without that mission, he lets himself go, as he did in the time prior to the novel. Then, when he decides to take over the world—and Wilhelmina "Mina" Murray, Harker's fiancée (see "Mina Harker: Dracula's Angel")—he is rejuvenated. The prospect of another life is enough to get him back into the world. As he feeds, the years fade away, bringing him back to the elegant, handsome prince he'd been before.

"I have crossed oceans of time to find you," he tells Mina, and that long journey blinds him to the dangers of changing so many people. Biting Mina's friend Lucy Westenra and turning her into a vampire cements the will of vampire hunter Abraham Van Helsing and his cohorts after they're forced to kill her. It drives them to destroy the collection of Transylvanian dirt in his home, ultimately robbing him of strength and rest. Rather than avoiding further confrontation, Dracula refuses to sway from his goal of having Mina.

Control Freak

Throughout his existence, Dracula has a strange and often passionate relationship with the women in his life. During the novel *Dracula*, his three "brides" are kept locked up in his castle. When the Count is buried in a tomb in the castle's chapel, his females are entombed beside him. Two may also be related to him and may, in fact, be his daughters, sisters, lovers, friends, vampire progeny, or different relations resulting from a combination of these. In any case, they share a close tie.

When the bloodthirsty trio tries to seduce and drain Harker, only to have the Count bust in and stop them, he physically attacks one of the women and chews out another. As if that weren't enough, he travels the seas in search of Mina, the bride of another man. The women at home are surely not allowed to do such things if they are his lovers. They will be, at best, considered secondary wives in his plan to bring Mina back to his castle.

The relationships appear to be abusive and one-sided, but there's more to it. On a deeper level, this anger and threatened loss of control go together in every instance. When the brides try to drink Harker, they threaten Dracula's plans. It shakes him on a very basic level, inciting his rage. This could be one of the reasons so many in the past were impaled.

Love and Symbolism

Dracula's journey is one of love. Ultimately, the beast needs his beauty to tame him. He craves it. Having once been truly in love, he will do anything to have it back. It's no coincidence that Mina, the picture of Victorian purity, is the one he desires. The Count is corrupted by darkness; Mina represents the light that he craves. He is the world, the power of men, and she is innocence longing for adventure. Dracula offers this, saying, "Then, I give you life eternal. Everlasting love. The power of the storm. And the beasts of the earth. Walk with me to be my loving wife, forever." He is happy to give her any and every thing she could desire, to share his power.

It's symbolic, not just practical, for Dracula and other vampires to be killed with a stake through the heart. When true love betrays or is taken away, the heart bleeds emotionally as it would literally, were it staked. The pain and hollowness that shattered love leaves in its wake is easily associated with the pain of being stabbed in the chest. At least a staking will kill its victim. A broken heart can last forever.

Companions

It's clear that not every relationship is "love" for him, and he knows the difference. Lucy is this difference, a relationship without love that is so common in life. Though he is on a mission to win Mina's heart, he visits Lucy's bed every night to feed from her (also infecting her). It's beyond symbolic. Just as Mina's innocence and devotion hold power of Dracula, so Lucy's submission to her passions allows him to take control of her.

Modern Life

Since the time of the novel *Dracula*, the Count has been busy. He's possibly the most well-known dark angel ever. His countenance is featured on boxes of Count Chocula cereal and as Count von Count of *Sesame Street*. There are even fuzzy slippers with his likeness.

Among probably a thousand movies, TV shows, and books, he is most notably portrayed in *Buffy the Vampire Slayer* during the "Buffy vs. Dracula" episode, which recounts when he visits the Slayer out of curiosity and attempts to change her. Then his visits are again discussed in *Tales of the Vampires: Antique*, in which he learns to ride a motorcycle. He is also mentioned in *Buffy* Season Eight: "Wolves at the Gate" and the comic book *Spike vs. Dracula*. Dracula has been a busy, busy guy!

Abilities

Poking fun at Dracula, Spike once said of his predecessor's powers: "Nothing but showy Gypsy stuff." That's not exactly the case. Dracula has several notable supernatural abilities. His strength and speed are enhanced. Drinking not only exsanguinates his victims but also infects them, as Dracula performs a series of nightly meetings on Lucy that turn her after death. He can shape-shift, becoming a wolf when he leaves the *Demeter*. At other times, Dracula transforms into fog or other animals, such as bats. He can control animals and the minds of humans, hypnotizing some and totally brainwashing others. According to the Romanian Tourism Board, "Transylvania sits on one of Earth's strongest magnetic fields and its people have extra-sensory perception." This may discount or add to the rumors of his ESP. And Dracula is said to somehow defy gravity, climbing upside down, like the Paris vampires in *Interview with the Vampire*.

There is some debate over the effectiveness of stakes on Dracula. In some stories he's staked and dies, but other stories tell that he changes into dust, perhaps willingly, and reforms. Garlic seems somewhat ineffective, and based on the various accounts, it seems that he is perhaps faking his aversion to the odor and its effect on him. He does seem to need the soil of his grave to empower him, and he does need to be invited into a home to enter in most cases. At one point Harker slices his throat and a bowie knife is plunged into his heart. It obviously doesn't work.

❧ FACTS AND TRIVIA ❧

- Unlike most vampires, Dracula has an affinity for the black arts in addition to his own powers. He is said to have studied at the Scholomance Academy near Sibiu, or Hermannstadt, in the Carpathian Mountains. The teachings versed him well in alchemy and magic. He has elemental abilities, controlling fog and storms as he needs through magic rather than vampiric power.

QUOTES

"*My revenge is just begun! I spread it over centuries, and time is on my side. Your girls that you all love are mine already; and through them you and others shall yet be mine—my creatures, to do my bidding and to be my jackals when I want to feed.*" —Dracula *(1897)*

"*To die, to be really dead—that must be glorious! There are far worse things awaiting man than death.*" —Bela Lugosi, Dracula *(1931)*

"*Listen to them: the children of the night. What sweet music they make.*"
—Gary Oldman, Bram Stoker's Dracula *(1992)*

"*Without me, Transylvania will be as exciting as Bucharest . . . on a Monday night.*"
—Love at First Bite *(1979)*

"*I shall rise from my own death, to avenge hers with all the powers of darkness.*"
—Bram Stoker's Dracula *(1992)*

"*I was betrayed. Look what your God has done to me!*" —Bram Stoker's Dracula *(1992)*

"*Do you believe in destiny? That even the powers of time can be altered for a single purpose? That the luckiest man who walks on this Earth is the one who finds . . . true love?*"
—Bram Stoker's Dracula *(1992)*

Select Bibliography

Books

Baring-Gould, Sabine. *Book of Were-Wolves* (London: Smith, Elder, and Co., 1865).

Cast, P. C., and Kristin Cast. *Betrayed* (New York: St. Martin's Griffin, 2007).

Burned (New York: St. Martin's Griffin, 2010).

Chosen (New York: St. Martin's Griffin, 2008).

Hunted (New York: St. Martin's Griffin, 2009).

Marked (New York: St. Martin's Griffin, 2007).

Tempted (New York: St. Martin's Griffin, 2009).

Untamed (New York: St. Martin's Griffin, 2008).

De la Cruz, Melissa. *Blue Bloods* (New York: Hyperion, 2006).

Masquerade: A Blue Bloods Novel (New York: Hyperion, 2007).

Misguided Angel: A Blue Bloods Novel (New York: Hyperion, 2010).

Revelations: A Blue Bloods Novel (New York: Hyperion, 2008).

The Van Alen Legacy: A Blue Bloods Novel (New York: Disney/Hyperion, 2009).

Hamilton, Laurell K. *Blood Noir* (New York: Jove, 2008).

Bloody Bones (New York: Jove, 1996).

Blue Moon (New York: Jove, 1998).

Bullet (New York: Berkley, 2010).

Burnt Offerings (New York: Jove, 1998).

Cerulean Sins (New York: Jove, 2003).

Circus of the Damned (New York: Jove, 1995).

Danse Macabre (New York: Jove, 2006).

Flirt (New York: Berkley, 2010).

Guilty Pleasures (New York: Jove, 1993).

The Harlequin (New York: Jove, 2007).

Incubus Dreams (New York: Jove, 2004).

The Killing Dance (New York: Jove, 1997).

The Laughing Corpse (New York: Jove, 1994).

The Lunatic Cafe (New York: Jove, 1996).

Micah (New York: Jove, 2006).

Narcissus in Chains (New York: Jove, 2001).

Obsidian Butterfly (New York: Jove, 2000).

Skin Trade (New York: Jove, 2009).

Harris, Charlaine. *All Together Dead* (New York: Ace, 2007).

Club Dead (New York: Ace, 2003).

Dead and Gone (New York: Ace, 2009).

Dead as a Doornail (New York: Ace, 2005).

Dead in the Family (New York: Ace, 2010).

Dead to the World (New York: Ace, 2004).

Dead Until Dark (New York: Ace, 2001).

Definitely Dead (New York: Ace, 2006).

From Dead to Worse (New York: Ace, 2008).

Living Dead in Dallas (New York: Ace, 2002).

A Touch of Dead (New York: Ace, 2009).

Kate, Lauren. *Fallen* (New York: Delacorte Books for Young Readers, 2009).

Rapture (New York: Delacorte Books for Young Readers, 2011).

Torment (New York: Delacorte Books for Young Readers, 2010).

Kenyon, Sherrilyn. *Acheron* (New York: St. Martin's, 2008).

Knibb, Michael A., ed. *Ethiopic Book of Enoch* (Oxford: Clarendon Press, 1978).

Mead, Richelle. *Blood Promise* (New York: Razorbill, 2009).

Frostbite (New York: Razorbill, 2008).

Shadow Kiss (New York: Razorbill, 2008).

Vampire Academy (New York: Razorbill, 2007).

Meyer, Stephenie. *Breaking Dawn* (New York: Little, Brown and Company, 2008).

Eclipse (New York: Little, Brown and Company, 2007).

New Moon (New York: Little, Brown and Company, 2006).

Twilight (New York: Little, Brown and Company, 2005).

Rice, Anne. *Blackwood Farm* (New York: Knopf, 2002).

Blood and Gold (New York: Knopf, 2001).

Blood Canticle (New York: Knopf, 2003).

Interview with the Vampire (New York: Knopf, 1976).

Memnoch the Devil (New York: Knopf, 1995).

Merrick (New York: Knopf, 2000).

Pandora (New York: Knopf, 1998).

The Queen of the Damned (New York: Knopf, 1988).

The Tale of the Body Thief (New York: Knopf, 1992).

The Vampire Armand (New York: Knopf, 1998).

The Vampire Lestat (New York: Knopf, 1985).

Vittorio the Vampire (New York: Knopf, 1999).

Shan, Darren. *Allies of the Night* (New York: Little, Brown, 2004).

    Cirque du Freak (New York: Little, Brown, 2000).

    Hunters of the Dusk (New York: Little, Brown, 2004).

    Killers of the Dawn (New York: Little, Brown, 2005).

    The Lake of Souls (New York: Little, Brown, 2005).

    Lord of the Shadows (New York: Little, Brown, 2006).

    Sons of Destiny (New York: Little, Brown, 2006).

    Trials of Death (New York: Little, Brown, 2003).

    Tunnels of Blood (New York: Little, Brown, 2002).

    Vampire Mountain (New York: Little, Brown, 2002).

    The Vampire Prince (New York: Little, Brown, 2002).

    The Vampire's Assistant (New York: Little, Brown, 2001).

Smith, L. J. *The Vampire Diaries: The Awakening and the Struggle*
    (New York: HarperTeen, 2007).

    The Vampire Diaries: The Fury and Dark Reunion (New York: HarperTeen, 2007).

    The Vampire Diaries: The Return: Nightfall (New York: HarperTeen, 2009).

    The Vampire Diaries: The Return: Shadow Souls (New York: HarperTeen, 2010).

Stoker, Bram. *Dracula* (New York: Signet, 1897).

Websites

charlaineharris.com (Southern Vampire Mysteries)

darrenshan.com (*Cirque du Freak*)

sherrilynkenyon.com (Dark-Hunter)

stepheniemeyer.com (*Twilight* saga home, and only place to find the unpublished manuscript
    of *Midnight Sun*)

theundercoverbooklover.blogspot.com (character interviews)

trutv.com (Visit the site library and look under "Serial Killers" for Elizabeth Bathory.)

white-wolf.com (White Wolf Publishing and *Vampire: The Masquerade* role-playing game)

Acknowledgments

This book has been a massive undertaking, and I couldn't let it go by without saying thanks to Jill Alexander and Will Kiester for their vision and guidance; to David J. Skal for his expertise; to Sandy Lu, agent extraordinaire; and to Clay and Malloree for their willingness to suffer through the months I worked on this. You two rock! Candy Grace and Mandy Vinyard for their invaluable opinions and help. Nicole Seales Ives, Megan Knotts, April Renee Symes, and Amanda Long Birdyshaw for being dark angels experts. And to my dad, for all the late-night vampire movies that fed this monster.

Photo Credits